He cli

the old boards of tl
his weight. When ne reacned the bottom, ne turned, held out his arms. "Come on down, Ashby. Just go slow."

"Not to worry. I've done this before." I reached for the first step with my foot, carefully moving toward the bottom, one step at a time, leaning against the wall for support. I was halfway there when it happened—so suddenly that I had no time to react. Frigid air swooshed down on me from behind, freezing my face, causing me to screw my eyes tight shut at the same time something strong and determined pushed against my back violently—so violently that I stumbled, then tumbled forward, to be caught in Luke's outstretched arms from several stairs below.

"Whoa!" He exhaled from the impact of my body on his. "My God, Ashby. What happened?"

I slumped against him, unable to utter a single word, my breathing shallow and rapid. At last I found my voice. "Something pushed me, Luke. I don't know what—or who—but it was powerful and deliberate."

Luke glanced up to the top of the stairs. "Nothing there. I'm going back to the loft to look."

I stopped him. "I doubt you'll find anything." I sniffed the air, expecting a new infusion of foul odor. "And what would you do if you did find anything?"

Just then we both heard it. Hollow, chilling, trailing away from us with every syllable: "Go away. He's dead. He's dead. He's dead…"

Praise for Susan Coryell

A RED, RED ROSE (The Wild Rose Press, 2014) was nominated for a Literary Award by the Library of Virginia.

~*~

"I really enjoyed the layers to [*BENEATH THE STONES*], including the young, rascally cousin Jeff, the M&M Wedding Express (bridal planners), and the interesting history tidbits. My favorite part was Ashby's interaction with the paranormal and what she learns about herself."

~Author Clifford Rush

~*~

"Fans of Victoria Holt and Phyllis Whitney will love *BENEATH THE STONES*. Ms. Coryell spins a tale in the tradition of the Gothic masters, complete with a ghostly mystery that'll give you the shivers. I'm hooked!"

~Author Jannine Gallant

~*~

"BENEATH THE STONES is a sequel to *A RED, RED ROSE*, but you don't have to have read the first book to enjoy this one. Coryell provides just enough background so we understand the story as a standalone novel. An interesting cast of characters is featured in this book, which is actually a story within a story—a mystery that dates back to the Civil War. Coryell combines humor, suspense, mystery and a good dose of the paranormal to entertain readers in this Gothic romance. A highly enjoyable read."

~Author Marilyn Baron

For Jennifer—
A good friend
and a kindred
spirit!

Beneath
the Stones

by

Susan Coryell

Susan Coryell

Beneath the Stones

Cover Art by *Tina Lynn Stout*

The Wild Rose Press, Inc.
PO Box 708
Adams Basin, NY 14410-0708
Visit us at www.thewildrosepress.com

Publishing History
First Mainstream General Edition, 2015
Print ISBN 978-1-62830-852-5
Digital ISBN 978-1-62830-853-2

Published in the United States of America

Dedication

For my family, with gratitude

Acknowledgments

I owe thanks to many who helped this book evolve: For equestrian expertise, Rick Caldwell and Lisa Dabareiner, who spent the day showing me around her horse farm.

For musical notes, Ron Goad and Ricky Ellis.

For out-of-this-world advice on the paranormal, Karen Wrigley.

And for a deluxe winery tour, Fred and Dreama Sylvester.

Also, I appreciate John and Margie Gibson for welcoming me to their historic home at Fort Stover—the model for the overseer's cottage.

For my readers and editors, Matt Uselton, Valerie Coryell, and Heidi Williams, who supplied the constructive criticism every writer needs.

For patience and understanding, my husband Ned.

A note from the author:

The Civil War letters included in *BENEATH THE STONES* are based on actual letters written from battle fronts by family ancestors, Joseph Franklin Stover and John William Stover.

After my mother-in-law's death, the family found a nondescript box in her file cabinet. Inside we were amazed to find fifteen letters hand-written in beautiful, flowing script.

Since this occurred as I was in the midst of writing *BENEATH THE STONES*, I immediately seized on the idea of using excerpts from the letters in the novel.

Though, for practical reasons, I omitted many details, overall the letters reveal a haunting picture of life for the Confederate soldier.

A final note: The flute mentioned in one of the letters is very likely the same flute on display at the Museum of the Confederacy in Appomattox, Virginia.

Chapter 1

The file folder was thick as a Manhattan phone book. I'd chewed over every form, notice and bill—calculated bank balances, cash reserves and expense projections. It was enough to make an English major pack up and run away. Any way I calculated it, we were in deep financial kim chee. Something had to be done, and, unfortunately, I was the one to do it. I closed my eyes and sighed, then, called out, "Monica, can you come take a look at this?"

My lovely, clueless aunt appeared in the doorway of our home office at Overhome. "Take a look at what, Ashby?"

"This file. The one the accountant left. Before *he* left, that is."

Monica's winged eyebrows rose. "Oh dear, Ashby. You know I have no head for figures." She lifted the file and weighed it in her slim fingers. "I know we are over-extended. Surely…surely you can find a way to fix it? Maybe Luke…when he gets home…?"

I wanted to shake her—to shout, "How could you let this happen?" In her early forties now, and a widow on her own for five years, Monica should have been able to deal with some of life's financial realities, but I discovered, too late, that that was the impossible dream.

It was unfortunate that Luke and I both headed off to our respective colleges so soon after my uncle died and Overhome became mine. For a while the horse farm continued to support itself, but when Aunt Monica hired the no-account accountant who speculated in a shaky stock market, we lost our reserve. Then the economy tanked. Luke, who had kept the books meticulously for so long, was deep into his studies in veterinary school. Meanwhile, Aunt Monica spent an awful lot of money updating the estate. Now we were in crisis mode. We either had to sell off the horses or mortgage the property or…what? Turn Overhome into a B&B?

I assumed my most serious look and tone. "There *is* a way to 'fix it,' as you say, Monica. I expect there'll be a period of adjustment, but I've come up with something just short of desperate."

Her look told me she felt both relief and trepidation. "Desperate?"

"Yes. We are in *desperate* financial straits. Now, the question is, do you trust me to find a way out?"

"You've always been very good at finding a way, my dear niece. Of course I trust you." She smiled with what appeared to be genuine relief, handed back the file and turned to leave. "Thank you, Ashby. Do whatever you deem necessary. I am sure everything will work out for the best."

I wished I shared my aunt's confidence *"Do whatever you deem necessary."* There would be battles along the way. That was the only thing I was sure of.

****

Saddling Sasha, my faithful dappled gray, now more gray than dappled, I inhaled the familiar scents of the stable. Hay and pine shavings and leather. Nowhere was I more at home than here on my beloved estate in

Southern Virginia.

Glancing toward the tiny office across from the horse stalls, my mind flashed back to my early days at Overhome five years ago—my first meeting with Luke, the groom who often worked in that little office. What a clash that was! Me—the city-chic Jersey Girl, self-absorbed and naive about what to expect from my summer visit to Overhome. Luke—the cynical hayseed with a thick drawl and bad hair who looked upon Yankees as invaders. It was more than a bumpy beginning. More like a Civil War skirmish! But the summer had led to romance, and the romance had turned to love. Soon, we would be man and wife.

Sasha moved quickly into a trot. Ever appreciative of the green, rolling landscape, my heart drew me to the wooded bridle path both Sasha and I loved. But today I had more than a relaxing ride in mind. Crossing the wooden bridge that arched over a merry stream, I guided Sasha toward the back section of the estate where there was minimal lakefront and the land flattened out, punctuated here and there with an outcropping of rocks or a tuft of scrub cedars. Overhome Estate included extensive acreage; it was many minutes before I reined Sasha in as we approached an old dirt road. I wanted to get a good look at the part of the estate I hoped to market.

From horseback, I took into account the saleable points as we moved slowly over the grounds. Though long unused, the road had been a thoroughfare for local travelers. It ran alongside the creek, which once fed into the river, dammed up over fifty years ago to create Moore Mountain Lake. Now overgrown with weeds and brambles and deeply rutted above the waterline, it was hardly impressive. But the creek bubbling in the background was surely an asset. I was ever more aware of the complexity of selling off a parcel of property; it was what I'd determined to do, and I knew I'd need expert help.

My horse and I moved toward a thick strand of cedar trees. Unlike the scrubs we'd already passed, these trees were healthy and bushy. As we brushed against the branches, I smelled Christmas in the summer air. Though the going was rough, I kept moving, urging Sasha forward. Well into the copse, I spied an unusual structure—bulky and largely covered in a tangle of kudzu. Sasha moved with careful steps over brush and vines into a partial clearing where I was surprised to find a weathered and stained stone building. An old tobacco barn? No, that would have been made of wood. A storage building, perhaps. Something long unused.

Dismounting, I led Sasha to what certainly appeared to be a house. Larger than I'd first thought, the building revealed narrow windows boarded up. The limestone walls might have been white originally, though now the building was brown and green with kudzu and stains. A stone chimney rose from the middle of a rusting metal roof; the whole structure appeared old but surprisingly sturdy.

The front door was blocked with a couple of warped boards, not that I'd have the courage to try to get in. Probably inhabited with wasps and spiders. Snakes, maybe. An expanse of rotting, splintering boards, all that was left of an ancient porch, stretched across the front of the house.

A sudden chill washed over me, as if an icy breeze

had sprung up. But nothing stirred. The kudzu could have been painted to the walls of the old place, the air was that still. Oddly, Sasha, too, seemed to sense something untoward. His ears flattened back and he pulled against the reins so hard that I had to forcibly hold him still—a completely alien reaction from my usually docile companion. "Whoa, Sasha. Steady, boy," I encouraged, standing my ground and holding on tight.

How had I lived at Overhome all this time unaware of this old house? Who had lived here and why had it been abandoned? It would have to be torn down for development purposes, I figured, though I'd seen a few housing tracts where vintage barns and tobacco sheds and such were left standing to lend an old-fashioned, down-home flavor to modern housing projects. Then, developers liked to give the area a nostalgic name— Heritage Acres or Colonial Crest.

If anybody could fill me in on the details of this ancient abode, it would be Miss Emma Coleville, the housekeeper at Overhome for so many years. She was the resident archivist of all things pertaining to the Overton family. "Well, Ashby," she'd say. "Let me tell you about that old house. Sit awhile. I'll pour you a cup of tea. Where shall I begin?"

I snapped to. I was hopeful that I could move ahead with my plan to market this section of the estate. It was, after all, mine to sell. Of course, as a courtesy, I'd just alerted Aunt Monica to my actions, without being specific. And I considered, briefly, consulting my dad who had grown up at Overhome. With Luke and me communicating in text bites the last few weeks, I couldn't figure out how to relay the news to him without causing panic. All in all, I felt it wasn't fair to

5

drop the responsibility in anybody else's lap. The reality: I was the one who inherited Overhome when my Uncle Hunter died. Now I had to save Overhome from financial disaster. And I had to move immediately.

Mounting Sasha, I realized he was still skittish from the aura of the old house. I called his name and stroked him lovingly. "It's okay, boy. We're leaving. We'll have our ride on the trail after all." We were off! Neither of us could resist the call of the wooded trail, and when I reined him in and led him to the stable, we both wore sweat on our flanks.

"Hi, Ashby!" My cousin Jeff looked up as he brushed the silky-pale mane of Sunshine, his palomino pony. "There you go, boy." He patted the horse, and Sunshine nibbled Jeff's hand. "You want a treat, do you?" Reaching into his pocket, Jeff pulled out a peppermint and offered it on his flattened palm. Sunshine gulped down the candy with relish and a look that asked for more. Jeff laughed. "That's all, Sunshine. We don't want to spoil your dinner."

As I began to brush Sasha down, I wondered where Jeff's friend Nick was. The son of our hired workers Carlos and Mariana, Nick had become fast friends with Jeff. Now that Nick and his parents were living in the guest cottage, one rarely saw the twelve-year-olds separated, especially when horses were involved.

Jeff read my mind. "Nick's helpin' his dad out in the pasture. One of the mares is acting up. Carlos says Nick's a natural. He understands how horses think."

My cousin's loving ministrations with Sunshine prompted the thought: Here is another one who understands how horses think. I marveled at Jeff's maturity. Five years ago I had been invited to

Overhome to act as a companion, an *au pair*, to Jeff, a cute, canny, freckle-faced dynamo who became more than a cousin to me, more of a younger brother to love and nurture. He still had the freckles and the permanently sun-streaked hair. His Overton blue eyes were as bright as ever, but he'd shot up like a magic bean stalk and his voice cracked appealingly when he was excited. The fact that he had Nick for a close friend, someone to share his love of horses with, warmed me as little else can.

"Well, that makes two of you. Horse whisperers." I leaned over to press a quick kiss on Jeff's cheek, knowing he was at the age of "E-W-W-W" at any such gesture from a female, even an older cousin. He had the grace not to brush it from his cheek.

Finishing up with Sasha, I turned to head up to the house. I'd need time to freshen up for dinner. Though she'd softened considerably over the years, Aunt Monica was always one to consider meals formal affairs. She'd not welcome a sweaty, disheveled Ashby at the table. I looked back at Jeff. "Hey, Jeff. Did you know there's a decrepit, old building over on the other side of our property?"

Jeff gave me a guarded look. "Um, decrepit? Not sure what you mean…where?" His eyes widened in feigned innocence.

I waved a finger in front of his face. I could always tell when he was fibbing. "Don't hold out on me now." When I could see him struggling with himself, I added, "You won't get in any trouble from me."

"Well, me and Nick, we…we…we kinda explored it…once." He fidgeted and shifted his eyes from mine. "We actually went inside, you know. Broke in, sort of."

"Okay. Breaking in might not be cool, probably dangerous for that matter, but I imagine finding an abandoned house like that would be irresistible. It would've been for me when I was your age."

Jeff brightened. "Wanna go check it out? You and me together? I can show you how to get in."

"Hah! Well, you've got me figured out. I'll take you up on that. Let's make it a date." I called a goodbye to Sasha before departing.

"Ashby? The truth is we've been there tons of times. We were lookin' for a Christmas tree last winter. And the house was just, you know, suddenly right there in front of us. Inside we found animal bones and old dishes and other stuff. It's kind of like a club house. We spent a long time sweeping up, dusting off cobwebs and bees' nests. We've stocked it with candles and peanut butter and sodas. What we'd really like to do is spend the night out there." He blinked, then gulped. "Rats. I wasn't supposed to tell anybody. Me and Nick pledged each other to secrecy."

I crossed my heart. "I promise not to tell." I thought that spending the night in a creepy old house would probably be the dream of every adventurous twelve-year-old.

"Let's keep our date to explore the place," I said. "Then, maybe...well, we'll see about anything else."

"There's one other thing." Jeff's freckles danced. "Nick and me—both of us—we think, maybe, there's something weird about the old house. I mean, we both get this whacked-out vibe in there—like somebody's watching us, or, maybe waiting for us." He shrugged. "Oh, I don't know. Nick was first to sense it, but then I felt it, too. But we've never seen anybody there."

Well, I'd had plenty of my own experiences with "something weird" afoot at Overhome. Believe me, I was not one to toss it off to adolescent fantasy. I didn't say anything about my own strange vibe upon visiting the abandoned structure. Or Sasha's, for that matter.

"I'd like to check it out for myself. See you at dinner, Jeff. Your secret's safe with me." For now, I added to myself.

"Ashby, you rock!" Jeff reached up with a high five.

Just then Samantha, our caretaker, jogged into view. "Hey, Ashby! I caught a couple mares cribbin' the railings and kickin' th' fence boards, too." She paused to light a cigarette. "We're gonna have to replace some planks."

Samantha—affectionately known as Sam—looked tough and sturdy in her "uniform" of jeans, heavy boots, man's shirt and baseball cap, but she actually baby-talked even the most stubborn steeds into doing her will. We were lucky to have Sam and our other loyal employees—yet another reason I was determined to keep Overhome going—not just the manor house and grounds, but the vital horse farm I'd come to appreciate over the years.

I meandered along the path to the house, pausing, as I frequently did, to marvel at the timeless beauty of the old place. I gazed over the panorama of the ancient estate, taking in the stone wall that clings to the rolling landscape as if it had sprung from the soil, arriving finally at a boxwood maze planted in the Colonial period. The maze twisted into itself like a kid's board game, exiting at a charming wooden gazebo where generations of Overtons had courted and kissed and reminisced—the gazebo where Luke and I were planning to recite our wedding vows. Down the hill on the opposite side lay Moore Mountain Lake—deep, clear and smooth.

Returning to the manor house, I thought how fortunate it was that Overhome itself stood high on a bluff—high enough to be spared when Moore Mountain Lake was created, over fifty years ago, by damming up the rivers and flooding the valley. Against a green background of stately trees, the mansion's bone-white clapboards served as a stark palette for rows of black-shuttered windows. From the slate roof, four stone chimneys rose, proud testaments to antiquity. Perfectly balanced wings settled into the contours of the yard like a roosting bird, supplying harmony to the solid bulk of the mid-section. Overhome, my ancestral home, never ceased to amaze me with its settled beauty, dignity and ageless grace.

****

Dear Diary:

I know a diary is an old-fashioned way of recording thoughts. But a blog just doesn't do it for me. All the Overton women have kept diaries—from my Grandmother Lenore all the way back to the 1800s. I've read many of them. Urged by my professors to journal my thoughts and activities daily, I've come to see my diary as an archive, a friend, my ear and my comfort—as well as a way to satisfy my need to write, write, write.

Unacceptable. Overhome is over 200 years old. Solid in Southern Virginia, it's survived the Revolutionary War, the Civil War and the construction of Moore Mountain Dam. Please tell me, how did I manage to run it into the ground in five measly years?

This was supposed to be my summer to shine. Luckily, I paid my tuition before our financial crash. And Luke was the grateful recipient of a private scholarship for community college transfers to Tech. So we have no college loans or anything like that to worry about. Now, with my writing degree tucked under my arm, I have a half-decent freelance career on the uptick and a novel working in my mind. Best of all we have our wedding to look forward to at summer's end. You know, Diary, how long Luke and I have waited for this—five long years. We're more than ready to begin our married lives together at Overhome. Luke has a promising future as a large-animal vet. Mom and Dad have retired from their educator jobs in Jersey and they're moving down to Southwestern Virginia permanently. Helping me plan for the Big Event. Oh, everything is in place. All my orbs in orbit.

Except for the future of my beloved ancestral estate, Overhome.

Well, my idea is not going to be popular, but it just might save us. I've contacted a real estate agent. If we can work out a deal, I should be able to sell off a fifty-acre portion of the fallow land which has not been used for years. Yeah, somebody will build shoddy tract homes on it, no doubt. That can't be helped.

We need the cash and we need it as soon as possible. Hang on, Overhome. Help is on the way.

Chapter 2

Dinner in the dining room at Overhome was always a production if my raven-haired, Greek goddess of an aunt could find a reason. Born to wealth, Monica knew how to set a table, and she rarely let an occasion to do so pass her by. Tonight she had a guest, so the best china and sterling silver and crystal were put to use along with the linen table cloth and napkins. Tall, lighted tapers rested in the candelabra. The ancient crystal chandelier glittered overhead. You'd have thought it was a formal banquet for twenty, which the venerable old table easily sat, instead of dinner for four.

"Ashby, darling, I want you to meet Hal Reynolds. Hal is the historian who has been researching Overhome's past, including the slave graves and headstones lost when the lake was filled."

Monica spoke with deliberation, enunciating each syllable as though she were studying it. She tilted her chin toward a pleasant-looking man wearing wire-framed glasses, a pastel blue Oxford shirt and a light sports coat. "Hal, this is Ashby Overton, my niece. Naturally, as the owner of Overhome, Ashby is interested in the historic aspects of the estate."

Hal smiled and nodded in my direction, but he looked a little uncomfortable. "Nice to meet you, Miss Overton." He fidgeted with his shirt collar, perhaps wishing he'd worn a tie.

"Call me Ashby, please. And I'd like to call you Hal, if that's all right." I smiled back at him. "Monica sets a formal dining table, but we're not so hung up on formality when it comes to names." This seemed to relax Hal somewhat; I figured the silver, china, and crystal might be a bit overwhelming.

"My son, Jefferson." Monica nodded toward my cousin.

"Hello, Mr. Reynolds," Jeff began, but Hal interrupted him.

"Ashby prefers to call me Hal, and I'd like for you to do that, too, Jefferson."

"In that case, Hal"—Jeff shot a brief sideways glance toward his mother—"please call me Jeff."

I covered my laughter with my linen napkin and a cough. Jeff had his mother's number. If she was over the top he'd bring her back to earth with a resounding thud. Sneaking a glance at Hal, I could see he was as amused as I was. I decided on the spot that I liked Hal. And if Monica's unusual spontaneity and high color hinted at romance, I'd award Hal my stamp of approval. It was good to see my aunt in a mellow mood. She'd had some rough times as a young widow after Uncle Hunter's death.

While Hal and Monica made conversation with Jeff, I looked around the room. Located in the oldest section of the house, the dining room, which lay directly under my bedroom, had once been a part of a barn. Built in the eighteenth century, the barn was converted to a house when the original home was partially destroyed by fire. With carpeted floor and silk wallpaper, the room certainly did not in any way resemble a barn. I'd always felt that the porous old barn board far beneath the ornate wallpaper must have trapped eons of Overton talk—of crops and lawn parties, horses and war. I could feel the murmur of their collective voices in the air.

"…Luke," Monica said.

I'd drifted off, but the name whipped my attention back to the present. "Sorry, Monica. What about Luke?"

Monica gave me a fleeting, skeptical look. "Your wedding, Ashby. To Luke. I am wondering when you expect him to return home."

"Oh. I'm not sure. Luke's awfully busy with his summer tracking program." And when she looked blank, I added, "You know, after graduation from vet school he works through a rotation—a few weeks with a veterinary clinic and then some required application at school and then back to a practice with an established vet. To gain experience in the field. It's called 'tracking.'"

"So your fiancé is a veterinarian?" Hal appeared interested. "Is he studying at Virginia Tech, by any chance? Tech happens to be my alma mater."

"Tech it is, and Luke graduated in May. Equine practice is his specialty. He's a wonder with horses." I turned to Monica. "Anyway, he'll get here at the first opportunity. But weekends are busy with the tracking schedule."

"I think you guys should get married on horseback." Jeff spoke without a hint of humor.

"Oh my goodness. That would never do!" Monica looked at Jeff in horror. "It's already been decided—Luke agrees. The ceremony will take place outdoors at the gazebo here at Overhome. NO horses allowed." She looked to me for corroboration.

I had to laugh. "Not a bad idea at all, Jeff. You know, since Luke and I first became acquainted over my riding lessons. But we're firm on the gazebo. Hey, we love horses, but the idea smacks of a low beginning or something. I can hear our future children's comments: 'What? Mommy and Daddy were married in a BARN?'" Then I saw the twinkle in Jeff's eye and knew he was taking the opportunity to push his mother's buttons yet again.

Just then Mariana arrived with the first course. She was a first-rate cook, whether the menu involved her native Argentinian cuisine or something else. "Avocado soup," Mariana announced, loading a tray full of bowls and a tureen onto the sideboard. Deftly she doled out the steaming liquid and placed a bowl in front of each of us. "Warm tortillas and goat cheese to go with the soup." She placed a fragrant basket in the middle of the table. "Enjoy!" Her diminutive figure retreated to the kitchen to prep the next course.

For a while everyone ate in silence. "Well, I made an interesting discovery today," I said when I'd satisfied my hunger with the creamy concoction. I reached for the basket of tortillas, took one and passed it on. "Roaming around with Sasha on the fringes of Overhome property."

Monica and Hal both looked at me with interest. Jeff kept his head bent to his soup bowl. I continued. "I found an old house, windows and door boarded up, roof still intact, but it looks quite ancient. I can't believe I wasn't aware of its existence until today."

Hal looked thoughtful. "House, you say? Not a shed or shelter for animals?"

I shook my head. "I'm quite sure it's a house. Even has a chimney. It's made of limestone—well-hidden by a grove of cedars and camouflaged with kudzu."

Hal's expressive face brightened. "You know, it might have housed an overseer. For the slaves. An estate this size would have had a number of slaves living on the property prior to the Civil War. The overseer would typically live apart from the manor."

The idea that my ancestors had owned slaves never ceased to bother me. Hal, the historian, accepted it as fact, no doubt. Certainly everyone else around here considered slavery to be an undeniable part of early Southern life. Unfortunate but undeniable. There was a huge difference for me between studying about slavery and sitting at a table actually once served by slaves. As I said, it bothered me.

"That would make sense." I chewed thoughtfully for a moment. "I wonder if it's been lived in since slave times."

"Miss Emma could answer that for us," Monica said to Hal. "She's from an old Virginia family herself. The Colevilles. The First-Family-of-Virginia Colevilles, and she is proud of that heritage. Over the years she made it her business to learn all she could about the Overton family history as well as her own."

"She knows the name behind every picture in our portrait gallery." Jeff pointed toward the portrait wall in the great room.

"The Colevilles fell on hard financial times and Emma came to work here when she was no more than a girl—the same age as Ashby's grandmother, Lenore. She and Lenore became fast friends," Monica explained.

"Miss Emma still lives downstairs. She doesn't work anymore, but we can visit her whenever we want. She bakes awesome cookies." Jeff gave an appreciative nod.

"Well, maybe we can ask Miss Emma if she knows anything about the overseer's cottage." Hal looked at me, eyes big as a child's. "Hope you don't mind my calling it that. You know, I'd love to see the place myself. We might find revealing relics."

Jeff's gaze lowered toward his soup bowl again. I knew he did not like this turn of the conversation.

"Let me take a closer look first, if you don't mind," I told Hal. "Jeff and I can explore it together. I need his young eyes and sense of adventure."

Jeff beamed. "It's all right, Mom, isn't it?"

Monica looked hesitant. "Ashby, just how safe is it?"

"We'll be careful, Mom. Real careful."

"Spiders or snakes, Monica. Nothing more dangerous than that, I'm sure." I tried for a light tone, knowing there might, indeed, be something a lot more dangerous than spiders or snakes. Something dangerous enough to spook both me and my horse, not to mention my cousin and his friend.

As Hal looked thoughtful and Monica looked unsure and Jeff grinned at me for keeping his secret and inviting him along, I became aware of something nobody else seemed to notice. It was the crystal chandelier hanging over the dining table. A barely discernible tinkling of the teardrop crystals. I resisted the impulse to look up, lest the others follow my gaze. But there was no denying it. Without any breeze or fan or anything else to stir up the air, the individual pieces of crystal bumped against each other ever so lightly, barely tinkling, like fairy wind chimes on a puff of magic air.

Laden down with a fragrant casserole, Mariana opened the swinging door from the kitchen. "*Arroz con pollo*. Rice with chicken. A family favorite."

****

For some reason I had a wakeful night. Exhausted as I was from a full day of riding, exploring and staying up late to talk with Hal and Monica, I kept waking up, turning over, plumping my pillow, only to doze fitfully until the next awakening. Something was up. I couldn't tell what, but I could feel the unrest in the air. I had sensed it at the overseer's cottage and with the tinkling of the chandelier, and I could feel it here in my room. I had developed a kind of sixth sense in my years of living at Overhome—a sense of immortality that lives in the molecules whirling about in the ancient air we still breathed.

Finally, toward dawn I began to dream. Luke and I were riding our horses in the pasture, having a race, actually. I was winning, galloping ahead of him on Sasha, until we came to the maze that ended at the gazebo. We dismounted to walk our horses through the maze, and Luke reached out and held me in a strong embrace. Just as he bent to kiss me, a Voldemort kind of character dashed out from the maze brandishing a whip. "Get to work! Stop wasting time and get to work!" he screamed. And then, from the gazebo, I heard the strains of a familiar song: "Flow Gently, Sweet Afton."

I sat up, my breathing shallow and quick. I was awake for sure; I could still hear the notes. The music had nothing to do with my dream. It was definitely "Flow Gently, Sweet Afton," an old Robert Burns poem set to music. "Flow gently, sweet Afton, among thy green braes," the lyrics went. It spurred vivid memories from my earliest days at Overhome years ago—memories I'd just as soon leave forever behind me.

I slid from bed, grabbed a robe and tiptoed to the hall outside my room. Looking over the high catwalk that encircled the great room below, I saw Jeff at the piano. After years of piano lessons, which he'd heartily resisted, he was able to read notes and play quite well, preferring to practice in the morning so that he could spend his afternoons with his friend and his horse. Fighting vertigo, I leaned over the railing, listening as his fingers flew across the keys. Then, he began to sing in that adolescent nether range between soprano and bass, "Flow gently, sweet Ashby, among thy green beans."

I could not resist calling out to my cousin. "Jeff. Hey, Jeff. Up here. Look up!"

Jeff followed my voice to my perch, looking up at me. "Hi, Ashby."

"It's Afton. Flow gently, sweet Afton. That's how the song goes. And it's among thy green braes—not 'green beans.'"

Jeff exploded with laughter. "Nah, Ashby. This is *my* version. I dedicate it to you 'cause you're so cool." And he began to play and sing again. "Flow gently, sweet Ashby, among thy green beans."

Chapter 3

Dear Diary:

Holy freaking cow! Could things get any more hectic? I've just hung up the phone with my editor at Blue Ridge Heritage *magazine. She wants a comprehensive, in-depth series of articles on the arts and artists in our area. To span the summer issues—we're talking serious dollars here. It won't finance the wedding, but it will sure help the bottom line. And it's going to mean a LOT of work for yours truly. I can't wait to tell Luke, who, BTW texted only minutes ago saying he'll be home this coming weekend. Good news all around! Now, I must get busy on yet another front. Mom and Dad will arrive here—at Overhome, in time to greet Luke's appearance. They're moving from New Jersey to Southern Virginia permanently, storing their household goods and staying at Overhome for the summer until they can find a house. I know Mom will be full of wedding ideas. She and Monica will hash out the details, and then Luke and I will do our own thing. Well, maybe not quite that drastic. But I know in my heart these two well-meaning creative artists will have much more elaborate plans for Luke and me than either of us could envision. Compromise will, no doubt, be the operative word.*

But first, I must talk to my Realtor. Saving Overhome is key.

****

"You may have a viable proposal here, Ashby." Paul Gordon peered at the old plat, along with a rough sketch I'd prepared showing the acreage to be sold. "I'll need to walk off the area, call for a survey and a soil test for the septic field site." He jotted a list as he spoke. "Fifty acres, you say?" He looked at the sketch again. "With R-1 zoning, we could find a builder to construct custom homes."

"Custom homes?"

"We're talking a quality builder who customizes each home to the buyer's wishes. Not one of those every-house-looks-the-same developments. If you know what I mean."

"I suppose that's the best I could hope for," I sighed. "I hate to do anything to compromise our family estate, but…"

The Realtor appeared sympathetic. "This economy is a challenge to all of us. A lot of home owners are making tough choices to stay above water financially." He looked at me thoughtfully. "If it's done right, the development shouldn't impact your own quality of life. A separate entrance, one house per acre, a group dock completely out of sight of Overhome itself."

I took a deep breath. "Can you keep this meeting under your hat, Paul? I haven't mentioned this to my family. Monica knows something's up, but my mom and dad get in mid-week and Luke, my fiancé, is coming home this weekend. I plan to tell everyone at the same time." I scooted back my chair and stood up. "Wish me luck."

Paul pushed back from his desk and stood. "You know, your dad, Madison, and his brothers, Washington and Hunter—we all grew up and hung out together. Madison and I graduated in the same high school class. Overhome's an important part of local history—not just for your family—but for many of us old-timers. We consider the estate a part of our heritage. A symbol of our strength and determination and ability to endure—the Old South personified."

I had to laugh. "Wow! You've expressed my feelings with more eloquence than I can call up myself. Thanks for understanding. You've made me feel better about the whole thing. Now, if I can gather my courage for the family pow-wow."

"I'm sure you'll handle it beautifully. In the meantime, I'll write up a contract that will work best for all concerned. Of course, I'll do my homework, check out the comparable sales and the county's Master Plan." Paul offered a hand shake. "Say hello to Monica. I know it's been years now, but what a shock Hunter's death was. Such a skilled horseman to die in a riding accident like that—so young. "He shook his head slowly, a look of honest regret on his features.

"Yes. We all miss Uncle Hunter." I let myself out of the realty office. And if my uncle were still alive, would Overhome be in jeopardy now? It was a question I'd asked myself more than once.

As I drove home, I mulled over different approaches for revealing my plans to the family. How would Luke react? Familiar as he'd been with the financial books all those years he served as "stable boy," he might be the most understanding. Or the least. Mom and Dad? Overhome was, after all, Dad's childhood home and family heritage, even though he'd left after a feud with his father and never returned.

Once there were the Overton brothers Paul had referred to: Madison, Washington and Hunter, born in that order. Washington married Marian Mills, a local girl, and they were my biological parents, but both were killed in a car accident near Overhome, leaving me orphaned at the age of two. Madison and his wife, Helen, adopted me. I have no memory of my birth parents; growing up in New Jersey with my adoptive Mom and Dad was a totally wonderful experience. Now, as the only surviving Overton son, would Dad consider selling part of Overhome's property a huge mistake?

****

Detouring the house, I stopped at the stables, looking for some comfort from Sasha.

"Hey, Ashby." It was Eddie Mills, the long-time neighbor I'd hired to work as a groom when Luke left. Eddie and I were cousins, but there had been a lot of bad blood between the families over the years and disputes over land boundaries. The Mills branch of the family had not fared well, and they, apparently, placed most of the blame for their situation on the Overtons, whom they considered to be land thieves. Conversely, Luke held little respect for Eddie, since he'd been a member of the Night Riders, a gang of local thugs who for years "specialized" in vandalizing estate properties, including Overhome, leaving Luke to clean up after them.

When Luke went off to college, and I offered

Eddie a job, he promised to turn over a new leaf, abandon all ties with the Night Riders, and he'd done a darn good job caring for the horses, minding the stables, keeping the barn ship-shape.

Eddie flashed his new, straight-toothed grin. Okay, I'd put some money into orthodontia for Eddie. I'd also funneled a bit of capital to the Mills family next door so they could improve their property, which had fallen into disrepair. I couldn't see perpetuating a state of disgruntled neighbors once I inherited Overhome. Did I regret that these gestures may have added to my current financial woes? Not really. Good investments needed no regrets.

"What c'n I do fer you?" Eddie's wide glance took in the whole area. He seemed quite proud of his spic-and-span stalls, feed troughs, and tack room.

"Hi, Eddie. I just want a little horse-love." I headed for Sasha's stall from which I could hear his welcoming whinny.

"How 'bout a lil' stable boy love?" Eddie leered.

I gave Eddie my sweetest smile. "Thanks, but I'll stick with Sasha."

Eddie laughed. He was really quite harmless when pretending to hit on me, knowing he had no chance for success. And he was a natural with animals. Eddie had brought in barn cats to keep the mice down, but I knew he fed them on the sly every day. And his dog, Barney, was constantly at his side.

Just then Jeff and his friend Nick trotted into view. Nick, though the same age as Jeff, was shorter by a head and wiry as a coat hanger. Jeff gave me a high five. "Ashby! Nick and me are saddlin' up for a ride. Wanna come along?" I wondered if the overseer's cottage was their destination.

"No, Jeff, but thanks. I have lots of work to do, I'm afraid. You guys have fun. Going exploring?"

Jeff turned to his friend. "Ashby knows about our club house. It's *muy bueno*, Nick."

I watched Nick's worried expression relax as Jeff looked back to me. "We like to check in—do a little clean up. It's just so cool." As my cousin and his friend trotted off, I noticed their pockets were bulging— probably filled with snacks for their club house pantry.

With a last pat to Sasha's neck and a kiss for his soft mane, I left the stable thinking about the overseer's cottage. I had a feeling it was more than an abandoned, forgotten structure. More than a long-ago employee's abode. Hal was all about the history of the place, but Jeff and Nick had other ideas: weird vibes, Jeff said, somebody watching. Me? If I'd learned one thing in my years at Overhome, I'd learned to pay attention to my sixth sense.

****

"Mom, Dad." I hugged one and then the other. "It's wonderful to see you again. You're here. I mean *really* here. Retired and ready to move on. It's goodbye New Jersey, hello Virginia." I'd been watching for them all afternoon, and we stood just outside the front door.

My mother laughed and threw her arms wide as if to encompass all of Overhome in an embrace. Mom is the kind of woman who grows more beautiful with age. I mean, she's always been slim and petite, but her naturally graying hair could have been one of those pricey frosted and highlighted jobs—it looks that good. And the tiny lines around her eyes and mouth added a merry look to her heart-shaped face—a face perpetually

26

ready for fun. It was the fun that her kindergartners recognized first. "Ashby, this place is just amazing. It never changes, yet somehow it gets better and better every time I see it."

"Just like you, Mom."

Her smile spread all the way up to her eyes.

Dad engulfed me in a strong hug. "You, my dear daughter, have done a magnificent job of maintaining the old family estate." He released me and looked around appreciatively.

Oh, Dad, you'll find out the real story soon enough was my thought, but I smiled bravely. "Thanks, Dad. Want to check out the stable?" My father's love of horses trumped any interest in the house or grounds.

"You bet!" He grinned, and I marveled, as always, at how much he and Hunter, my dead uncle, looked alike. Dark hair, navy-blue eyes, cleft chin—all the Overton traits.

Just then Monica emerged from the house. "Welcome! Welcome!" More hugging and exclaiming ensued. "Come in. You must be tired. Let me get you some refreshments. Mariana has the guest room all fresh and ready."

Dad nudged Mom toward Monica. "Go on in with Monica, Helen. I'm sure you're not nearly as interested in the horses as I am. We'll get the luggage later." Dad slung an arm around my shoulder and took a deep breath. "Virginia—I'd forgotten how pure and sweet country air can be."

"We're all really excited you and Mom decided to move to Virginia now that you've retired. And Miss Emma is probably the most elated of all. She says it's natural and right that the Overtons, at long last, are gathering at Overhome."

"I expect she considers New Jersey alien territory—that we've come to our senses and returned to the native land." Dad chuckled.

I nodded. "On to the stables."

"How about Luke? When do you expect him?"

"This weekend. Monica's planning a big dinner party to celebrate everyone's homecoming."

"Monica's doing well, is she?"

"She may even have a boyfriend. Hal Reynolds—a historian who's looking into Overhome's past. Not sure, but the two of them seem pretty chummy to me."

"Well, I'm glad to hear that. I know it took her a long time to achieve any kind of balance after Hunter's death." Dad looked pensive. "So much death at Overhome. Accidental death. First my mother with that freak riding accident. Then Washington and Marian…" Dad brightened. "But that's how Helen and I got you, dear girl. And life without you as our daughter is unthinkable." He squeezed my shoulder.

"I know. You and Mom are the greatest parents. As Jeff would say, 'You rock!'"

As we made our way to the stables, I thought about how different my life would have been had my birth parents survived and raised me at Overhome. As much as we adopted kids love and appreciate the parents who chose us, we cannot help but wonder about the life-line of birth—a tie most of us can never really know first-hand. I've seen pictures of Washington and Marian—looked through their trunk of keepsakes in the attic. Gazed upon their wedding photos and read their love letters. But I never knew them. I never will know them. It's a huge loss. An unexplainable, indescribable emptiness to be kept at a distance—a bittersweet corner of life to be visited, sometimes when we least expect it, but never banished completely.

We caught Carlos as he was preparing to give a riding lesson. Limping slightly, he moved toward Dad and extended his hand for a shake. "*Señor* Overton. Welcome back. We all looking forward to your arrival."

"It's good to be home, Carlos." Dad moved from stall to stall with an appraising eye, all the while chatting with Carlos. "The horses look healthy. And happy. Even more important." It was one horse aficionado to another; the two men were instantly on good terms.

"I have student for riding lesson in five minutes," Carlos said. "Will you return later so that we can continue our horse talk?" His dark eyes glowed with anticipation.

Dad laughed. "I'll probably still be here when you're done, Carlos. This is where I'm most at home." He turned to me. "How about a quick canter, Ashby?"

I'd moved automatically to Sasha's stall. "Gee, Dad, I'd love that. But I feel I should go back to the house. I've barely had a chance to talk to Mom, you know." I gave Sasha a longing look and stroked his neck. "Later, Sasha, boy," I murmured. He whinnied his response.

"You're right, of course. Your mother is champing at the bit to catch up with you." He caught my eye to see that I appreciated the horse analogy. "And then there's the wedding. I can only imagine the mother-daughter bonding that goes with that scenario." Dad rolled his eyes, then, looked at Carlos. "How about I saddle up?"

"Sure, *señor.* I'll let Eddie know. He keeps—how you say it—he keeps taps on all the horses."

"Good for Eddie. See you back at the house, Ashby." Moving toward the tack room with a huge smile on his face, Dad said to me in an undertone, "Taps, tabs, whatever. It's good to hear Eddie is taking his job seriously."

I gave Dad a thumbs-up. "Yep. All's well with the horses." I only wished I could say the same for the rest of the estate.

****

Dear Diary:

I'm feeling all warm and fuzzy about Mom and Dad's arrival. There's so much to look forward to and to worry about, as well. Mom and Monica (I call them the M&M Wedding Express) are already deep into nuptial plans. They insist I get serious about finding a bridal gown right now. Me: There's plenty of time for dress shopping. M&M: Oh, but you'll need time to find exactly the RIGHT dress. You won't know it until you've tried on dozens. And after you've found the perfect gown, there are the alterations, fittings, accessories...Sigh. There are a million other things I need to do right now.

And I have another little bothersome issue to deal with. I know it sounds adolescent, but I'm wondering where Luke and I will be able to—you know—meet. Talk. Plan. Make love. OK, that's the major point, isn't it? Where will we be able to be alone together? The guest cottage is out. The hayloft, scene of our first romantic tryst, is right above all the barn activity—Carlos, Eddie, Jeff and Nick and the riding students and Sam, constantly in and out. Even at night sometimes with the lighted riding ring in frequent use. And Luke and I certainly cannot meet in my room. Too obvious to the entire household what with both of us climbing the stairs to the catwalk that leads only to my room. Luke will stay in Miss Emma's second bedroom on the lower level, she's his great aunt and dearly loves my guy, but she'll be right across the hall from him— and she rarely leaves her apartment. So that's out for a meeting place. Needless to say, I am counting every minute until Luke arrives and we can be together after weeks apart. The question is: How?

Chapter 4

"Babe! I've missed you." Luke drew me into his arms and held me to his chest where I inhaled his familiar scent hungrily—earthy and clean as country air. He pulled away and looked at me. "God, how I have missed you." He bent to kiss me.

I caught my breath. "Oh, I've missed you, too, Luke Murley." I took in his square shoulders, nutmeg-brown eyes and infectious grin. I found it interesting that over his years at college Luke had lost most of his Southern drawl.

Luke ran his fingers through my hair, stroking it back from my face. "I don't know how it's possible, but you are more beautiful than ever." He kissed me again. "I have so much to tell you—about school and vet practice…"

"Well, I have a lot going on, too." I took Luke's hand. "Some things are just too complex. Texting—email—doesn't work for everything, you know. " We began walking toward the house. "My folks are in. They're dying to see you. And Jeff's been dancing around all day he's so excited about your coming home. I think they all begrudged my insistence on being first to greet you. All by myself, I mean."

Luke's face lit up. "A grand home-coming, for sure." He hesitated. "But, first, could we…"

"Check out the horses?" I finished his sentence.

"You and Dad—two of a kind!" Hand-in hand we jogged to the paddock.

"Luke! Luke!" Jeff intercepted us before we could reach our destination.

Luke wrapped my cousin in a bear hug, lifting his feet off the ground and twirling him around. "Look at you, buddy! You've grown a foot since I last saw you."

Jeff puffed out his chest and stood tall. "I'm the biggest kid in my class. Uh, for boys, that is." He blushed. "There's a couple of tall girls."

"And who's this?" Luke suddenly noticed Nick standing back a bit.

"My *amigo*, Nick," Jeff said. "You know, Carlos is his dad. They live in the guest house."

"Well, Nick." Luke extended a handshake. "Good to have you on board."

"Thanks," Nick murmured, making brief eye contact with Luke before ducking his head shyly.

"I grew up in that little house myself, with my grandpa, Abe. It's good to see it being used as a home again."

Sadness stabbed me at the mention of Abe who had died shortly after Luke left for college. Abe who loved to sit in the gazebo and reminisce about the old days when he was caretaker and trainer for my grandmother Lenore. It was common knowledge that Abe had been in love with her.

Luke moved toward the barn. "Now, who's going to show me what's going on with the horses?"

Jeff and Nick both jumped at the chance to show off their knowledge and expertise and, as they moved from horse to horse pointing out this and that, I used the opportunity to scout out Eddie to let him know Luke was home. I found him in the tack room cleaning up. Girths, long lines, saddles and bridles hung in an orderly fashion from hooks all around the walls of the small space. Eddie looked up from a show bridle he was cleaning.

"Ashby. What's up?"

"Luke's home for the weekend. The boys are showing him the horses."

Eddie carefully hung the bridle on its hook, then, turned a serious look on me. "Well, now that Luke's a certified vet, I guess he'll have a lot to say about how we're runnin' things."

I put my hand on his arm. "Don't worry, Eddie. I know Luke will appreciate the job you're doing. And he'll have a lot of work on his own dealing with farm animals and horses all over these parts. Are you afraid he'll try to run interference with you?"

Eddie looked sulky. "I jest don't think Luke was too happy about me takin' over his job here in th' stables. That's all."

I patted his arm and turned to leave.

"Ashby? Just remember…If Luke ever treats you bad, I'm here for ya."

"Thanks, Eddie." I worked hard to keep from smiling. Would poor Eddie ever give up the torch he was carrying for me?

****

Hours later, after the grand reunion between Luke and everybody else, and with some time left before Aunt Monica's family dinner party, I looked for Luke but he was nowhere to be found. I poked about the grounds, hoping to find him alone—maybe a chance to talk. Stables? Nope. Gazebo? Not there, either.

Thinking he may have gone to look at the lake, I headed down the steps to the dock.

Moore Mountain Lake took advantage of both man's ingenuity and nature's bounty. Formed by damming up three river valleys and flooding the land, the huge body of water meandered into dozens of coves along a cookie-cutter shoreline. Forested mountains encircled the cobalt waters like an emerald necklace. Great blue herons, hawks, osprey and American eagles flourished in the lush waterscape, undeterred by seasonal boaters, fishermen and water sports of every sort—for sure, peaceful coexistence of man and nature.

With the creation of the lake, many farms and other properties had to be inundated, but Overhome remained high and dry, for the most part, losing only some low-lying areas used primarily for family and slave cemeteries. We were left with a unique property: a lakefront historic plantation still functioning as a horse farm.

As I approached the dock, I noted a pair of kayakers in their low-slung, bright-yellow slipper-crafts sneaking silently along the shoreline. Dashing from the big water into our cove was a young girl on a jet ski, her ponytail flying behind her like a flag. A pontoon boat full of waving people lumbered placidly across the mouth of the cove. Summer at the lake! Hearing the whirring sound of a boat lift, I turned toward the dock. Sure enough, I found Luke standing atop a ladder positioned under the shaft that operates the cables to lift and lower the boat. In one hand was a grease gun and in the other a rag. Hanging in the lift was Uncle Hunter's beloved teal and cream-colored ski boat, still shiny and streamlined, despite its age.

Susan Coryell

I peered up at Luke. "What..?"

"Oh, hey. You found me. Caught me at an awkward moment."

"Luke! What are you doing up there?"

"Just applying a little oil to the lift cables."

I must have looked confused, for Luke laughed heartily. "I know, I know. With all there is to do." With a final swipe at the shaft, he climbed down the ladder and began to fold it up. "See, I've been thinking. I mean...where...how...?" He gave me a sly look. "These cables can be very noisy when we lower and raise the boat, ya know?"

It was my turn to chuckle. "Oh, Luke. I'd never have thought of it. What a great idea."

"Well, we can't use the guest cottage..."

"And we certainly can't meet in your room in your Aunt Emma's apartment."

"The hayloft is definitely off the list. I'm not into swatting wasps."

We fell into one another's arms. "It's perfect!" I said.

"We wait for dark—lower the boat in the lift. Quietly, now that I've oiled the driveshaft."

"Then we slip into the boat—do you like the pun?"

"Raise the boat with the lift remote...and we're out of sight and home free."

"Free and alone. You are a genius." I nudged him toward one of the wooden posts that supports the dock roof. When we were semi-blocked from view, I pulled him close and kissed him hard. Luke responded by hugging me so tightly I could feel the rapid pumping of his heart beneath his shirt. We kissed again.

A shrill wolf whistle from the direction of the lake

broke our embrace. Startled, we both laughed when we saw that one of the kayakers had noiselessly sidled alongside our dock, apparently approving our kiss. Moving on, he raised his paddle in the air and twirled it like a baton.

"That's why we wait until dark," Luke said.

Arm in arm we mounted the steps to the house. One little problem solved, I thought. Now, for the big one. Revealing my plan to save Overhome. I hoped it wouldn't ruin Monica's dinner party.

****

Monica had outdone herself. The dining room table sparkled with silver and china settings artfully arranged around bowls of fresh flowers, and candles, candles everywhere. The crystal chandelier centered above the table glittered like its own bright constellation. It was a picture for the cover of a glossy decorator magazine.

Everyone had dressed up for the occasion—the men in light-colored jackets and the ladies in summery dresses. Even Jeff had observed the dress code with a sky-blue polo shirt and khaki pants. But all eyes were on Miss Emma Coleville. Sitting tall and straight-backed, she looked elegant in a silver-gray shrug that somehow perfectly matched her hair. A strand of pearls encircled her neck, casting a creamy glow onto her pale features. Her cheeks sported a faint, pink blush of excitement.

"Miss Emma!" Dad took her hand and raised it to his lips. "You are a wonder. How lucky we are to have you grace this table."

"Thank you, Madison. Monica and Ashby and Jeff—they've made me feel like family."

"Family. Yes. Exactly that, Miss Emma. We are all

family here. And glad of it."

Miss Emma nodded and smiled, and I thought how kind she had been to me when I first arrived at Overhome five years ago. How thoughtfully and patiently she had helped me through that first rough summer when I was searching for self—trying to find the true identity of Ashby Overton—born at Overhome, adopted and raised up North.

With a twinge, my thoughts turned to my mission for tonight's event. Should I announce my bad news with the appetizer and get it over with, then try to enjoy the rest of the meal? Or should I let everybody chow down and savor the reunion through the main course before hitting them with my intentions to sell off the tract of land? The more I thought about it, the easier it was to put it all off until dessert. Replete with good food and mellow homecoming feelings, my listeners might react less negatively to such a jarring proposal. And maybe, by then, my nerve would be geared up for the ordeal.

"A toast!" Dad held his champagne flute high. "A toast to the soon-to-be bride and groom, Ashby and Luke!"

Glasses clinked all around the table. Luke, sitting across from me, caught my eye and pantomimed a kiss.

"To the Overton family," Mom called out.

"And to Overhome," Monica added.

More glass-clinking. I squirmed. What an ironic toast I could make myself: "To Overhome Junior Estates—fifty custom homes and a group dock!" But I kept quiet. Now was not the time.

Mariana's wonderful food almost got me through the meal without thinking of my mission. Roasted beef tenderloin, creamy mashed potatoes, grilled asparagus, dinner rolls so light they had to be anchored to the plate with butter to keep them from floating off into the air.

And the conversation any other time would have been enchanting. Tales of teaching from Mom and Dad, funny vet school stories from Luke, memories of Miss Emma's youth at Overhome. I chimed in myself with vignettes from college, and Jeff kept up a constant chatter about his and Nick's adventures on horseback.

"Ashby has discovered something quite interesting," Monica said with a suddenness that brought the table to a hush. "An old house near the edge of the property. Hal Reynolds, a friend of mine who happens to be a historian, thinks it may be the overseer's cottage from back before the Civil War."

Dad cocked his head. "I remember it—made of limestone? Remote from Overhome proper."

"Mostly covered in kudzu now, Dad. It's pretty dilapidated."

"We boys used to explore it until our father boarded it up and forbade us to go near the place. It's still standing, you say?"

Mariana arrived with a platter containing a molded flan and a plate of cookies, which Jeff recognized as Miss Emma's.

"Yay! Miss Emma's cookies!" He clapped his hands and everyone laughed.

I knew I could put it off no longer. "Yes, Dad. The cottage is still standing." I stood up, looking around the table, gaining eye contact from each and every one. "Concerning that, I have an announcement." Luke shot me a questioning look, which, any other time would have made me laugh. "This has been a special evening.

Monica, I thank you for the lovely table setting, the wonderful meal. Every significant, important person in my life is gathered here tonight. I love you all."

All eyes were on me, the room silent. Their looks—puzzled. Curious, for sure. "There's something you all need to know, something I've known for some time. I wanted to know my facts before sharing this…this bad news. There's no other way to put it. Bad news. Terrible news."

The curious looks turned to alarm. Luke stood up and walked around the table to my side. "Ashby, what is it? What's wrong?"

I wanted to cling to him, throw myself on his neck and weep, but I stood strong. "Overhome is broke. Our income no longer supports our expenses. I've eked out the money for this year's taxes. I can't apply for a mortgage until I have full-time employment. We have to do something very soon, or we'll be in serious financial trouble."

They seemed to exhale in unison. Dad was the first to speak. "You're sure?" He shook his head, "Of course, you've gone over the books, checked it out with an accountant…."

"Damn." It was Luke. "I don't see how…when I left off doing the books…what? Five years ago? We were solvent—better than that. We were in the black. The horses, brood mares, the riding school…."

"Oh, this is my fault," Monica wailed. "It was that accountant I hired after Hunter died. He assured me we could double our money with his investment strategy. The money disappeared almost as fast as he did. I should never have allowed him to talk me into his schemes. And all of my personal funds are tied up in a trust for Jefferson. For when he turns twenty-five."

"What's your plan, Ashby?" Miss Emma's quiet voice intervened. "I'm sure you have one, dear."

I stood up straight, finding Luke's hand. I held it tight. "My plan is to sell off a fifty-acre plot—the land on which the old overseer's cottage stands, actually. I've already spoken to a Realtor. He says it can be developed and sold to a builder of custom homes. Fifty of them—one per acre."

I waited for the reactions, but it was a long, silent time until someone spoke.

"I realize I'm the only one here without a long-time personal connection to Overhome," my mother said. "So, in a way, that makes me more objective. Right?" She did not wait for an answer. "From a practical standpoint, Ashby, will we see these homes? Will they obstruct our view of the lake? Will they in any way devalue the property? And won't there still remain over five hundred acres of Overton land untouched?"

My mother, the mediator. The peacemaker. Always the voice of reason. I opened my mouth to answer her, when I became aware of a tinkling sound emerging from the crystal chandelier. The teardrop crystals shook, rubbing against each other. Louder and louder. Everyone looked up as the lights blinked and the ceiling began to vibrate like an upside-down earthquake. There was a crackle and a flash as the huge fixture centered over the dining table began to swing, then dropped from the ceiling, caught by a single slender wire which saved it from crashing to the table. There it continued to hang and swing, the crystals rattling against one another like chattering teeth.

"My God!" Dad cried. Mom covered her head

protectively with her arms. Jeff stared in stunned amazement. Monica put her head on the table and wept silently. Luke and I just looked at each other, wide-eyed.

"Oh no." Miss Emma spoke so quietly that I was not sure anyone except Luke and I heard her. "Not again."

Chapter 5

"Why didn't you tell me?" Luke sounded hurt. He pulled me closer, kissing my ears and neck. "Maybe I could have done something to help."

We lounged against the soft, cream-colored boat cushions, snuggling beneath a light blanket Luke had thought to bring. Suspended in the lift some seven feet above the dock, we could enjoy everything about the mild summer night and nobody would ever suspect us of being there. Overhome slept silently from her hill high above.

"Why didn't I tell you? Some things are better left for face-to-face communication. Anyway, the damage was done long before anyone knew; it was simply too late and the knowledge that Overhome is broke would only have worried you—maybe thrown off your exam grades or something. We hired Carlos, who has done such a good job these past two years…I've been hoping for a miracle that didn't or couldn't happen." I sighed. "I just didn't want *you* to feel responsible."

Luke stroked my arms. "And you're a big girl now and maybe don't need my help with such things as family finance."

"Luke Murley! You know that's not the issue." I sat up. "Sure, it's my responsibility. And you would be the one best person to act as a resource on the family finances. Uncle Hunter always praised you for your 'impeccable' book keeping." I lay back and nestled comfortably under his chin. "Once I discovered there was no hope, I knew I had to act on my own to find a solution. If there's any blame for selling off the piece of land, there's no need for you to share in it."

"Well, we're in this together, babe. And I, for one, think your plan is solid."

"I've been counting on your support. We'll just have to wait—see how the others weigh in. But I can't project any better means of salvation, and I doubt anyone else can either. You know, it's odd, when I think of it. First, I fell in love with the house and grounds, then with the horses, and now I am all about the entire estate. Overhome, the horse farm."

"Didn't you forget something? Something else you fell in love with?"

I smacked him hard on his arm. "You big lug. That goes without saying. And I can't wait until you get your practice up and running; we'll be in a much better place financially."

"Believe me, babe. I'm working toward that goal every single day."

We lay comfortably in each other's arms. Night sounds on the lake surrounded us: the gentle lap-lap of water against the shore, the occasional slap of a fish breaking the surface, a peeper choir chorusing in the trees around the dock. It almost seemed sacrilege to bring up the crashing chandelier, but I took a deep breath and pressed on. "Well, what do you think about the dining room drama?"

"Been thinking of nothing else, to tell the truth."

"You heard Miss Emma's comment: 'Oh no, not again.' You know what she meant, don't you?"

"'Fraid so. It was my thought, too."

"I doubt the others have a clue, though. I mean, Monica never knew about…and Jeff was too young. Except for brief visits the last few years, Dad and Mom have been away from Overhome for so long…"

"Do y'think it's Rosabelle again? Voicing her opinion in a—a dramatic fashion?" Luke frowned. "That was such a turbulent time for you, Ashby, your first summer at Overhome. Until you figured out there was a family ghost who only wanted to protect you."

"This is different." I chewed my lip in thought. "I don't know who, but *somebody*, it seems, does not approve of my proposal to sell off fifty acres. That chandelier—a violent reaction to my announcement— too timely to be dismissed."

"Somebody or some*thing*. Have y'seen any evidence…any other evidence, I mean…"

"As a matter of fact, yes. The day I explored the overseer's cottage. Even Sasha seemed to sense something out of the ordinary. Who knows, it could have been an other-worldly presence. And Jeff tells me he and Nick experience 'bad vibes' there. As for that chandelier, well, I've noticed it tinkling before tonight. For no apparent reason."

"Well, I have to agree. A crashing chandelier doesn't fit Rosabelle's M.O. She was more into making nice—leaving you roses, as I recall. Humming that old tune…what was it? Flow gently, sweet…something, I forget."

"It's 'Flow Gently, Sweet Afton.' We'll just have to be on the alert, I guess. As if the wedding and the real estate deal weren't enough to fill our time and attention."

"Hey! Don't lump our wedding in with a financial bailout scheme," Luke protested. "I can't believe my good luck—becoming a real veterinarian and marrying my beautiful babe all within a few short months." He brought my face to his and kissed me warmly. "I say we move on with your real estate plan. Who knows? The chandelier could've been a one-time thing."

I took a couple of yoga breaths. "Okay. New subject. Tell me about this vet tracking program you're involved in. I heard a couple of snippets at dinner, but I want more details, please. If I'm going to be the vet's wife, I need to become acquainted with the culture."

"It's some culture, believe me. Large animal practice is about the messiest, muddiest, dirtiest job on the planet. And I'm lovin' it!"

"So give me an example. What've you learned from the tracking practice?"

"Okay, you asked, so here's an interesting story. A horse owner calls Doc Forest, the vet I'm working with—says his horse has hives. We get there and the poor animal is so swollen that huge red bumps are showing through his hair. Doc Forest lets me give the injection and do the follow up. Next day I go see how the horse is doing. He's improved a lot—so much that I notice something odd on his lower left leg now that the swelling's gone down. Two tiny bite marks. I ask the owner if he noticed anything unusual yesterday and he said, 'Oh yeah. Found a dead copperhead in the horse's stall.'"

Luke snorted. "I felt like Sherlock Holmes. 'That's what caused the hives,' I told him. 'Your horse was bitten by the snake and then he stepped on it and killed it. The hives were a reaction to the venom.'"

"That's a great tale! Tell me more!"

"You're not going to put this down in one of those romance stories you're writing, are you?"

"Not much romance in a copperhead biting a horse, now is there?" I laughed. "More!"

Just then a beeping sound broke in. "What's that?" I looked around. "A boat alarm or something?"

Luke reached into his pocket. "Oh. That's my beeper. I forgot all about it. They always give the new kid on the block weekend on-call duty. Let me check this out."

After a moment of fiddling with the device and listening, he stood up. "Sorry, babe. I've gotta leave— gotta go check this out."

My face must have shown my disappointment, for Luke took me by the hands and pulled me to him, kissing me gently. "Seems Dr. Forest is more than ready to turn this one over to me. It's that cantankerous old horse Cupcake over at Hadley's farm. Dr. Forest is half afraid of Cupcake, she's so mean. But there's some problem, and the owner thinks it can't wait for morning. So, I'm off."

"There's always tomorrow night." I tried to sound upbeat. "Same time? Same place?"

Luke kissed me again. "Yep. Tomorrow we'll— you know—get in some *us* time. Not so much talk-talk-talk." Returning the beeper to his pocket, Luke pressed the remote and the boat slowly descended to dock-level. We walked hand in hand up the stairs to the house.

****

"I've wracked my brain, Ashby, for details about the old cottage." Miss Emma poured a cup of hot tea for me. "Lemon, no sugar?" she asked, looking up briefly.

My gaze took in the familiar surroundings of Miss Emma's cozy apartment. Flowery slipcovers, over-stuffed furniture, gingham draperies—all in soothing pastels which softened and warmed the compact space. Warm and completely comfortable—just like Miss Emma herself. I accepted the china cup and saucer with a contented sigh.

She poured herself a cup before settling back into her arm chair. "What's the old proverb—'the devil is in the details'?"

"Details. Absolutely! You have always been one for remembering little things long-forgotten by everyone else. Important things." Over the years, Miss Emma had filled me in on so much of her life as confidante to Lenore that I felt I knew my grandmother intimately, though she died in a bizarre riding accident before I was born.

"Well, you see, as girls, Lenore and I were always alert to any tidbits the grown-ups tried to hide. And in those days, believe me, anything the least bit spicy was hushed up. Big time, as Jeff would say."

I smiled, imagining Miss Emma as a sprightly, curious young girl, boon companion to Lenore, the two of them pricking up their ears for juicy news around the estate. I knew they spent many hours perusing the family diaries in the attic where they discovered long lost loves and fears and feuds among the generations of Overtons as recorded by the women of the family.

"There was something 'spicy' as you say regarding the overseer's cottage?"

She was quiet for a moment, so I added, "Was the cottage actually used by the slave overseer, as Hal seems to think?"

"I don't know. Slavery was long gone by the time Lenore and I were coming up. Though descendants of those slaves live all around us now." She reached for a plate of cookies and offered it to me. "Just baked this morning."

"Ummm. I can't resist your chocolate chip wonders, Miss Emma. Thanks." I bit into one of the rich confections. "Yum! Now—about the spicy tidbits involving the cottage?"

"Yes, all hush-hush, of course, but I distinctly remember that there was a parade of folks who stayed in that house. Used for tenants who worked at Overhome, it became a revolving door. A worker would rent it for a few months, then, disappear mysteriously—often in the middle of the night—leaving no forwarding address. I remember one fellow particularly because he seemed to be overly interested in Lenore. She was quite the beauty, you know." Miss Emma smiled, perhaps at the recollection of my grandmother.

"Go on, please."

"Well, said admirer went galloping off on his horse one afternoon, white-faced, carrying a single suitcase, and muttering under his breath, with nary a backward glance at Lenore or me or Overhome itself. He looked downright terrified. We never saw him again."

Miss Emma sipped her tea and looked reflective. "After that the family seems to have quit renting out the cottage. It fell into disrepair, and we girls were warned to stay away."

"Did you? Stay away, I mean? Adventuresome as you and Lenore were, I'd think you might take that as a challenge."

Miss Emma rocked back in her chair. "You're

right. In those days it was easy to get to the cottage by road. We played house there, had tea parties for our dolls in the kitchen, even sneaked in the ancient family diaries from the attic for secret reading. Heaven knows we might have used the place for teenage trysts...but..."

She paused so long I wondered if she had lost her train of thought. "I guess you'd say we discovered what might have caused the tenants to run off with such regularity. At any rate, I was scared enough to refuse to go back to the place ever again. Lenore would have continued sneaking in—claimed to have a theory about how to confront whatever it was. But she was reluctant to go back to the cottage without me."

I sat up straighter. "What did you discover, Miss Emma? What scared you?"

Miss Emma shut her eyes and began to recite, trance-like: "Once upon a midnight dreary, while I pondered weak and weary, over many a quaint and curious volume of forgotten lore—While I nodded, nearly napping, suddenly there came a tapping, as of someone gently rapping, rapping at my chamber door."

When she paused to take a breath, I placed my cup and saucer on the coffee table with deliberation. "Miss Emma, there are details and then there are details! Whatever are you talking about?"

"Sorry, Ashby. I had to get that out of my system. You see, Lenore and I agreed to meet at the cottage late one night for a forbidden sleepover. We'd stashed blankets and pillows and candles and some food. It was a fine summer night, I recall. A sliver of moon shone through the window, and there were friendly night sounds—you know—crickets—moths fluttering around the candles. We were settling in, taking turns reading those famous lines from Poe's 'The Raven,' to set the mood for a scary night. 'The Raven' was our favorite because of Lenore's name and Poe's '…sorrow for the lost Lenore.'"

She looked at me to see if I was following her and I gave her an encouraging nod. "We'd just gotten to that part that says '…Quoth the Raven, nevermore,' when, suddenly, all sounds evaporated into a deadly hushed void. Lenore and I looked at each other, hardly breathing in the silence. It was like a tornado had sucked the air right out of the place. Then, the noises began. Odd noises. Frightening noises. Certainly none of Poe's 'tapping' at the chamber door. More like moaning. Crying. Then crashing, thumping sounds. The candles flickered, and went out, all at the same time. It was unbelievably dark, but we stumbled our way to the door, desperate to get out. Then we heard it. The voice. Barely a whisper, like it was emerging from the depths of a well, but I clearly remember the words."

Maddeningly she paused again. If Miss Emma was trying to be dramatic, she had my attention, for sure. I looked at her, my eyes big, waiting. She tilted her head, shaking it slightly. "It made no sense. But it was frightening, nonetheless. That coarse whisper in the dark of night."

"Miss Emma! You're killing me. The 'coarse whisper.' What did the whisperer say?"

Her eyes shut briefly again, as she remembered. "'Go away! He's dead.' That's what we heard. Then just the two words repeated: 'He's dead.'"

I stared at her in silence. Finally I offered, "Do…do you think someone was living there on the sly—without renting—a squatter? Trying to scare you two off or something?"

"That did occur to us. But we couldn't broach the subject to our elders without giving away our own misdeeds—sneaking into the cottage. Besides…"

"You two thought it was a spirit, didn't you, Miss Emma?"

"Naturally. We were young and impressionable."

"And you'd just given a choral rendition of one of the creepiest poems in American literature." I crossed my arms and leaned back into the chair.

"It was long ago, Ashby. Long ago and, probably best forgotten."

"Well, I'm planning to tell Luke your story. That all right with you, Miss Emma?"

"As you like, dear."

"One more thing. Do you think there's a connection. Between the overseer's cottage and the…the free-wheeling chandelier?"

"The past is always with us. We cannot escape it, even if we desperately want to. Especially at Overhome." She gave me a clear-eyed, head-on look. "Now be on your way. You'll want to spend every minute with Luke before he has to go back to school or his next veterinary assignment or wherever. Oh dear. What bad timing this all is." She shook her head sadly. "Long ago and best forgotten," she said again.

****

Dear Diary:

I'd love to report that Luke and I had better luck our second night in the "Love Boat," but—sigh—the damn beeper interrupted us once again. One or two kisses

52

in—and there it was—calling the novice vet to duty with its implacable bleep, bleep, bleep. I am now calling it that "blessed bleeping beeper." Though I tried valiantly to stay awake for Luke's return, I awoke at dawn swaddled under the blanket and in danger of rolling off the long seat onto the floor of the boat. Where was Luke? Turns out he'd been out all night with the cranky old mare Cupcake again. He arrived home after breakfast, bleary-eyed and disheveled. "First, she tried to head-butt me and then she swished her tail back and forth, letting me know for sure a kick was coming. She slung me around for a while, but I hung on 'til she stopped from sheer fatigue." Poor Luke. "Good thing she's so old," he mumbled over his cold toast. "I don't know if I could've outlasted her in her prime." Then he gave me a sour look. "And I have to get back to school before lunch time. My advisor wants a run-down on my adventures with Cupcake, the Culinary Catastrophe."

So—long story short—Luke's back at Tech, and I'm wondering what to fix first. I have an interview with a local pottery maker for an article for my Blue Ridge rag, and Jeff is salivating for our visit to the overseer's cottage, and the Realtor wants to share details about the sale. Dad would like to go over the books to see if there's any other recourse for financial rescue than selling off the land parcel and the M&Ms are sidling in for bridal dress shopping. All I want now is a nice, long, relaxing canter with my sweet Sasha. Fat chance, eh?

Oh yeah. How could I forget the thought that haunts me. Another ghost at Overhome? What are the chances of that? Can I take Poe literally? "Quoth the Raven, nevermore."

Chapter 6

We'd been driving for what seemed like ages and my sweet mother had hardly paused for breath. "Now, don't worry about finding the perfect gown on your first outing. Not that you'll have any difficulty with size. You've exactly the right figure. Tall and slim— just like the models."

"Mom, I swear, you're more psyched about my wedding dress than I am."

She laughed. "Guess I have been going on and on. Sorry. But it is deliciously exciting, isn't it?"

"I've lost my knack for shopping. I never had much spare time in college. And living miles from malls all these years at Overhome—well, as I said, I'm out of practice."

"Too bad Monica couldn't come along. I can just imagine what elegance she would work into the formula for finding the ONE."

I snickered. "Yeah and we'd have to win the lottery to finance it. Monica's taste is pretty high-end. I was thinking of getting her input on something impossible to jack up the price on—say a hair clip? Oh no. She'd definitely go for the diamond and ruby model. I'm gonna need your help, Mom."

My mother patted my knee. "Well, anyway, it's nice that Hal invited Monica to accompany him. She told me he's discovered some Overton ancestry information up in Page County—in the Shenandoah Valley. Thinks it can shed light on Overhome's history."

"Hal and Monica are spending a lot of time together," I said, turning into the bridal shop parking lot.

My mother giggled. "Looks like a budding romance to me. But I think Hal's still at the 'I-need-an-excuse-to-see-you' stage. Also, he's looking into that old house you discovered—what did he call it?"

"The overseer's cottage."

"Yes. As I said, though, maybe it's just an excuse to spend time with Monica. Who knows?"

Finding a parking space, I pulled the key from the ignition and let off my seat belt. "Okay. Here we are. Let's see what Bradford Bride has to offer."

Nothing with diamonds and rubies, was my silent hope.

"Too frou-frou—too dazzlingly white. Wrong neck-line, and I hate the bustle on the back of that one." I eyed the line of hanging gowns I'd already tried on—each one a reject—despite what my mother calls my perfect figure. I looked like some version of Prom Queen Ashby in every single one. "I want something simple."

"But elegant," Mom finished. "I told you, we need Monica."

The sales clerk removed several hangers from the rack. "There are still a few gowns from last year's bridal line back in storage. I always like to show the prospective brides what's newest in the fashion world first, but I remember there were several 'simple but elegant' dresses left in the back. I'll just be a moment, if you'll excuse me."

Mom and the sales lady were completely unhurried and unruffled, but I was growing frustrated. Part of me was saying, It's just a dress, but I really did care about Luke's viewpoint. I didn't want him on our wedding day to think, *Oh no—am I marrying marshmallow fluff?*

The sales clerk returned, hefting a huge box. "I just remembered this designer number. It's from a season ago, and it's a classic."

Slipping into the creamy satin folds, I twirled in front of the multiple mirrors, leaning this way and that, bending, dipping. "Well, Mom. What do you think?"

My mother's rapt expression said it all. "That color—ivory—is perfect with your blonde hair. Adds a little cream to your cheeks—points up your eyes of blue. It is absolutely *you,* Ashby. The lean lines cling to your figure like…like they were painted there by a master artist." She made a complete circle around me, her smile increasing until she was positively beaming. "The neckline is perfectly sculptured for a single strand of pearls. Even the length works—touches the floor with just room enough for heels. Oh my! I think I'm going to cry."

The clerk nodded knowingly. "Designed by Patricia of Boston—the very best when it comes to simple but elegant." Then, as if anticipating my concern, she added, "And since it's been in storage for a while, we can offer you a very nice discount—to include any alterations necessary."

Mom clapped her hands. "I can't believe how lucky you were to find the ONE so quickly. Why, I must have gone to a dozen shops before I found my own perfect wedding gown."

Unbeknownst to Mom, I already had my accessories—the delicate wedding veil with its crown of seed pearls and the matching pearl necklace—like she said—a single strand. They were in my hope chest where they've been lying in wait for my wedding day. My mother—that is, my bio-mother, Marian, had worn them when she married Washington Overton. I'd discovered them in a trunk in the attic my first summer at Overhome. I've always felt she left them there for me.

"Thanks, Mom." I turned to the sales lady. "Thanks for locating this gown. I love it."

My mother did, indeed, brush a few tears from her cheek. "I'm afraid Monica will be disappointed. She let me know there was no possible way you would find anything remotely suitable on your first trip out, and she has every intention of helping you shop for your bride's dress."

"She'll get over it." I sincerely hoped she would not try to make up for missing the event. Monica did tend to over-do things.

Mom brightened. "Lovely! Now let's do lunch." She looked at her watch. "Oh, it's already one o'clock. Hurry now."

I laughed. "Let me get dressed, first."

By the time I reached the cashier's counter, my mother had already taken care of the deposit on the dress. When I protested, she gently but firmly indicated that this was to be her contribution to the wedding expenses. "I insist, Ashby. I am paying for your wedding gown, your accessories, and your going-away outfit as well. I've been saving a little money from each paycheck for years. Some folks have a Christmas fund.

I have a *wedding* fund—for you. I *am* the mother of the bride, you know."

I hugged her and shed a few tears of my own. "I'm so glad you're here for me, Mom," was all I could get out. "To have your support. Yours and Dad's. I love you guys."

I felt a hundred pounds lighter as I drove home. I hadn't realized how burdensome shopping could be. Before I came to Overhome, where I grew up in New Jersey, my best buds and I lived for mall-hauls—though I never had as much to spend as most of my friends. I worked odd jobs for my own spending money, so I was pretty thrifty. A handy habit—especially now.

"…worried about Nick," my mother was saying. Deep in my own thoughts, I'd missed what she was talking about.

"Nick? Jeff's friend Nick. I didn't realize you'd even met him. Why the worry?"

"It's almost impossible to interact with Jeff without Nick—they're thick as thieves. And I certainly wouldn't know much about either one of them, except for the backseat confidential."

"Sorry, Mom. You lost me. Backseat confidential?"

"Oh, it's a great technique for finding out stuff kids wouldn't otherwise let on. When you were a 'tween' I used to offer to drive you and your girlfriends places just so I could get in on the backseat talk. It was as if you forgot the driver had ears. I learned all kinds of things I wouldn't otherwise have been privy to."

"Really!"

"For example, one day when you and a friend were in the backseat, I heard about your first kiss—that cute soccer player—Nibsy, I think you called him. And another time I learned how you got caught trying to skip school the day you had to share your…um…*disappointing* sewing project with the Life Studies class, only the young math teacher sneaking a smoke outside the door coaxed you into returning to class. He said he wouldn't tell on you as long as you didn't tell on him. Oh, and…"

I held up my hand in protest. "Okay, okay. I get it! So, what did you glean from the backseat occupied by Nick and Jeff?"

"I offered to take them to see a movie. You know, since school will be out for the summer in a matter of days. Sort of a reward. Anyway, I heard Nick telling Jeff that his report card was going to get him in trouble with his parents. Seems he's having a problem with reading and it's affecting his grades in several classes, including English and history. And he most definitely does *not* want to have to attend summer school."

"Jeff goes to a private school, but I assume Nick's in the local public middle school—what? Seventh grade?" I asked.

"Yes. Oh, I've read about the local budget crisis in the public schools and how the reading teacher was cut. Reading is considered a frill, I suppose. Class sizes are huge. No doubt Nick's English teacher is already overwhelmed with a packed classroom and no aides." She shook her head sadly. "I've been involved in public education for thirty years, you know. All of these budget cuts just make it that much harder for everyone—especially the teachers and the students who struggle—for whatever reason." She frowned. "I don't need the backseat to tell me that."

"With Nick—his reading problems—do you think it's a language thing?"

"He's certainly fluent in English, but if Carlos and Mariana speak Spanish at home or are not able to offer Nick help with homework—well—it could contribute to the problem."

"Nick was born in the U.S.—lived here all his life. Carlos and Mariana are studying for citizenship as we speak. Years ago, they came from Argentina on a work visa—got their green card—completely legal."

"I'd wondered about their legal status," Mom said. "How did they end up at Overhome?"

"It was quite a process. Aneesh, Luke's college roommate, comes from a long line of vets—in Northern Virginia. His dad knew about Carlos' reputation as a trainer in the hunt country up there. We knew we needed to do something to bring in more cash. So, on the advice of Aneesh's dad, Luke brought Carlos to Overhome, showed him around, interviewed him. When Carlos saw that he and his family could use the guest house and that Mariana could work for us, too, he came on board. That was two years ago."

"Interesting," Mom said. "I forgot that they're from Argentina. I only met them once, I believe, on a quick trip to Overhome over a year ago."

"Carlos Vasquez was a well-known young rider in the Argentine hunter-jumper amateur circuit. He was getting quite a name for himself when he suffered a terrible injury."

"What happened?"

"I got this from Mariana. Carlos is reluctant to talk about his past. Mariana says he'd started over a jump when his horse stopped short—spooked by a camera flash. The horse left long, scissored the rail, did a rotational fall and landed on Carlos. It crippled him for life."

Mom flinched. "So that explains the limp."

"Afterwards, he apprenticed with expert trainers in Argentina and became so accomplished, he never lacked for employment. But coming to the U.S. had been a life-long dream for both him and Mariana."

"Argentina's loss and our gain."

I nodded. "We wanted to bump up our training and riding lessons. For income purposes. Our idea was that Carlos would bring in more boarders and riders. And it worked—so well that we hired Julio as an assistant trainer and Sam. Then, in the economic upheaval, we lost business. With our money reserves gone, the expenses just got to be more than we could handle. And now there's nothing left to operate on a day-to-day basis."

"Which is why you're looking to sell off some of the property."

"If we can just back up our current operation— maybe expand it—and Luke can get a toe-hold with his veterinary practice, we'll eventually be able to move into the black."

Mom stroked her chin as she thought. "I may not be able to help Overhome, but I might be able to lend a hand to the Vasquez family—offer to work with Carlos and Mariana on their upcoming citizenship tests and tackle Nick's reading problems at the same time. That way it wouldn't seem like I'm singling out Nick as needy. And the citizenship process can be tricky." She frowned. "I'll tread lightly. Could be a sensitive issue for all of them." She looked at me, her eyes bright.

"What do you think, Ashby?"

"I think that you've barely retired from education, and you're about to plunge in again. Teaching is as natural as breathing for you."

Mom looked thoughtful. "Literacy has a life of its own. I'm just an enabler."

"Yeah—well—I have my own literacy assignment to deal with. Going to interview the folks who run Moore Creek Pottery for an article in *Blue Ridge Heritage*. I have a tight deadline, so I'm actually thrilled the dress is a done deal. One less thing to worry about."

"Remember, Ashby. You yourself said it. We're here for you—Dad and I. We're your moral support, if nothing else. Don't ever hesitate to call on us. No matter what."

"How's Dad when it comes to real estate? Do you think he might go along with me next time I meet with Paul Gordon?"

"I think he's been hoping you'd ask!"

I managed a high five from the driver's seat. "Right on! I'll talk to Dad as soon as we get home. Thanks, Mom. Did I tell you I love you guys?"

****

Dad stood at the base of a ladder, looking up and talking to an electrician. "So you can't find any reason for the fixture falling down, you say?"

"It's old, for sure. Can't say I've ever seen a chandelier older'n this one. Look, Mr. Overton." He moved aside so that Dad could peer at the ceiling opening he'd created. "This beam it's hooked to is solid as Gibraltar."

"And the bolts?"

"Again, old, a bit rusty, but solid. So tight I had to use a ratchet to get 'em off." The electrician tapped the beam. "I got no idea what caused it t'fall." He tapped the beam again. "Anyway, it won't happen again, I can promise you that. I've double bolted it with new, heavy-duty bolts. And I've completely re-wired it to code." He closed the hole up and descended the ladder. "A 300-pound gorilla could swing on this here light fixture and it wouldn't give an inch. Guaranteed."

"Thanks, I appreciate your candor—and your expertise. Now, what do we owe you?"

"I'll take care of it, Dad," I interrupted.

Dad gave me his don't-argue-I'm-the-dad look. "We can discuss that later," he told me, taking the bill from the electrician's hand.

He waited for the worker to leave, then, looked at me. "Ashby, your mother and I are staying here until we can find a permanent home. And until we do, we intend to pay our fair share of bills."

"But, Dad...."

He put his index finger gently to my lips. "Food, utilities, and, yes, upkeep. We're getting decent retirement pay, between us, you know, and we have no intention of mooching off our daughter—taking advantage of your natural generosity. End of discussion." Before I could protest, he walked past me and out the door. He didn't say anything about how I could ill afford upkeep for Overhome myself.

Just then Jeff peered around the dining room door. "I heard what the guy said about the chandelier." With a puzzled expression, he looked up at the magnificent crystal fixture. "So...why did it crash?"

"Very curious. We'll probably never know—just a

fluke or something, I think."

Jeff's quick mind ricocheted in another direction. "Hey, Ashby, wanna go exploring? Now? Could we?"

"Sure, why not. I've been craving a little horseback time."

"Can Nick come, too? We both dig the place."

"Sounds like you've put your claim on the old cottage."

"It's our clubhouse. Our *casa*."

"Will you be totally bummed if we have to tear it down? For the sale of the property?"

Jeff gave me a sidelong look. "Well, it's been there a long time, right?" He did not wait for my reply before hurrying on. "There's just something *different* about it, ya know?"

"Let me say—we need to be watchful. And careful—not to go blundering into a situation we may not fully fathom."

"Well, then, let's explore! Meet you at the stables." Jeff trotted off to find his friend.

I thought again about Miss Emma's recollection when she and Lenore had camped out in the old cottage. Now, in the same space, all these many years later, Nick and Jeff had experienced…what? I looked once more at the chandelier, hanging stately and pristine as though it had not done an acrobatic feat of its own volition a few days ago. I would have to follow my own advice: Be watchful. Be careful. I could see the ad Paul Gordon would write up: *For sale. Fifty acres wooded property with lake view. Ghost thrown in for free.*

Chapter 7

"Nick's dad wouldn't let him come with us," Jeff grumbled. "Says he can't go anywhere or do anything fun until he's finished studying for final exams."

"Well, I can see why that's important." I urged Sasha over the rough ground, avoiding rocks and ruts as best I could. Jeff followed on Sunshine.

"Nick's parents are gonna make him go to summer school if his final grades aren't good. That sure would wreck our plans for summer." My cousin looked so glum I felt the need to cheer him up somehow.

"Maybe there's something we can do, Jeff. To help Nick avoid summer school."

Jeff flashed a hopeful look. "For real?"

"You know, my mother and father are both retired educators. My mom told me she'd be interested in tutoring Nick—to help him with reading and language and any other academic problems he might have." I checked for Jeff's reaction before continuing. "Seems she overheard you two discussing Nick's school troubles."

"That'd be awesome, Ashby! No summer school!"

"Don't get your hopes up yet. Carlos and Mariana have to agree to the plan. And Nick would have to be completely on board—willing to cooperate—work hard over the summer."

"He'll do it! They'll do it! I know they will!"

"Mom only mentioned it as a possibility. It's by no means a done deal."

Jeff was not hearing me. Too late, I realized I should have kept my mouth shut until all parties were in accord. "You have to promise not to say anything until the adults have worked out the details. Promise, Jeff?"

Jeff nodded so vigorously that his freckles bounced. Then his face lit up. "But I can't wait to tell Nick!"

I gave an inward groan. No way to stuff this genie back into the lamp.

We left the horses to graze and made our way to the cottage. Sasha did not display any skittishness this time, perhaps because of Jeff's horse, Sunshine. The two stood in contented companionship, cropping grass.

Following Jeff to the front door, once again I marveled at the sturdiness of the old building. That's stone for you. However, the rotting porch floor offered precarious footing. Carefully, Jeff stood at the front door. "We loosened these boards over the entrance. Left the nails in, though." Moving trailing stems of kudzu aside, he wrenched several warped boards loose and pushed in the door. "When we leave, we just press them back like they were. You can't tell they were moved." He looked pleased with himself. "Come on in!"

Stepping inside, I looked around cautiously, peering into corners for any lurking snakes. There wasn't much to see from this vantage point. Interior stone walls, once covered with some kind of paint or whitewash, showed peeling and flaking here and there. Scuffed wood floors, recessed windows, some cracked, a few scattered, broken-down chairs and a table with one side of its drop-leaf gaping floor-ward like an open mouth completed the gloomy scene. A stone fireplace climbed from floor to ceiling on the central wall, its rock face smudged with ancient smoke residue. I rubbed my arms to smooth out the goose bumps caused by the damp chill.

I sniffed the air. "Ugh. That's a nasty smell. You and Nick leave something in here that might have rotted?"

Jeff wrinkled his nose. "Nope. It always smells funky. Like something died, maybe."

"More like rotten eggs." I exhaled. "Phew! Gross."

"You get used to it after a while."

We picked our way across a pitted floor to the room on the other side of the chimney. A few door-less cupboards and a dried-up counter topped with ribbons of age-dried paint of at least five different colors were the last remaining remnants of what must have once been the kitchen. Cobwebs and dust were the only decorations.

Jeff beckoned. "Come here. I want to show you some stuff." Leading me back through the main room to a smaller one, he pointed out a narrow, curved staircase, very steep, leaning against one wall. "It leads to a loft," he pointed up. "I'll go first, then, you can come. One at a time."

"Good idea. It looks pretty sturdy, but do you think it's safe? There're no railings to hold onto."

"Me and Nick use it all the time." Nimbly he ascended the steps. Peering down from the top, he encouraged, "Your turn. Piece of cake."

"Here goes nothing," I muttered. Clinging to the wall on the left, I fought off vertigo. The stairs were incredibly steep.

Jeff reached for my hand. "Here, I'll help you." He reeled me in and I stood, steadying myself before brushing off my jeans.

"Here's our clubhouse," Opening his arms expansively, Jeff offered me the view of the good-sized space. The ceiling sloped on both sides from a peak barely above our heads. "We've tried to make it homey," he said with an embarrassed laugh.

I took it all in. "Okay. Not bad for two guys. I dig the folding chairs and pillows. Nice use of a crate for a table, with candles. Supply box with flashlights, batteries, matches, some bowls and spoons." I sifted through the contents of a cardboard box, then, pointed to one wall. "And a shelf of books! *Boys' Club Series*, *Horse Sense*, *Black Beauty*, *The Black Stallion*, *The Red Pony*, a pile of Spiderman and Superman comic books and a vintage copy of *Huckleberry Finn*. Very nice, indeed."

"I love to read, but Nick—well, you know, it's hard for him. I thought if we had comics and books and stuff in the clubhouse he might get better at it. We both love horse stories." I made a note to tell Mom this nugget of information, thinking it might help her with the tutoring project.

I surveyed the space again. "These beams in the ceilings—the paneling on the walls—I'm amazed at what good condition they're in. Have you found any evidence of critters?"

"Lots of little bones. We got rid of 'em." Jeff reached for a small cup with a handle on each side. "We found this cup under the eaves when we were clearing out the bones." He shifted the receptacle from side to side in the light. "I think it's made of tin or something."

"May I take a look?" I examined the cup, rubbing my fingers over the surface again and again. "Know what, Jeff? This cup may be silver. It's darkened with age, but it's definitely not tin or pewter." I handed it back to him. "Run your finger over the front there. Feel the slight indentations? It could be etched underneath the tarnish."

"So—what do you think, Ashby?"

"I think we should give it a thorough cleaning with some silver polish. Do you mind if I take it back to the house and work on it?"

"Cool! It might be a clue to the past or something, you know?"

Cool indeed. I sniffed a few times. "Funny. Up here there's no bad smell. Or, maybe like you said, I've gotten used to it."

"Have a seat." Jeff gave a gracious bow. "I'd offer you a snack, but we need to stock the pantry. Would you like a comic? A book?"

"I'll take the *Huck Finn*, please. I'm a huge Mark Twain fan." I settled into one of the chairs, arranging a pillow beneath me. Jeff lowered himself to the other chair.

"I can see why you guys like coming here. But, where's the 'bad vibe' you talked about?"

Jeff shrugged. "No tellin'. Sometimes we feel it and sometimes there's nothing."

"Can you describe what you've experienced?"

Jeff chewed his lip. "Well—it usually starts with some kind of noise. You know, a thud. Or a crash. Or rattling." He demonstrated by rattling the arms of his folding chair. "Last time we were here we heard a voice. A creepy voice. A voice like it was deep down inside a…a…"

"A well." I finished Jeff's sentence.

His eyes opened wide. "Yeah. That's it. Like way down a well. Hollow. Echoing."

"Words? Were there any words from down in the well?"

"For sure, we did hear words." He looked at me as though I might be able to explain. "*Go away. Go away, he's dead*." Then, for emphasis, he cupped his hands and intoned, "Gooooo awaaaaay. Heeeeeee's deaddddd."

It took me several seconds to steady my thoughts and voice. The exact same words Miss Emma and Lenore had heard so long ago. "You and Nick—you weren't frightened by this creepy voice?"

Jeff's eyes sparkled. "Spooky! Sure. But *spooky* is what keeps us comin' back! Nick calls it—the voice—our *fantasmas.*" He stopped abruptly, looking directly at me. "Do you believe in ghosts, Ashby?"

"Do you?"

Jeff ignored my question as easily as I'd ignored his. "What do you think it means? '*He's dead*'?"

"I suppose you—you and Nick—would like to find out the answer to that." I chewed my lip before adding. "I'd like to find out myself." I cradled the little cup under my chin.

Just then my cell phone buzzed in my pocket. It was a text from Luke. I read it quickly, then, looked up at my cousin. "Luke's been working on a horse at the Hadley farm. Says he's not going back to school tonight. He'll be here for dinner."

"Super! I can't wait 'til Luke's living here full-time again," Jeff said. "I miss him."

I flashed back to my earliest experiences at Overhome, remembering how envious I had been of Jeff's easy relationship with Luke.

"I'm with you. But I guess we'd better get back home now." I stood, handing the *Huck Finn* book to Jeff. "Let's plan to come back. Do some sleuthing." I looped the cup handle on my finger.

"There's something else I want to show you, Ashby."

I checked my watch for the time. "Can you put it off until next time? I need to see about dinner, get cleaned up before Luke gets here."

Jeff looked disappointed. "Okay. Maybe next time we'll hear something." Jeff reached for the Twain book and returned it to the shelf. "Goooooo awaaaaay," he droned, heading for the stairs.

Carefully replacing the boards and kudzu cover, Jeff nodded toward the corner of the house. "It's back there. What I want to show you. Me and Nick thought we'd explored everything, but we found something we'd missed."

My curiosity perked up. "All right. You got me. Hard to believe you guys could miss anything."

Jeff led the way and directed my gaze to the foundation. "It's there." He pointed to the ground.

"What? I don't see anything, Jeff. Just weeds and briars, that's all. Honeysuckle taking over."

"Yeah. That's why we missed it, too." He moved in closer to the house and approached the tangled mass of honeysuckle. "We were looking for a ball we'd lost when we found this." Pulling the vines back from the exterior wall, Jeff brought my attention to a tiny opening in the foundation, about the size of a nickel, and partially obscured by packed dirt.

"What do you suppose it is?" I knelt, running my hand over the hole.

"We think it's maybe an opening to a space under the house." He picked up a pebble and pressed it through the small opening, then waited until it landed with a faint plink. "Hear it land? It's a ways down to the bottom." He repeated the process.

I rocked back on my heels. "Isn't there's some kind of root cellar under the back of the house? Where the land slopes."

"Yeah. We've been in it. The old door is half broken in. It's just a space with a dirt floor." Jeff squatted down beside me. "This is different."

I saw what he meant. "Let's take a quick look at that room around back."

We entered the crude room without any problems. It was, as Jeff said, just a small space with a dirt floor. Stone, whitewashed walls like the interior of the cottage and a high, beamed ceiling. On one wall, hung a slightly sloping wooden shelf with pegs attached. A tapestry of cobwebs completed the picture. A few broken crocks and an ancient basket covered in dust were the only apparent inhabitants of the space, which was obviously situated the length of the house away from the small aperture Jeff and Nick had discovered.

"The opening in the foundation you found—it may turn out to be nothing but a hole in a plugged air vent to a crawl space—something like that," I told Jeff, as we mounted our horses. "But you're right. It took those pebbles a good long time to reach bottom. Very curious. Very curious indeed. It merits further investigation."

Jeff looked pleased. "Investigation? Great! Nick and me love to explore."

"Thanks for the tour, Jeff. Just promise me you won't be too disappointed if—when—your clubhouse—your *casa* has to go."

"Yeah—well—it might not be so easy to get rid of this place, you know?"

We ambled toward the cedar copse. I wasn't sure what my cousin meant, but I was formulating some ideas. There was, for sure, much work to be done if I was going to pull off this sale.

****

Luke tossed the anchor into a shallow, deserted cove and joined me on the bow seat of the ski boat. "There's nothing to beat a sunset cruise. Unless it's a sunset cruise with my bride-to-be." He wrapped me in his arms.

I leaned into his shoulder and purred. "Ummmm. How is it somebody who mucks around huge, filthy animals all day smells so good?"

"Baby powder. My secret weapon." He kissed my hair, then turned my face to his and kissed my lips. "Baby powder for my babe."

"And didn't we hit the lucky strike tonight?" Reluctant to move, I spoke, still snuggled into his shoulder. "Mom and Dad out with Miss Emma for a movie and dinner—Monica and Hal arriving back from their jaunt very late tonight. And Jeff having dinner and a sleep-over at Nick's."

"We have the boat—the lake—the dock—and dinner to ourselves. What a miraculous turn of events."

"All I can say, Luke, is—I love you. And I love Cupcake, too, for acting up again and forcing you to come home. What a horse!"

"If the old nag would quit eating foreign objects—ping pong balls, for example—she might have a more cooperative digestive system." He chuckled. "But, don't tell her. She probably wouldn't listen to you anyway."

"Did she treat you better this time?"

"Oh, I still got the laid-back ears and the twitchy tail. And I tell you, she can roll her eyes like a teenager. But I do think she's mellowing. No kicking and only a few attempts to bite this time. Doc Forest has completely turned Cupcake over to me."

"Doc Forest is a brilliant man." I lifted my face for another kiss.

We sat for a long time, watching the sun descend slowly, a flaming ball nestled in a bed of pink, red, orange streamers reflecting on the chrome-mirrored lake. At last we stirred. "Gettin' dark," Luke said. "Pull out the anchor light, please. We'll need it for our return to the dock."

"All good things most definitely do not have to come to an end." I rummaged in the storage compartment near the floor of the boat. "Here it is." I inserted the long pole handle with the white light at the end into the stern fitting. "You think the sunset was magical? Wait 'til you see what we're having for dinner!"

"What's on the menu?" Luke lifted the anchor, then slid into the driver's seat and turned the key, looking back to see that the anchor light was working. He pushed the throttle and the boat rolled into the channel.

I raised my voice to be heard over the hum of the

engine and the wind. "Actually, you're the cook tonight. I've defrosted some striper that was in the freezer. I believe you were the one to pull in that 36-inch beauty over spring break. Or was it striper break?"

"Ha. Good pun. The stripers were breaking, for sure. It took me a half hour to lug the sucker in. What a fight." He smiled at the memory. "I'll use the grill on the dock."

"A chilled chardonnay and my famous tossed salad to round out the feast—already in the dock fridge prepped to go. Magic."

Luke pulled his eyes from the lake and looked at me. "And will the penthouse lounge be available? The one with the wrap-around lake view?"

"The one with the open-air, wrap-around lake view? Maybe we should call it some kind of code name—the penthouse at the 'Yacht Club,' exclusive membership of two." I raised one eyebrow. "It is available, but there's a condition."

"Let me guess. No beepers allowed?"

"Exactly! Any beeper confiscated will be thrown into the lake. It's in the by-laws of our Yacht Club, you know."

"For once, I'm not on call." The motor slowed and Luke eased the boat into the slip. We climbed onto the dock.

While Luke puttered around the boat, I uncorked the wine and filled two plastic goblets. I pulled the striper from the small dock fridge and placed it on the table. "Do you think we need the dock lights?" I handed Luke a glass.

Luke put an arm around my shoulder. "Forget the lights, and put the fish back, babe. It can wait—but I can't." He led me back to the boat.

Just before we stepped in, Luke grabbed the wine bottle. "Are you settled? Up we go." He pressed the button on the remote. "To the penthouse lounge." As we ascended noiselessly, he murmured, "Like magic."

****

Dear Diary:

So much to do as the days fly by. Mom had a long talk with Mariana and the two of them convinced Carlos that Mom should tutor Nick this summer in place of summer school. Mom's still working around the idea of helping Nick's parents with their citizenship courses. She says there are some matters of pride involved, and she has to tread carefully. Jeff is delighted with the plan.

My interview with the aging hippie couple who run Moore Creek Pottery was crazy fun, and the article is a winner! They actually began by making and baking their own bricks—then branched out to pottery. They married, divorced, and continue to live in the same house and work the pottery business. It's gorgeous stuff, too—all hand-fired and hand-painted and the designs change seasonally year after year. Moore Mountain pottery is shipped all over the world. One of their favorite vignettes: a special order of pottery sent to China, imprinted with the words: "Made in Virginia." My editor loved my story!

The M&M Express is chugging along with wedding details. They try hard to include me in the plans, but, honestly, they're doing such a good job and having so much fun that I haven't intervened much at all. They bring me computer images of flowers and cake toppers and such and I try to keep Luke abreast of everything, but he's perpetually on-call, it seems. He buzzes in and out like a honey bee looking for a swarm. Honestly, without the M&M Express, I cannot imagine how we'd be able to plan the wedding in such a short time frame.

Monica and Hal continue to run off on mysterious jaunts over the Virginia countryside—supposedly gathering historic information to be shared with the family when they're finished—if that ever actually happens. Is it just an excuse to spend time together? I wonder.

As for the overseer's cottage, Jeff, Nick and I are working on a time we three can meet and continue to explore. Oddly enough, the little two-handled "tin" cup Jeff and Nick discovered cleaned up well enough to reveal a big O and the date, June 1, 1840—no doubt a baby cup belonging to some Overton ancestor. Sterling silver. Wonder what it was doing in the cottage? After showing it to everyone, I gave it back to Jeff who was quite pleased to return it to the loft clubhouse where it sits on a crate along with some candles.

Oh, Dad and I are to meet Realtor, Paul Gordon, to walk the plot we plan to sell. I admit the prospect makes me nervous, but having Dad on board is a comforting thought.

Which leads me to the chandelier with a life of its own...thus far the electrician's promise has held. But then, no 300-pound gorillas have showed up to test his theory. I'm a bit more concerned about the machinations of a zero-pound ghost (with havoc on its mind.)

Chapter 8

The library had long been one of my favorite rooms, and I'd always felt more comfortable there than almost anywhere else on earth. I stood looking at the neatly organized books lining the shelves—a surprisingly extensive collection for a private home. The library spanned many decades of book-loving Overtons. One entire shelf was dedicated to Civil War books, and I made a note to show the collection to Hal.

My thoughts returned to the business at hand. I had called our very first family meeting in the library after dinner. Smiling, I greeted each one who filed through the doors and waited until everyone was seated.

Though I was tempted to ask Dad to lead, I knew this gathering was mine to deal with. I took a few yoga breaths to steady my blood pressure before I spoke. "Thank you all for coming." I looked from face to face with studied eye-contact. "The needs of Overhome are so pressing and so important to each and every one of us that I feel we must work on some money-saving plans. Until we can sell the tract, we're going to have to exist in a state of semi-austerity."

No one said anything, so I pressed on. "Luke and I plan to keep the wedding small. Just family, a few neighbors, the staff here at Overhome and some friends."

Monica gasped. "Oh no! Ashby, a wedding is

special. A once-in-a-lifetime happening. To scrimp on such a sacred event…" She trailed off, then, brightened. "Interestingly, I have been considering canceling my membership at the country club. It is outrageously expensive, what with monthly fees, dining minimums, green fees, pool membership." Monica looked around the room. "I would like to donate whatever thousands of dollars that saves to Ashby and Luke's wedding."

I gave an inward sigh. My aunt, as usual, had missed the point. "Monica, I appreciate your generosity, and I applaud your move to cut the country club from your expenses, but we need money to keep Overhome going. Day-to-day expenses. Not for the wedding."

"I understand," she said, but she did not look happy about it. "I truly do want to support the cause."

"Actually, Monica, your country club membership may be exactly what we need to promote our proposed expansion. We're looking for the cream of the crop, so to speak. If you're able to spread the word about our expert horse trainer and excellent boarding facilities, for people who are interested and can afford it—people like your club members—who knows? Our business could take off."

"Oh." Monica brightened. "Power golf. Hunter told me all about how he would settle financial deals over eighteen holes and a glass of bourbon at the club. In fact, he said he'd sealed more deals on the golf course than in his office."

"That's what I'm talking about!"

"I'll be happy to attend public school," Jeff blurted out. "My private school must cost a bundle."

Monica frowned and shook her head. "Private school is an express stipulation of your trust, Jefferson.

It is already funded."

"Aww, shoot. I wanna go to school with Nick." Jeff stared at the floor and scuffled his feet. He murmured almost to himself, "What can I do to help, then?"

Dad raised his hand. "Let me get this right. The plan is to ask Carlos to bump up the riding lesson business? And, maybe, add clientele to the boarding and training? Wouldn't that be a lot of extra work for him?"

Jeff sat up straighter. "Nick and I can muck out the stalls, groom the horses, help Eddie with the feeding and watering. And we can ask Sam if we do some caretaking stuff. Maybe we could even help Carlos with the pony-riding lessons." He beamed.

I gave Jeff a thumbs up. "That could work."

"Do you think Eddie could take over some of Carlos' duties with the boarding horses?" Dad asked. "Maybe cover Sunday for Carlos' day off?"

"I think Eddie is definitely ready," I approved. "He's come a long way from his Night Riding days."

Mom caught my father's eye. "Dad and I intend to pay for the upfront costs on the land sale. No, don't stop me," she insisted, when I tried to protest. "We are in for the surveying costs, the soil tests and other preliminaries. We've saved for a down payment on a home here, and we can always get our money back for that after the sale of the tract at Overhome goes through. It will give us time to look around, see what's the best buying option for us. Who knows? We may even buy one of those 'custom-built' homes Paul Gordon is talking about."

I struggled to speak without the trembling of

emotion I felt. "Once Luke gets his vet practice up and running, and as my writing begins to pay off, we'll be in much better shape financially. Until then, I do believe we can make it—thanks to all of you," I managed to get out.

Just then Mariana arrived with a tray of tea and cookies. "I am sorry," she demurred. "I...I overhear..." She looked embarrassed, and her voice was hesitant. "I want to help. Carlos and Nick and I...we feel that Overhome is ours to care for, too."

Maybe Mariana was only worried about her own employment—hers and Carlos'—but she seemed entirely sincere. "I know Carlos will love to teach more riding lessons, to have more training responsibility. And I...I would like to cater the wedding...to prepare all the food." She stopped. "If is okay with you, Ashby."

I took the tray from Mariana and encircled her in a hug. "I can think of nothing I would like better," I told her. "As for Luke, he's so in love with your cooking, Mariana, I can assure you he, too, will be honored and delighted."

"Thank you! Thank you!"

"It is we who thank you," I murmured above my tightening throat which threatened to choke off my words.

"Oh, wonderful! We must get right to work on the menu," Monica pronounced, with such eagerness that it broke the tension in the room and everybody laughed.

Munching on cookies and sipping tea, we sprawled in the overstuffed chairs chit-chatting about nothing important. Everybody seemed on deck with the new expansion plan for the horse farm. For that, I was grateful. But I knew it would not be enough. I would have to put a lot of faith into Paul Gordon's real estate savvy. For sure, I was glad Dad would be traversing that thorny path with me. But something Jeff had said simmered on the back burner of my mind. "It might not be so easy to get rid of this place." He meant the overseer's cottage, of course. And he might be right. But it seemed to me that we'd have to demolish the place to make way for fifty new homes.

Everyone left except Dad.

"Care to take a stroll with your old dad? There's only one better use for a fine Virginia evening like this."

"And that would be a horseback ride. Sure. Since the horses are all put up for the night, let's go for a walk."

We ambled alongside the old stone wall in the warm fragrance that descends after sunset. "To the gazebo?" Dad asked.

"Why not?" We walked in companionable silence, tracking the ancient stone wall, until we came upon the matching lampposts at the entrance to the maze. Lifting the latch to the iron gate, we moved down a short flight of steps into the labyrinth of boxwoods which had been wild and untrimmed when I first arrived at Overhome five years ago. Monica had since hired a landscaper to tidy up the whole maze and the result was worthy of Williamsburg.

Dad and I had no problem solving the boxwood puzzle whose exit merged with a path of periwinkle. The ground-cover fed into a charming gazebo, also restored, thanks to Monica. Painted snow-flake white, the wooden structure perched like an ornament atop a bed of what had once been a wildly prolific bed of red rose bushes, now, sadly only a tangle of thorny vines. We seated ourselves so that we faced each other.

"You did a fine job with your family confab tonight, Ashby. I was proud of you."

"Thanks. I doubt you know how hard I worked to convince myself it was *my* job to lead, not yours."

"I understand. And I respect your decision."

I collected my thoughts as we sat in silence. "You know, Dad, a lot happened my first summer here at Overhome. Things I never shared with you and Mom."

"Your mom and I knew you must have gone through trials—solved some problems we might not be privy to. We knew—well—because you *grew* so much. Life's challenges have a way of maturing folks. Building character."

"Trials? Problems? Challenges? For sure. But there's another whole aspect of that summer...Luke knows. And Miss Emma, and Abe." I brushed back an unexpected tear. "I think of Luke's grandfather every time I'm at the gazebo. Abe loved to sit here and reminisce."

"Tell me about your first summer at Overhome. Do you want to talk about it?"

Looking over the bloomless rose vines, I couldn't help but feel sad for their fate. Monica had told me that somehow the painters who spruced up the gazebo had trampled the bushes and cleaned their paint brushes with deadly chemicals nearby. Or, she thought, perhaps the gardening crew that trimmed up the maze had disturbed the roses' growth. Always before, the blossoms had been so beautiful. Lush and aromatic. I looked at Dad. "Abe once told me right here at the gazebo—he picked a rose and handed it to me and told me it reminded him of Lenore because she loved roses so much."

Dad nodded without speaking. Swallowing hard, I continued. "Abe said it was because of Rosabelle. That's why my grandmother loved roses." I looked into Dad's eyes. "Did you ever hear your mother say anything…did she talk about…Rosabelle?"

Dad appeared deep in thought. "Your grandmother—was a wonderful story-teller. When we three boys were growing up, she was forever making up tales and poems and proverbs, usually designed to give us a conscience, I think, or help us make a moral decision of some kind. I do remember that name—Rosabelle. It's quite unusual, memorable. But I couldn't tell you anything about the context. Was it a story about a flowery nymph? A poem about a garden?" He shook his head.

"Did your mother deal in ghost stories?"

"You mean—Rosabelle was a…ghost?"

"A family spirit. Hanging around Overhome for the longest time. Waiting, apparently, for me. The rose was her sign—her symbol—her way of telling me and, before me, Lenore, that she was with us. That first summer I was here? Roses, roses everywhere—even in the most improbable places."

My father gave me an incredulous look. "Roses? The sign of a ghost named Rosabelle? And you say Abe and Emma and Luke all knew? You can't be serious."

I sighed. "Yeah. Unbelievable. But real. There was plenty of evidence. You'll just have to believe me. She was buried right here at the gazebo, back in the 1800s." I pointed to the small marker that was her gravesite.

"But her spirit is gone now."

"Gone?"

"To the other side. Once she was sure I was safe."

Dad continued to look at me as if I'd just dropped down from Mount Olympus. "Well! Of all the trials and problems we imagined you might have faced, I must say dealing with a ghost was never on the list."

"Rosabelle was not exactly a *problem*, though I must say she put me through many a trial. But in the end, she turned out to be more protective than harmful—at least to me. She's no longer with us, however. I firmly believe that."

"You say the spirit protected you? From what?"

I straightened on the wooden bench. "Someday I'll tell you. But for now, you can read about how it all began in the family diaries. I've moved them from the attic to the library. I suggest you and Mom dig them out and settle in for some highly entertaining reading—of a historical nature, of course. The Overton women believed in preserving the family heritage for posterity."

"Sounds fascinating. I'll tell your mother. Sometimes I think she's more interested in the family tree than I am." Dad gave me a sideways look. "By the way, shall I share your story with your mother?"

"By all means. And read the diaries. Then the three of us can talk."

Dusk descended, softening the verdure of the evergreen maze and the pale emerald rose vines and variegated periwinkle until their hues merged into one rich, dark tone. "So beautiful, Dad. The house, the gardens, the horses, the lake." I moved my arm in a wide, encircling gesture. "How could you leave it—

never to return—until now?"

"To borrow a phrase from you, dear daughter, someday I'll tell you. Tell you everything. For now, I'll just say that while my mother was wonderful, my father was a mean brute—in every conceivable way. I vowed that if I ever had a child, I would do and be the exact opposite of my father. I wanted nothing but space between him and me."

"So you never talked about your years at Overhome because it was too…"

"Painful. Yes. And because I wanted to shield you from my father's aura. Even after he died, I was reluctant to revisit the scene of all the pain he'd inflicted on the family."

"I think I understand. Between Miss Emma and Abe I've heard quite a lot about Grandfather Thomas' ugly side." I stood and stretched. "I guess we'd better get back. There's no moon to light the way tonight."

"You know," Dad said as we meandered home beside the stone wall, "I've never been a believer when it comes to ghosts. I'm a trained scientist, you know. We pride ourselves on dealing with facts—observable facts."

"Luke was skeptical, too, at first. But…sometimes things happen. It's hard to explain."

Dad slung his arm around my shoulder and gave it a squeeze. "At any rate, I'm glad you told me about your first summer at Overhome. And I'm *really* glad that spirit, whatever, or whoever, it was, is *no longer with us*. No more ghosts for Overhome, eh?"

How I wished that were true. With another specter on the prowl, would Dad have a chance to observe the facts for himself, trained scientist that he was?

As we entered the house, Dad said, "Tomorrow we meet together with Paul Gordon. I remember him as a good guy—when we were kids. Makes me optimistic—about everything." He turned to go to his room.

"See you tomorrow, Dad. I'm optimistic, too, and ready to move on with the project." As my father departed, I darted a hasty look into the dining room before ascending the stairs to my room. My family was ready to get on with business, but there might have been an exception with a certain resident of Overhome. An exception that could turn my father into a believer.

The chandelier tinkled ever so slightly.

****

Dear Diary:

I suppose the family meeting was successful; however, Dad and I both know the austerity plan is but a band aid. A call for solidarity? Yes. A chance to get everyone on the same page? Of course. A rally-cry for the troops? By all means, and any other trite phrase designed to promote a win. But it is a mere drop in the bucket when the bottom-line accounting looms large and menacing. We need a good-sized influx of cold, hard cash to counteract the black cloud of deficit looming on the horizon.

I can only hope and pray that Paul Gordon is a sorcerer of a Realtor.

Speaking of magic, Luke texted that he'll be home by week's end. How I miss his powerful shoulder to lean on, his dancing eyes to find some humor in our grim financial situation, and his quiet assurance that things will all work out for the best. I know he has crucial work to do to complete his vet's certification. Still, I want him here now. Thank God Mom and Dad, my family support, are so willingly involved.

Which brings me to Eddie Mills. When I reflect on the damage to the Mills family that Grandfather Thomas inflicted, I hesitate to ask any favors of Eddie. Through his own devious methods, my grandfather and his lawyer friend managed to steal a good bit of Mills land by moving the property lines to Overhome's advantage, claiming the acres to be "worthless." Yes, Eddie and I are cousins, something he will never let me forget. It makes any move on my part even more delicate, now that I am going to ask Eddie to take on more responsibilities without any more pay. We shall see just how thick family blood is.

Oh, my next arts article involves a family bluegrass band. I can't wait to interview the leader of the talented crew, which includes several of his family members. Word is they can sure put on a hoedown. Should be another winner for my editor! And now, to bed. I am exhausted, both mentally and physically. Being a home-owner is entirely overrated.

****

When I was over-tired, I liked to meditate, taking in my surroundings and reflecting mindfully, as I learned to do years ago in yoga class. Before I turned off my bedside lamp, I let my eyes wander around my room in the oldest wing of the house. Square, low-ceilinged, with creamy stucco walls outlined with dark wood moldings, my room was somehow spacious and cozy at the same time. Wooden floors shone with aged patina, and a four-poster bed and a heavy chest of drawers topped off with a pitted oval mirror supplied heft and bulk that was somehow feminine and delicate, too. On the outside wall leaded-glass French doors led to my private balcony with a high view of the grounds and lake. From my very first night in this room, I felt a warm acceptance, knowing that I belonged here. Tonight was no different. Breathing yoga breaths, I relaxed until my eyes shut and I knew I would sleep.

I do not know what time it was that I awoke. I had been in deep, dreaming sleep, when a noise aroused me. It took a while before I rose into consciousness; even then, I was groggy with sleep. I'd heard a sharp, slapping sound. What? Thunder? Something falling to the floor? In the brief silence that followed, I yearned to return to my peaceful slumber and almost succeeded, when it hit again, this time louder. Sharper. SLAM! SLAM! SLAM!

A spark of fear jumpstarted my heart and I sat up, rubbing my eyes and trying to activate my brain. SLAM! There it was again. It had to be the French doors opening and closing. But they had been shut tight. Locked, the nighttime ritual I never neglected. No wind, no storm, no natural element could possibly open those doors.

High on adrenaline, I slipped to the floor. Moonlight filtered through the French doors, casting geometric patterns onto the floor. I followed their hopscotch pathway, then, reached for the handle. Locked, as I had known it would be. Turning the key, wrenching open the doors, I stepped onto the balcony and gazed out. The yard below glittered with moon-tipped dew. The tiny guest house peeked over the horizon. In quiet symmetry, the fences encircled the pasture and barn. Off to the side the lake lay flat and ebony-dark. Nothing moved. Silence settled over the scene.

How long I stood, watching, waiting, I do not know. My heart rate slowed to a normal pace, and my heightened senses calmed until I found myself back in my room, climbing into the high bed. Though my fear had subsided, I wondered. What? This was no dream. That was all I knew for sure.

As I dozed off, I was aware of the light but unmistakable stench of rotten eggs.

Chapter 9

"The tack room looks perfect. And the stables. Not to mention the horses themselves. You get an A-plus." I'd found Eddie in the stable office. I'm always struck by the colorful display there, wall-to-wall ribbons and trophies won by our horses in shows from all over and going back to my grandmother's time, some of them faded and tarnished with age.

Eddie grinned, proudly flashing his new, even smile. "Why, thank y', ma'am." He bowed. "I do take some pride in my work, y'know." He leaned down and to pet one of the barn cats.

One thing I'd learned about Eddie long ago was you could catch this fly with honey, not vinegar. "You've done *such* a good job," I went on rather hastily, "that we—I'd like to ask you to take on a bit more responsibility."

Gullible as he appeared to the naked eye, years of fending for himself throughout a hardscrabble youth had engendered in my cousin a sharp, shrewd edge. It glittered just now in his steely eyes—the what's-in-this-for-me glint.

"You're doing a stellar job as our stable hand. Sam appreciates the way you work with her on caretaking. Ordering the grain and hay, repairing broken equipment—you are surely a jack of all trades." Realizing I was laying it on too thick, I toned down a notch. "Now I have a favor to ask."

I couched a quick look at Eddie to see if his expression had changed. Too soon to tell. I went on. "We need to ramp up the business. More horses for boarding and riders for training. More riding lessons. Carlos won't have time to deal with all the extra work without help. From you."

"So…y'want me to help Carlos? In addition t'what I'm already doin' in the stables 'n out in the fields?"

I tilted my head as if sizing up Eddie's potential. "Jeff and Nick have volunteered to work the jobs you can trust them to do. I have faith in you, Eddie. I think you're ready to take on more responsibilities. My dad agrees."

Eddie looked sullen. "So you and Mr. Overton thinks I'm good enough? What about Luke?" His expression darkened. "Damn Luke. He still don't trust me. Right?"

"You have to understand, Eddie. Luke did it all when he was Overhome's senior groom—taught riding, trained horses and riders, even took care of the books. It's not a fair comparison."

Eddie jerked his chin up defiantly. "I can do it. A'course I can! I'll show 'im. Jes' let me try it fer a while. Y'don't even have t'pay me more or nothin'. I'll show you. I'll show Luke. I can do it and I can do it good."

"You know this may mean more hours— unscheduled hours. Sunday duty."

"I'm up fer it, Ashby. I swear. They ain't no problem about stayin' late or comin' in early." He hesitated. "Excep' fer Tuesday nights. I got a engagement Tuesday nights."

Surprised, I hesitated, thinking. "Um…it wouldn't have anything to do with the Night Riders, would it, Eddie? Do they meet on Tuesday night? Because everything is off the table if you have any involvement with them." I gave him a hard look.

"Cross m'heart. I'm done with that lot," Eddie said with just enough gusto to make me question his veracity.

"You're sure? When we hired you, you promised you were no longer with the Riders."

"I know, I know. It took me a while to shake free a'them scoundrels. But scout's honor," he saluted, "Tuesday night's got nothin' t'do with Night Riders."

"You have to understand, Eddie. We're going for the wealthiest sector of society, telling them boarding their Thoroughbreds at Overhome is worth the money. The biggest estate owners around here. We can't have them worrying about any connection with the Night Riders." I could picture some Barn Queen screaming in my face about just such a scenario. "Night Riders! Vandals! Your groom is a member of that gang of thugs? Horrors!" Yes, horrors.

Eddie squirmed as he strove for an honest face. "I'm tellin' the truth, Ashby."

"Okay. I believe you. You will expand your duties and will work Sundays. We'll go over the details next time Luke gets in. Get it in writing."

"Except Tuesday nights." Eddie met my outstretched hand for a shake.

"We'll work out the details." I smiled my biggest smile. "And I accept your offer to put off a raise."

As I bid Eddie goodbye, I wanted to ask him what it is he does on Tuesday nights, but I decided it was none of my business, and, anyway, I'd eventually find out. I moved to Sasha's stall to stroke and talk to him. He'd been whinnying at his first detection of my voice as I talked to Eddie. I held a peppermint below his lips. "I promise you, Sasha. Luke and I will do some riding when he gets home. We'll have a good, long run on the trail." With a final caress, I turned to leave. "I promise." I blew Sasha a kiss.

"*Adios*!" Eddie called after me.

I left the stables with ambiguous feelings. I'd managed to talk Eddie into working more hours for no additional pay. But I'd dangled his jealousy of Luke as the carrot. I admit I was pleased but not exactly pleased with myself. I vowed to make it up to Eddie as soon as possible. Unless, of course, he really was still affiliated with the unsavory Night Riders. I had vivid memories of their wanton destruction—breaking up boards in the bridge, opening the barn doors to let out the horses in the middle of the night—moving water troughs around the fields and other annoying "pranks" that cost us time and effort. Their symbol, the Confederate flag, was tattooed on Eddie's arm. Eddie ran with this gang, happy in those days, perhaps, to get back at the rich estate-owners who had cheated his family. If he was, in fact, still involved with the vandals, that would be, as they say, "a whole 'nother thing."

****

Dad and Paul Gordon drove up in Paul's Jeep. Dad jumped out and opened the back door for me. "Hop in, Ashby."

"'Morning, Ashby." Paul turned to look at me from the driver's seat. "Buckle up. This'll be a bumpy ride. I know. I've been out here several times to look over the

96

general acreage." He maneuvered a sharp turn of the wheel. "It's like an obstacle course—big rocks, deep ruts. Probably easier by horse."

We lurched to a start and headed past the barn. Winding around to the back of the property, we bumped along the outer acres of Overhome Estate, dodging ditches and deep ruts and berms while trying to keep to the old road when possible. It seemed to take forever. As Paul had said, it was much nicer on horseback, I thought, as I clung to the strap attached to the ceiling.

Almost entirely covered over by water, the old road, which once led to the back of the property, had not been used since the lake was created. Now, we were forced to drive cross-country. This accounted for my being unaware of the cottage's existence, isolated as it was. Paul stopped the Jeep, and we got out. He took his time eyeing the parameters of the property, making notes on his electronic tablet. At last he spoke. "Okay. This is your biggest selling point." He swept his arm in a wide circle over the long view. "Water-access lots here. Water-view and off-water lots over here." Again he bent to his tablet. "Doing a quick price calculation." He looked up. "Not bad! Not bad at all. I think you'll be pleased. 'Water' is the magic word."

Dad raised his eyebrows. "Are you going to share the details?"

"Not until I do more research. I'm just letting you know there's good value here." With another satisfied look, Paul inclined his head toward the Jeep. "Let's go see the rest of the plot." He spoke to me. "You said there's an abandoned structure still standing on part of the property for sale, right? Which way, Ashby?"

I directed the Realtor over several serpentine bends

before we found the clearing in the grove of cedars where the overseer's cottage stood.

"Can't say I remember much about how the old building looked so many years ago," Dad said, climbing from the Jeep and brushing himself off. "I'd completely forgotten about it—it's certainly overgrown." He headed for the boarded-up door. "Where does this structure stand in relation to the total fifty acres we mean to sell?"

Paul flipped through his papers. "Not central, but definitely within the property lines. Let's take a look at the grounds first. Ostensibly, these would be the least expensive lots."

"Ostensibly?" I asked.

The Realtor hesitated. "You never know what you're going to run into with an old property like this."

The three of us paced off a large hunk of ground, Paul with his head down and his calculator in hand while Dad and I exchanged cautious looks over his head and behind his back. Until we came to a halt, I had not realized how tightly-clenched my fists were, how clamped my teeth. I calmed myself with a few deep-belly breaths before speaking. "What do you think, Paul?"

"Some surprises, of course." He indicated the cottage. "I'm wondering why the house would be out here in the first place. There must be a reason...how long has it been here?" He bent his head and went back over a portion of the yard. "Looks like there might've been some other smaller buildings clustered around the house. See the remains of foundation over there—and there? I wouldn't be surprised if we didn't dig up something else. That one there might have been an early kitchen. Kitchens were usually detached from the main house due to fire hazard, you know."

"Then you do think the plot can be developed?" Dad shifted his weight nervously. "I realize this may be premature…"

"Oh, no question. It's excellent land overall—gentle slope, a scenic creek, and, ultimately, the lake, of course. But, we'll have to do some detective work on the structure here."

"Why, Paul? I mean, obviously, it will have to be demolished. So, why the 'detective work,' as you put it?" Dad wanted some concrete answers.

"I'll have to check with county regulations before I do anything else." Was he being deliberately evasive? Or was he in typical reserved Realtor mode? "This building is probably historic. Let's take a look inside—see what we're dealing with."

I'd been thinking about the same thing—fresh eyes to see what we're dealing with. I ushered them over the porch and showed them to the door. Before I could remove the boards, Paul backed up and looked at the roof. "This is not the original roof. It's not exactly new, but this metal roof probably replaced the original chestnut shingles used in these parts. That's kept the structure standing. Also, the stone is a factor in the long life of this building." He lowered his gaze. "Okay. Let's go in."

No sooner had we entered the space than an overwhelming foul odor hit with such force, I felt knocked back. It was as though something had slapped me in the face and I staggered.

"Whoa!" Dad held his nose. "Did something die in here?"

"You...you get used to it after a while," I choked out.

Paul seemed unperturbed. "Critters of every sort make their way into old places like this all the time. They get comfortable, make a nest, feed their young and die of old age."

Jeff had mentioned finding animal bones, though there were none in evidence now. And I hadn't seen any signs of animal decay when Jeff and I had explored the place earlier. Whatever the source, the smell was enduring.

Paul and Dad made a quick survey of the interior, neglecting the staircase, to my relief. It looked like I wouldn't have to explain Jeff and Nick's *casa* after all. At least not yet. I suspected the smell was a contributing factor to their hasty preview. As we exited, I suggested we take a look at the room at the back of the house.

"Let's see it," Paul said.

So, we tramped around to the back of the cottage where I showed them the ramshackle room under the main floor.

"This type of storage room was standard," Paul said. "A root cellar."

I thought about showing him Jeff and Nick's discovery of the little hole in the foundation on the side of the house, but decided it could not be of much importance now. Later, I'd get Dad's take on the little opening.

"Overall, what do you think, Paul?" I was feeling better and better about my real estate rescue plan.

"There are a couple of things working for you here." He looked at me, then at Dad. "Ashby, the good news is that the housing market is on the uptick at long last. And the custom home market is usually a very good money-maker."

"So what's the next step?" I was more than ready to move on to the business of selling.

The Realtor looked thoughtful. "You've got a valuable piece of property here. You could simply sell the land to a developer—for streets, utilities and such, which makes the land even more valuable."

The good karma was fading rapidly. "Sounds like a lengthy process." I raised my shoulders and let them fall with a loud exhale. "I mean, if we need the money quickly…"

"Hold that thought," Dad said. "We'll talk about it later, Ashby."

I sensed a plan behind Dad's comment, but I knew there was no way to hurry it out of him. "Okay." I met Paul's handshake. "Thanks, Paul. Time is of the essence. Let's get together soon."

The two men climbed into the front seat of the Jeep, talking. As I opened the back door, I was aware of something tugging at my shoulders, pulling me back. When I turned to look, I felt a sharp slap on my cheek. There was no voice, but if there had been, I knew what it would have said with its bad breath spewing into my face: "Go away. He's dead." With that, the smell faded and, since there was no further aggression, I decided not to let the men know what had happened. No sense in alarming them now. A glance into the side view mirror before I slid into the backseat showed a bright red stripe burned into my cheek.

****

Luke and I stood shoulder to shoulder watching

Carlos work his wizardry on the sleek chestnut Thoroughbred in the round pen. A circular enclosure in the field, our round pen's footing was made from recycled tires. The cost was astounding, and I'd originally wondered if this was a place we could scrimp and save, but our trainer appreciated keeping the horses sound.

"Carlos is so gentle with the horses. So kind," Luke commented. "Frosty is absolutely putty in his hands."

Luke and I had often discussed Carlos' outstanding training techniques. We approved of his training mantra which could be summed up in one of his favorite words: supple. "The body, the mouth—making the horse supple is *muy importante*," is how he put it.

"Out in the field," Luke gestured, "I wish I'd known more about his kind of training when I was working the horses here. Running the horses over the tires and schooling fences and baskets, again and again—it's an excellent method for training the best hunter-jumpers. Takes a lot of patience."

For a while, we looked on appreciatively. "You know, Luke, it's not just the horses. It's also the way he coaches the riders 'No heavy-handed pulling! Gentle! Gentle!'" I laughed. "And, 'Balance! Remember your impulsion.'"

Luke nodded. "Once I saw him instructing a rider to place a crop in the back of his pants. Talk about sitting up straight in the saddle! And all the while, he's encouraging, 'No slumping! No slumping!' Now, that's gotta rub the skin off your back after a while."

"Oh yeah. 'Close your leg! Squeeze the horse forward.' I love to watch and listen when he's giving lessons. Let's face it: He gets results. Calm horses and competent riders." I smiled. "And Julio—his assistant? Same techniques. Carlos insists on that."

Leading a frisky gelding from the outdoor ring with a long-line, Carlos called to us. "*Hola*! Ashby and Luke." He patted the horse's neck. "This one fine animal, eh?"

"Lookin' good!" Luke gave him a thumb's up.

"Here's hoping Carlos will have a boatload of newbies to train with his wonderful Argentinian methodology," I said. "Let's saddle up. It's about time I showed you this mysterious overseer's abode."

"After I talk to Eddie about the new work plan." Luke grimaced. "You know how to sweet-talk him, but he dries up like an old sponge when I try to tell him anything."

"He's just jealous of you, Luke. He wants to do a good job but knows you're a hard act to follow." I stroked Luke's cheek. "If you start off with an honest compliment about his work—maybe that'll soften him up."

"He's jealous, y'say? Ha! That's because he's in love with you." Luke's lips formed a grim line. "I've conferred with Carlos. Now, hopefully I can outline Eddie's extra duties and somehow make him eager to comply."

"You can do it. Just remember: Find the good in Eddie. It's there if you look hard enough." I pulled his face down toward mine for a kiss. "By the way, have I mentioned how glad I am you're home for a spell?"

"Yeah. You can thank Doc Forest for that. He keeps requesting me for my tracking hours, for some reason."

"It might have something to do with your being a

wonderful vet. Now, I'll be puttering around here while you talk to Eddie. I want to make friends with the yearling in the paddock. We haven't weaned her yet since she and her mom are still bonding beautifully. I'm working on a good literary name for her. How do you like Flannery?"

Luke rolled his eyes, and I waved as he wandered back toward the barn. Luke would handle Eddie just fine, I knew, and Eddie would be more likely to stay the course with Luke's seal of approval. I was much more worried about what would transpire at the overseer's cottage.

Chapter 10

We rode our horses at a leisurely pace, enjoying our time in the saddle together. "You think Eddie's on board for our great expansion?"

"So he says. We'll see when the time comes." Luke let the reins relax in his hands. "Just how do you plan to go about 'expanding' the training here?"

"Oh, the usual routes. Advertising in local papers and magazines. Updating our website. Notifying all the Pony Clubs. And we may have a secret weapon at our disposal."

"Do tell." We stopped to let our horses graze.

"Evidently, Uncle Hunter was well versed in what Monica calls 'power golf.' He'd pay green fees for business clientele and schmooze them over eighteen holes. Monica thinks she can use her country club connections to do something similar. What do you think?"

"Golf is a complete mystery to me."

"Well, Monica certainly runs with an elite crowd, when it comes to money. Not just with her country club, either. She's been a Junior Leaguer for years. She's active on the board of Jeff's very swishy private school, and she's headed up I don't know how many charity fund drives. Whatever her plans, I think her connections with the wealthiest horse people in the area can only help the cause."

Susan Coryell

Luke nodded. "So we all do our part. In the meantime, we hope to sell off some property. Who knows? It might work."

And it might not. But what choice did we have? "Let's pick up the pace. I have some rather special plans in mind for tonight. But first, you need to see the overseer's cottage with your own eyes."

"Special plans? Other than an evening in our penthouse suite at the yacht club?" Luke raised a quizzical eyebrow. "So, is this 'special plan' to be a surprise?"

"I'm not telling. But, certainly, we'll retire for our airy tryst afterwards. Let me just hint that my plan for the evening involves a bit of multi-tasking. On my part, that is."

"I must say I'm mystified—but intrigued. Let's get going." Luke clucked his horse to a trot, then, motioned me to go ahead of him. "Lead the way, babe."

Beginning with the root cellar and working our way through the stinky interior of the cottage, Luke and I found nothing I had not already noted.

When we climbed up to Jeff and Nick's clubhouse in the loft, Luke pointed out that, though the ceiling was low, there was really quite a lot of floor space. "Wonder what this was originally used for?" he mused. "No fireplace. Must've been mighty cold in the winter."

"I'll bet there are some interesting stories about this place." I thought for a moment. "Hal—Monica's historian friend—you've met him in passing—is researching our history. He and Monica have been up and down the Valley of Virginia and elsewhere looking into archives and museums and I don't know what all. Monica has hinted that Hal has unearthed some good

106

stuff, especially about the cottage here."

Luke tapped his forehead. "Now, what d'ya say we get out of here? The smell is giving me a headache." He moved to descend the stairs from the loft. "Let me go first."

He climbed down cautiously, the old boards of the steps groaning and creaking under his weight. When he reached the bottom, he turned, held out his arms. "Come on down, Ashby. Just go slow."

"Not to worry. I've done this before." I reached for the first step with my foot, carefully moving toward the bottom, one step at a time, leaning against the wall for support. I was halfway there when it happened—so suddenly that I had no time to react. Frigid air swooshed down on me from behind, freezing my face, causing me to screw my eyes tight shut at the same time something strong and determined pushed against my back violently—so violently that I stumbled, then tumbled forward, to be caught in Luke's outstretched arms from several stairs below.

"Whoa!" He exhaled from the impact of my body on his. "My God, Ashby. What happened?"

I slumped against him, unable to utter a single word, my breathing shallow and rapid. At last I found my voice. "Something pushed me, Luke. I don't know what—or who—but it was powerful and deliberate."

Luke glanced up to the top of the stairs. "Nothing there. I'm going back to the loft to look."

I stopped him. "I doubt you'll find anything." I sniffed the air, expecting a new infusion of foul odor. "And what would you do if you did find anything?"

Just then we both heard it. Hollow, chilling, trailing away from us with every syllable: "Go away. He's dead. He's dead. He's dead…"

Luke held me close, stroking my back. "I wonder if Hal's research will turn up something to explain this…we smelled, we heard, but we saw…what? Nothing. That could only mean…" Luke bit his lip. "Well, you know what that means."

We moved away from the staircase. "Promise me you won't ever come back here alone, Ashby. Better yet, don't ever come without me, specifically. If I hadn't been standing there to catch your fall—I hate to think…"

"I'll avoid solo explorations, sure. But with your schedule—well—it's probably not practical to always wait for you to chaperone my visits. Unfortunately, visits may be necessary if we want to sell the property." And if we want to get to the bottom of our invisible opposition, I thought.

We boarded up the door and prepared to mount our horses. Sasha had turned skittish—just as he had on my very first encounter with the cottage, though Luke's horse remained quietly cropping grass.

"Even Sasha knows something's not right here. How are we to sell this land, demolish this cottage when we have to deal with…with…what looks to be a mean and angry spirit." I quieted Sasha as best I could while looking at Luke for answers.

His expression was grim. "Beats me. Beats the hell out of me."

****

"Tell me, are we still in Virginia?" Luke looked out the window on his side as I drove and drove and drove, gathering altitude slowly but surely into the mountains west of Overhome, the Virginia Highlands.

Ever since we'd turned off the Interstate, I noticed, the scenery had grown increasingly beautiful. Virginia mountains, never terribly tall, could be deceptively and seductively treacherous, nonetheless. With their gradual rise, lushly forested valleys and mossy overlooks, they lured a driver higher and higher until, ears popping and stomach dropping, one realized it was a long, winding, scary way down. I always kept my eyes on the road directly ahead when driving the mountainous byways; otherwise, my natural tendency for acrophobia could stop me cold.

"Trust me. This is worth our time," I ground out between clenched teeth. I had no intention of turning over the wheel when it was *my* surprise outing.

"Can't you give me a hint? I mean, other than your smug, 'I'm multi-tasking.' We're just about at the top of what might be the tallest mountain in the state."

"No need. We're here!" I slowed, allowing Luke to zero in on a huge sign attached to the wooden gates of a campground: Fiddlers' Convention—Old Time Bands and Bluegrass Competition.

We drove to a parking area and got out. Row after row of camping trailers greeted us as we made our way to the welcome booth at a pavilion where I gave a worker our tickets. "Band competition starts at 7:30," he said. "Set up yer lawn chairs over there, if y' like." He pointed to a grassy area roped off in front of the roofed stage front.

I drew my hoody in tight and shivered. "Whew! It's cold up here! Crisp—the air smells so clean— nothing like the good old summer-humid Virginny we know down there in the flatlands." I pointed toward the slope. "We can eat dinner while we wait, and I'll fill you in."

Luke hefted the picnic basket onto his shoulder and we ambled over to a spot not far from center stage, all the while, taking in the crowded venue: hundreds of trailers and what looked to be impromptu bands jamming at every campsite. Luke gazed at the panorama. "This is huge—there must be—what—twenty thousand people here?"

We set up our chairs and dove into the fried chicken and biscuit dinner I'd purchased at a trendy little shop called Oar Knot on our way out, serenaded all the while with random riffs of music from various areas of the campground. As we chowed down, I offered an explanation. "I'm doing an article for *Blue Ridge Heritage* on one of the bands here—they call themselves Solid Ground—a local family bluegrass group. I'm profiling them for my piece on arts and artists."

"Bluegrass, eh? I thought you consider yourself an ABC girl. Anything but country." Luke looked skeptical.

"Yeah, well that was a long time ago. Anyway, bluegrass and country are entirely different types of music. Country is usually s-l-o-o-o-w. Bluegrass is fast. 'Smokin' fast,' is the official terminology. Another difference—modern country music is all about electricity. Electric keyboard, electric guitar...not so with bluegrass. It's just natural sound, and it takes hard work and skill to achieve the right tone."

Luke looked impressed. "You say? When did you get to be such a music expert?"

"I've been listening to CDs nonstop, and I interviewed Robby Mitchell—the leader of Solid

Ground. Specializes in mandolin—he's been playing since he was eight years old, Luke. Robbie's won a ton of trophies and ribbons—his first when he was only ten years old. He's been named national champion mandolin player five times." I held up my hand and counted off five fingers for emphasis. "And many years later, he's still pickin'. Now, his three daughters do all the singing for Solid Ground." I nibbled on a biscuit. "Oh, most of the band members play multiple instruments. They'll switch from fiddle or mandolin to guitar just for variety."

"I'm impressed." Luke began gathering up the remnants of our repast. "So you dragged me up here to witness bluegrass performance up close and personal?"

"Hey! You're gonna love it, Luke. Just wait and see. I can understand how bluegrass gets such a huge following. It takes tremendous talent to churn out such up-tempo tunes. *Hard-drivin'* bluegrass is what the judges look for."

"Well, I've heard of Solid Ground. The group's been around for a long time. They played for a high school grad party that I attended." Luke grinned. "I danced all night with Loretta Dobson, the class beauty and a self-professed bluegrass lover."

I gave Luke a narrow look. "Thanks for that blast from the past." I finished my biscuit and dusted my hands together. "Robbie's band has been jamming since long before your high school days. Since the '70s. Evolving over the years, of course. They've played in competitions and festivals from the Berkshires in New York to campgrounds in Florida and in every state in between."

Luke looked at his watch. "Just about time for the

competition to begin." He reached for my hand. "This could be fun. Thanks for bringing me, Ashby."

I squeezed his hand. "It was serendipity. Perfect timing, for once—you're home, I have a deadline—complimentary tickets from Robbie and we got in a cool road trip to the highlands." Even if I'm not the class beauty, I thought.

Though night had descended, the stage was lit up bright as noonday. The crowd stirred, then hushed, as the first group trotted onto the stage to scattered applause. The competition had begun.

It was all good, I had to admit, with each band putting an individual stamp of personality on its performance, but Solid Ground was my reason for being here. I hoped we wouldn't have to stay until midnight for their turn, as group after group moved onto the stage, did their thing and slipped off. No sooner did this thought flit through my mind, than Robbie and his gang bounded onto the platform to thunderous applause. Dressed casually in jeans and unmatched flannel shirts, Solid Ground was truly on solid ground here. People stood, clapping and stomping and calling out the names of the band members. "Hey, Robbie!" and "You go, Laura! Sing it, baby!"

The high-pitched, squeaky fiddle charged hard into "Orange Blossom Special." Robbie was a mandolin magician, his fingers flying too fast to be detected by the human eye and I knew, then and there, he'd win the solo competition. It was absolutely impossible to sit or stand without tapping something or clapping or just plain moving to the fast and furious beat—an adrenaline rush that left me breathless.

Dancers thronged the dirt floor between the seats

and the stage, stomping out the flat-foot, clogging and gyrating with wild variations of Western swing and shag. The whole scene shook as Solid Ground rocked the rafters. If the crowd had had its way, the group would have played on into the night, but the one-song rule of competition prohibited that. As the next band in line hopped onto the stage, Luke and I began packing up to leave.

"Wow! Absolutely amazing! Loretta would have loved it!" Luke gave me a sly smile.

I headed for the stage exit. "Let me see if I can touch base with Robbie before we leave."

Just then Robbie jogged over and shook my hand and then Luke's. Luke introduced himself. "Great job! I'm sure your band will win."

Robbie put a hand on my shoulder and squeezed gently before answering. "Thanks. An' thanks for comin' tonight. Hope you got what you needed for your article, Ashby." He grinned and then added, "Oh, by the way, there's a fellah backstage who'd like to meet you." He waved at a figure behind him, then jogged back to his crew.

A middle-aged man wearing a wide-brimmed hat and a string tie stepped into the floodlights. "Hey, Miss Overton?"

I nodded, giving Luke a sidelong puzzled look.

"Name's Kyle Stover—that's Kyle Overton Stover, from Luray, Virginia. My group performed earlier tonight." He shook hands with me and then with Luke. "Robbie and I was talkin' before the show opened. When he told me about your interview with him, I let him know we're most likely related."

"Kyle Overton Stover," I said. "Interesting."

"My great uncle—name's Isaac Stover—is doin' a genealogy on the Overton-Stover family connection. A Stover relative married into the Overton clan way back before the Civil War. Isaac about drives us crazy askin' for family photos and stories and all, and he talks on an' on about the family connection at Overhome."

"You say you're from Luray?" Luke asked.

"Yep—the other side of this here mountain range, in Page County," Kyle answered. "If ya'll're interested in learnin' more about your ancestors, y'might give ol' Isaac a call." He chuckled. "Might help us out, too. Give us some relief with his never-endin' search for family ties."

"Thanks, Kyle. We actually *are* looking for any and all historic information on the Overtons, as we speak. I'll give Isaac's name to Hal Reynolds, the historian who's helping us. He'll be delighted, and I'm sure he'll contact your uncle soon."

"Good t'meet ya," Kyle said. "If you're ever in the Valley, look us up." With a wave, he retreated into the shadows.

It was a long way home, and I was more than happy to turn over the driving to Luke. "Well. Can you believe that? A family connection on top of a mountain. How random is that?"

"Yeah. It's a small world. Hal will be overjoyed." Luke touched my knee. "Were we thinking of hiring a band for the wedding?"

"Mind-reader! Robbie's already agreed to the deal. He's even giving us a bit of a discount, considering my article to be free advertising. One reason I wanted you to join me—a sort of preview for our wedding." I punched his shoulder. "You're such a good ole' boy.

Why am I not surprised to learn you've heard them play before? Sometimes, I think you should be writing these 'local arts and artists' articles."

"Too bad writing isn't one of my talents. If you can catch the spirit of that sound...the article will be amazing."

Luke pulled me close. "Come on, babe. Snuggle up for these COD curves ahead of us."

I moved to Luke's side and nestled under his arm. "Come-Over-Dear curves. How I love 'em."

****

Dear, Dear Diary:

Having Mom and Dad here has been a godsend, for sure. Mom's handling dozens of wedding details for Luke and me while steadily and gently guiding Carlos' entire family toward their assimilation and education goals. The underlying calm and esprit de corps are subtly working for the entire estate. Dad has fallen into the role of accountant. You'd think he was born to the task the way he's finding all kinds of money-saving and money-making avenues for Overhome. But get this! The latest boon: Dad plans to function as our developer for the sale property, saving us a bundle and hopefully expediting the operation! He's already talked with several engineering firms to find the most workable plan.

ME: "Dad, you were a career chemistry teacher. Where ever did you acquire these skills? Accounting? Developing? Did you have a secret life somewhere all those years we lived in New Jersey?"

DAD: "Little did you know. School teachers have to make that lauded 'summer off' a 'pay-off.' For many Julys and Augusts of my career I worked for new homes developments where I learned to read plats and topo maps. I saw what worked and what didn't for start-up projects. And many of my supervisors were more than glad to turn over the accounting to me. They were more interested in using their time to sell, sell, sell!"

ME: "Glory be! We may pull this off yet, Dad. Thanks to you and Mom."

DAD: "Just don't ask me to sell anything. A salesman I am NOT."

Seems Dad sold a lot of his students on chemistry, but I know he'd consider that to be an entirely different kind of salesmanship. And I do remember his working summer jobs. I guess I never paid much attention to exactly what he did.

Luke's off on another tracking assignment. We had a wonderful send-off in the remaining hours of his leave after the bluegrass concert. I will only say one thing: I did not get much writing done.

Chapter 11

Dad, Monica and I stood in the yard behind the cottage as Hal flipped through a bristle of papers attached to a clipboard. We had made a thorough tour of the inside, where Hal had peered up and down the walls, scrutinized the stairway and examined every window, ceiling beam and floorboard.

"The structure could have been built as early as the 1700s—an overseer's cottage, all right. But the original overseer was all about the furnace rather than the fields. Overhome once housed a furnace for making pig iron." He paced over an area of the yard. "See? Here are stones—evidence of a foundation. Your contact, Isaac Stover, has all the documentation."

So those stone foundations our Realtor noticed were from an old furnace. I was surprised—nothing in my database about pig iron.

"With the shut-down of the furnace, a slave overseer and his family occupied the cottage. But when the Civil War broke out, the man joined the Confederacy and his wife and children moved away. The cottage remained unused until at least 1863— before the war ended." Hal flipped a few pages on his clipboard. "Yes, here it is. At some point in that year, twenty-three year-old Raeford Overton moved into the cottage. Raef, as he was called, came home from the war and lived in the cottage until he died years later."

Monica spoke up. "Raeford's mother, Hannah, lived in the manor house at the time. Raeford's two older brothers had joined the Rebel forces. His father, Burwell, had also gone off to war."

Hal took up the narrative. "Burwell was injured at Gettysburg when one musket ball grazed his cheek and another shattered his left leg. He came home to recover and stayed for good." Hal smiled sheepishly. "Sorry. I'm a boring Civil War buff. Hannah, Burwell and their daughter Angelina remained at Overhome for the rest of their lives, but the two brothers were killed in the war."

I puzzled over this before asking, "So, why would Raeford, Raef, live in the cottage instead of joining his parents and sister in the big house when he returned? Was he a loner or something?"

"And why is Raeford Overton's picture not included in the portrait gallery?" Monica shook her head. "He was a Confederate soldier. All the Overton Confederate soldiers are immortalized in our portrait gallery. It doesn't make sense."

Hal tapped the clipboard. "A mystery. Raeford Overton definitely served in the Confederate forces. He joined the 7th Virginia Cavalry along with his first cousin, Jeb Stover, out of Page County. What was Raef doing at Overhome when the war would continue for more than a year. Was he ill? Injured? Suffering from PTSD?"

"Wouldn't he convalesce in the manor house?" I mused. "Wouldn't his family want to nurse him back to health?"

"We just don't know. That's the fascination of historical research—a bunch of puzzles with dozens of mismatched pieces that you eventually hope to put together for a complete picture." Hal looked cheerful. "I'm—we're working on it." He turned to Monica with an affectionate look, and I noticed how she naturally wafted to his side.

"I never suspected that chasing after history would be such fun—full of surprises," Monica gushed.

"Like discovering Isaac Stover, who's almost as nutty about the Civil War as I am." Hal cast another fond look at Monica. "Thanks for that connection you found, Ashby. At a fiddler's convention, no less."

"Old Isaac seems very lonely. Nonetheless, he is an expert genealogist. He has spent years and years gathering information on both the Stovers and the Overtons. Hal and I make an appreciative audience. He welcomed us with open arms."

"Well, we're an appreciative audience, too," Dad said. "I've spent a lifetime denying my heritage, but now I'm ready to learn all I can."

What I didn't mention is that I knew a bit about Burwell and his family from reading the Overton women's diaries. One particular diary, written by Angelina Elisabeth Overton, covered the four years of the Civil War. She mentioned her father's injuries at Gettysburg and his return to Overhome to heal. She talked about the deaths of her brothers Robert and Johbe—both casualties of the war. But she never mentioned a brother named Raeford. Not a word. I made a note to show the diaries to Hal and Monica. We kept them in a glass case in the library in an effort to preserve them. Raef Overton—another history mystery. Hal would surely be in seventh heaven over the diaries. I didn't know why I hadn't thought of them earlier.

As Monica and Hal departed, a truck wheezed into

view. Dad waved it to a stop. "I've hired Lewis and Elders Engineering firm. These must be the surveyors they promised to send out," he called to me over his shoulder as he jogged toward the truck.

Two men dressed in brown workpants and wearing baseball caps emerged, then unloaded equipment from the truck bed—a surveyor's tool on a tripod, wooden stakes, hammers and markers and other materials. "We're here to do a boundary survey," one of them said, shaking Dad's hand, and then mine. He unrolled a large slab of paper and other documents. "My name's Vince. My partner is Calvin. We'll plot the points. Would you like to take a look at this old deed which describes the boundaries?"

Dad and I moved in for a closer look, and I puzzled over the ancient document. "I'm not sure what I'm looking at—rock pile? Large red oak? Creek? What's all this mean?"

"In the old days they used trees and rocks and creeks to mark the boundaries—all of which can and will change, of course. That's why we need a new survey." Vince unrolled another document. "Here's the one that was updated when the lake was formed— what—about fifty years ago. After we complete the boundary survey on the part of land you want to sell, we'll come back to plot the topography for a topo map." Calvin removed his cap and scratched his head. "I've gotta tell you, this is the oldest piece of property I've ever worked on."

"What about the cottage?" It was my original worry: Would the cottage affect our development project? Would the development affect the cottage?

"Oh, the structure is here on the old map." Vince

pointed. That was not what I meant when I asked my question. He walked back to the truck and Dad headed in the direction of the cottage, leaving me standing there thinking that my father and I were surely both wondering the same thing: Would the cottage have to be torn down?

For a moment, I stood, watching the surveyors work. I realized the historic nature of the cottage could be a problem. And the ruins of the furnace? Could some hysterical historical society get in our way? Oh yeah. What about old Rotten Eggs, the unfriendly ghost? Of course, Dad didn't know about that little problem. Not yet.

As if on cue, the familiar chill emerged out of nowhere—a gust of wintry wind. I glanced at Vince and Calvin, in the distance, just in time to see both of their ball caps simultaneously fly off their heads in the sudden burst of air. Flailing their arms like windmills, they turned their backs and ran after their whirling headgear. So, I should have braced for what came next, but it happened so fast I was blind-sided. A black shadow swooped to within inches of my face. Cold, dark and foul-smelling, it wrapped around my throat like a tightening rubber band. "Raeford!" I managed to scream through my gurgling vocal cords. "Raef! Stop! Leave me alone!"

Dad, who had reached the cottage, turned around at the sound, then, ran back toward me, looking frantic. "Ashby! What is it? What's wrong?" Reaching me, he reeled back as the frigid blast turned onto him. "What in God's name…"

Then it was gone. Dissipated into the warm summer air, leaving only a faint odorous reminder of its existence. My father and I looked at each other, gravitating between shock and horror. He was the first to find voice. "It looked like something was going after you, Ashby. It only stopped when you called out *Raeford*. Its name?"

I was unable to control my trembling voice. "N-n-not my first encounter with…with…whoever he is. Though it *is* a first to be able to put a name to it…to him…going on Hal's history of Raeford Overton. I don't know what made me say that name—Raeford. Impulse, maybe." I fingered my throat tentatively. "Remember the chandelier? I suspect the same force had a hand in that curious event—the night I told everyone about my plan to sell off fifty acres. And last time I was here along with Luke, it tried to push me down the stairs. There've been other incidents." I looked at the two workers standing in the distance, staring at us in open-mouthed surprise. "In fact, the day we rode out here with Paul, it slapped me as I was getting into the back of the Jeep. You and Paul were unaware of it."

Dad pulled me close and gave me a fatherly hug. "Looks like Raeford, or whoever it is, has a bone to pick with us. With you. For whatever reason, this…this *entity* is not happy about our interest in the cottage."

"You think?" I managed a feeble smile.

All the way home Dad grilled me on the ghosts of Overhome. Skeptical as he wanted to remain, he kept returning to the evidence he'd witnessed with Tornado Raef. By the time we reached the house, he was beginning to accept that something oddly unscientific and unexplainable was definitely afoot. He placed both hands on my shoulders and looked me in the eyes. "Is it worth it? Worth the danger this force presents to continue with our development plan?"

I put on my bravest look. "I hope we can work through this. See, I know I'm the target for all the attacks. As I told you, Dad, I've experienced the…the unpredictability of the spirit world at Overhome before." I attempted a smile. "And I am convinced there's a reason for this—this hostility. My thought is if we find the reason, we'll solve the problem."

He shook his head. "I don't know. I just don't know. Promise me one thing, Ashby. Promise me you'll stay away from the cottage. Let me or Luke, or Paul deal with whatever it is that's so hell-bent on destruction."

"Luke feels the same way. I appreciate your both wanting to protect me, but I'm afraid I'm the only one who can get to the bottom of this." I wrapped my arms around my father. "I'll take every precaution I can, Dad. That I can honestly promise."

As we parted ways, I knew my father was not satisfied that I could take care of myself. I admit that I had sounded more confident than I actually felt. This spirit was one mean, mad entity—unpredictable and dangerous. I'd have to be constantly vigilant.

****

"Carole Norton," Monica said. "Do you remember Carole, Ashby? They summer at the lake. Her daughter Tiffany used to ski with you."

My aunt and I sat on the sun porch sipping iced tea. "Sorry, Monica. I was daydreaming." I forcefully cleared my mind of the latest spirit assault, then made eye contact with my aunt. "I do remember the Nortons. Carole and Tiffany: two bubbly blondes. In fact,

Tiffany and I stayed in touch while we were both in college—an email now and then. She graduated from Duke last year—married a doctor she met through the medical center there—but we lost contact with each other. I believe they moved somewhere up north."

"Carole and I were golfing the other day and she told me that Tiffany and Brad have recently relocated to Moore Mountain Lake. Not just a summer home, but for year-round residence. Brad landed a good job with Central Health." She paused. "How would you feel about inviting them to your wedding?"

"Sure, Monica. Why not? I'd love to see Tiff—meet her husband. Catch up. Carole and Tiff's dad could attend, too."

"I thought it would be all right. It might even help our cause."

I must have looked like a deer in headlights. "What cause?"

"More boarding horses. More riding lessons. That *is* the plan, I believe."

"Oh, yes. I remember that Tiffany talked about her horse—how she missed it when they were at their summer place here."

"The Norton family has multiple horses—on their farm in Northern Virginia."

"And they want to board them here? Because Tiffany is here?"

"Exactly. It seems Carlos' reputation has caught their attention. Carole and Tiffany have made an appointment to talk with him, observe his techniques. If they like what they see, they will be boarding and training their horses at Overhome."

"Why don't Tiffany and Brad just buy a farm and

live on it here at the lake? Then they wouldn't have to board their horses."

"Well, they could do that, of course. Not good for us, though. They might even try to lure Carlos away from us for themselves." Monica shuddered at the thought. "I believe they far prefer to live in a nice residential lake community rather than on a farm."

"Whew! That's a lucky collusion of the planets."

"Carole and her husband own a young gelding ready for hunter-jumper training, and Tiffany and Brad have invested in two Thoroughbreds. Tiffany wants to work closely with them. They hope to move the whole operation to Moore Mountain Lake. Next step? Overhome."

"Wow. That will keep Carlos and Julio busy. We might even have to look for more help." I sighed. "Better not count my chickens before they hatch."

Monica leaned toward me and lowered her voice as though she were confiding in me. "Ashby, the Nortons have friends. Lots of wealthy, horsey friends. And Brad is—well—he's a bit older than Tiffany—and he grew up with horses—knows all about showing and racing and such. It's a connection we could tap for more clients." She sat back and resumed her normal voice. "I was never really a part of that crowd myself, and when Hunter died—well—I lost all ties. But the Nortons are the hub of the horse set, believe me."

"Looks like a good time to practice your power golf, Monica. Those wealthy, horsey friends of the Nortons—invite them to join you at your club for a friendly little round of golf, or lunch, or whatever works. What do you say?"

"I'm polishing up my putting," she said with a

laugh.

Clattering and chattering noises ushered in Jeff and Nick, playing at punch-and-run. "Oh, sorry, Mom," Jeff apologized. "Didn't know you were out here on the porch. Nick and Aunt Helen just finished their reading lessons."

Nick looked pleased. "Miss Helen's teaching me phonics. In elementary school we never learned about sounding out words. We just memorized them. *Sight-reading*, Miss Helen calls it—the look-say method. That's how I learned to read. I never knew you could sound out the hard words you didn't already know."

"Show them what you're reading, Nick." Jeff poked his friend. Nick pulled a worn paperback from his jeans pocket. "*Harry Potter*." He looked both proud of himself and slightly surprised.

"Now Nick's got me hooked on *Harry Potter*. The books are awesome!" Jeff eyed the frosty pitcher of tea.

"If you and Nick wash up and come back out in a more civilized manner, you may have tea and some cookies, if you like." Monica patted Jeff's arm. "Miss Emma baked a fresh batch for us this afternoon. They're on the kitchen counter."

"Oh, man! Totally awesome!" The two boys scuttled into the house, fighting to beat each other through the door.

"Awesome." Monica looked bemused. "I'll tell you what is awesome, Ashby. Your mother, Helen. Anyone who can get twelve-year-old boys to read during summer vacation is beyond awesome. Does she practice witchcraft, by any chance?"

Chapter 12

"Who's that?" I whispered to Luke, pointing to a man and a boy who were following caretaker Sam to the paddock. "New customers? I've never seen either one of them before."

We stood in the cool shadows near the barn door admiring our farm. In full bloom, the trees and flowering bushes, the neatly trimmed grassy areas radiated a healthy summer glow. The barn smelled sweet and fresh with clean straw and clean horses. Eddie's cats meowed and wound themselves around our ankles, ropes of soft fur and sinew. Even the pigs in one of the stalls, thanks to Sam's animal-loving heart, grunted peacefully as they slept. It was a scene straight out of *Charlotte's Web*, within a natural picture frame of mountains. "It's all so beautiful," I breathed.

Luke drew me in for a strong embrace. "Can you believe I pulled two full days without duty? I want to be here. With you. All the time."

I rested my head on his shoulder. "Mmmmm. Perfect. It can't come soon enough for me." We hugged, rocking back and forth comfortably until Carlos and the two visitors appeared from the distance walking back toward the barn. They could not see us, but they stopped close enough for us to hear parts of their conversation.

Evidently the two were father and son, and it

seemed that the father was interested in his son taking riding lessons. "His mother babies him," the elder was saying. "…he just wants to play video games all day…can hardly get him off the couch…need to toughen him up. I'm an outdoor dad with an indoor kid." The man, much taller than Carlos, had a tendency to thrust forth his rather large, florid jaw when he talked, as a way to project his voice, or, perhaps, to emphasize the importance of his words the way some people jab their fingers while they talk.

The boy looked on sullenly, alternately kicking at the ground and casting snake-eyes at the beautiful chestnut on Carlos' lunge-line, as though he wanted to kick him, too. Caught without an escape route, Luke and I backed into the shadows, hoping to remain undetected.

Carlos tried to make eye contact with the boy, whom I judged to be about Jeff's age. His arms and legs rolled with soft, spongy skin that looked unmuscled, almost girlish. Petulant, the boy refused to accept Carlos' overtures.

"I don't like horses. They stink," he muttered, not quite under his breath.

The father ignored his son. "Kicked out of that expensive private school his mother insisted on sending him to. Bullying the younger kids or some other ridiculous infraction." He tilted his head and narrowed his eyes, giving Carlos a once-over. "You come highly recommended, says my wife. Wife's awfully particular, y'know. She'll be in later today—wants to see about boarding her horse at Overhome." The man glanced dismissively at his son. "But *he's* the reason I'm here." Back to the shrewd look at Carlos. "What do you think?

Can you make a man of him?"

I watched our trainer's face for signs of disgust or dismissal—anything akin to my own negative feelings, but he was stoic as a gladiator. "The horse, *señor*. The horse will decide that."

Luke and I locked eyes and simultaneously produced thumbs-up. "Good luck," Luke whispered. "Looks like Carlos has his work cut out for him with these two."

"I can't wait to meet the kid's mother. Want to bet she's a real sweetheart?"

Approaching the entrance on the opposite side of the barn were Jeff and Nick. I stepped out of the shadows just far enough to get their attention, wave my arm silently and place a finger to my lips. They slowed down, all but tiptoeing their way to our corner.

"What's up?" Jeff's voice was so low I could barely hear him.

"Sh-h-h, new blood for Overhome's horse business." I pointed to the pair still standing in the yard beside Carlos.

Nick stared, shook his head, then stared some more. "Oh, no. That's Winn Davies. He was in my homeroom and my English class last year."

It was Jeff's turn to stare. "Y'mean the guy…the one you told me about…the…"

"The bully," Nick said through tight lips. "Called me the Wetback Kid. Made fun of my reading problems. Thought he was a hot shot, talking trash all the time. 'Hey, Wetback, your momma send tortillas and hot peppers for your lunch?' Stuff like that."

"Jeez. That's mean." Jeff eyed his friend sympathetically.

"We heard he was kicked out of his other school for bullying. I guess he learned to be quieter about it at my school. None of the teachers caught it, and he was always trying to grab me outside of school when his buddies were around so they could beat me up. But I was too fast for them." Nick looked woebegone. "Now he's gonna be here all summer?"

I had been thinking as the boys talked. "You know, Nick, it might not be all bad having this guy take riding lessons with Carlos."

Luke took up my argument. "I agree, Nick. This kid—name's Winn? That's ironic. I mean, he's obviously a Loser, not a Winner. And he won't have any of his jerk friends around to back him up if he tries his bullying around here."

"Yeah," Jeff put in with a show of loyalty. "He might just get what's comin' to him."

Still whispering, we watched silently from our corner until they left with a slam of their car doors and the revving of the motor. "Let's see what Carlos has to say in the matter." Luke took my hand and we strode out to the yard. "Carlos, *mi amigo*! Ashby and I caught some of that conversation. I must say, you handled the situation very well. But are you sure you want to take on this crew? You are not obligated to do so, you know."

"Ah, Luke, Ashby. *Hola. Gracias.* I have handled similar situation many times. Sometimes the rich...well, they have their own problem, yes? This youngster, he will not get his own way. It does not work like that when it comes to horses. They are a better judge of us than we are of ourselves."

"How wise you are, Carlos." I shook his hand to

show my appreciation. "I'm sure you'll do well with the boy."

"Is your work all done?" Carlos called to Nick as he and Jeff ambled out of the barn and into the yard to join us.

Nick nodded. "We've been helping Sam all morning."

"Sam's easier to work for than Eddie," Jeff chimed in. "Eddie likes to boss us around too much."

Luke and I looked at each other and suppressed our smiles. No surprises there.

Just then Eddie appeared, looking frazzled. "There's a lady in th' office—Ms. Somebody Davies—wants a complete tour of th' barn—tack room—paddocks and round pen. Says she *might* consider boardin' her *extremely* valuable imported warm blood with us."

I gave our groom an incredulous look. "So, show her around, Eddie. What's the problem? You've surely done that dozens of times with other prospective clients."

Eddie straightened his shoulders and drew in his chin. "Says she cain't understan' me an' she needs somebody speaks English fer a tour guide."

"I would volunteer," Carlos spoke up, "but she might have same complaint about me, eh?" He bowed, then, opened an arm in invitation. "*Si, señora, vamanos!*"

We all laughed raucously and, suddenly, I knew this Davies family was not going to be a problem for us.

"Luke, shall we conduct the grand tour ourselves?" I gave him a wink.

Luke bowed in imitation of Carlos. "*Si, señorita.*

Vamanos!" Together we walked to Eddie's office.

"Mrs. Davies, I'm Ashby Overton. My fiancé, Luke Murley." I forced my most gracious voice and manner.

Mrs. Davies reeked of money. She had enhanced her pudgy figure with a nicely-tailored jacket that nipped in at the waist. Ropes of gold jewelry somewhat camouflaged her thick neck, but her buttery-smooth leather boots, climbing almost to the knee, only emphasized her short stature. She looked pointedly at her diamond-encrusted watch. "Well, I haven't all day. Show me what you've got, please. I'm used to only the very best facilities. My Adonis is high-strung and requires expert handling." She sniffed, looking for something to complain about, no doubt. Finding nothing, she went on. "I've heard quite good things about your trainer. What's his name? Jose? Hector? Something Hispanic." She wrinkled her brow; the heavy makeup intended to hide the frown lines on her forehead failed to do the job.

"Carlos. His name is Carlos Vasquez. You've heard right, Mrs. Davies. Carlos is both experienced and skilled, and he is especially effective with high-strung horses." Luke's own attempt at graciousness was strained.

"I must say I am *not* impressed with your stable boy." Her nostrils flared as she pointed in the direction of Eddie's office.

"Eddie Mills is our groom, Mrs. Davies. He is quite knowledgeable. You needn't worry about that." Luke's decisiveness would have made Eddie glow.

"Yes. I believe you'll find our horse farm here at Overhome to be an excellent placement for Adonis.

And Carlos is a fine teacher. Is Winn your son? We just met him."

She nodded.

"Both your horse and your son will be in good hands." I glanced at her expensive boots. "Do you ride yourself, Mrs. Davies?"

"I don't have time for horseback riding," she huffed.

"By the way, Mrs. Davies, would you mind telling us where you heard about our trainer?" I could not stifle my curiosity.

She compressed her thin lips into an unattractive line. "I have my sources. Can we discuss the costs?"

"Eddie will give you complete details. And a contract if you decide to board Adonis here." I looked steadily into her close-set eyes. "After our tour of the facilities, I'll show you back to his office."

****

Dear Diary:

I know we have a Barn Queen on our hands, but the fact that Eddie has taken an instant dislike to Mrs. Davies comforts me no end. He will not let this chick get away with lording it over his barn, no matter what her horse is worth. It'll be Virginia Country-Boy vs. Princess Haughty Horsewoman Wannabe. I say, let the games begin!

I am a bit concerned, however, that the Disastrous Davies family may be a referral from Tiffany Norton or Carole. If all their "wealthy horsey friends" are like this, we may be in for more trouble than the new clientele is worth. Monica has never heard of them, but I intend to ferret out Mrs. D's "source." They're all coming on deck next week—"Loser" Winn and Adonis and Mrs. Davies—a trifecta of trouble?

On a pleasanter note, after our encounter with the Davies crew, Luke and I took Jeff and Nick out on the boat for a glorious afternoon ski run. Nick is just learning how to wakeboard and ski on a pair. Luke and Jeff are wonderful teachers—patient and helpful. Nick is glowing with all his accomplishments. No way can we allow a spoiled brat like Winn Davies to upset such positive momentum. I wonder if Nick will tell his parents about the bullying. I sincerely doubt he's said anything to them up to now. Boys are like that.

Needless to say, Luke and I had to hastily "clean up" the ski boat before our run. A blanket here, a pillow there, a couple of plastic champagne stems and a few (ahem) under garments. I wonder if we're fooling anybody, though. Jeff's offhand comment raised my eyebrows a notch, something about our boat looking "lived in."

Luke and I make the most of our time together, even though he is working frantically to set up his future practice at Overhome while finishing up vet school, and I am using every spare minute to write my articles for Blue Ridge Heritage *and plug into the M&M Express about wedding details. Both Luke and I have asked our college roommates to stand up with us—Aneesh Gopul and Danielle*

Rollins. And both have graciously accepted! It's probably a good thing that so much is going on lest I obsess over the nuptial plans. The very thought of our future as husband and wife revs up my heart rate! We simply cannot allow a spiteful spirit to interfere. There. I've written it, Diary. My greatest fear: Luke and I will have to delay the wedding for a reason completely beyond our control. I dare not say it aloud, lest it come true. Okay. Now I am banishing any such thoughts from my mind.

Did I mention I'm covering wood-turning in a future article? Somewhat different from wood-carving, I'm learning. This place is crawling with art and artists—fortunately for me! You see how scattered and random my thought pattern is, alas.

The surveyors are doing their thing as we speak. There are a lot of technicalities and uncertainties about selling the tract, but we're determined to remain optimistic. We've got a fighting chance, though there's a definite sticking point. You know what I'm referring to, Diary. Mr. Mini-tornado, who is, quite possibly, the spirit of Raeford Overton. What's his problem, anyway? What's he up to? Why is he concentrating his energy on me? At a loss to explain it, I am certain of but one thing: Whatever Raef is about, it is connected to the overseer's cottage. And, ultimately, it's connected to me. Does this scare me? Unqualified YES is my answer. Truth be told, I am terrified. But I will not let my fear stop our progress. Luke—Dad—they both worry for my safety because they love me. And Mom keeps giving me sidelong looks and random pats on the back, hugging me while murmuring, "Be careful" or "Watch your step," or "Oh dear, oh dear." I'm pretty sure that once we solve the mystery of Raeford Overton and the overseer's cottage, we will be home free. Until then, I admit how aware I am of this fact: Each incident with this rotten-spirited spirit has become increasingly aggressive. Next time, who knows, he may seriously injure me— or worse.

Chapter 13

Dad and I dismounted and let our horses graze. Walking to the now-familiar site, we found the surveyors, Vince and Calvin, standing, caps in hand, staring at the grounds around the cottage. Vince leaned over and picked up a broken survey marker. "I'll be dogged." He showed the damaged stake to his partner. "Look here." He began walking and gathering up stakes scattered randomly about the ground. "Every one of 'em. Pulled up. Broke in half. Thrown down every which way."

"Never seen anything like this before." Calvin scratched his head. "Looks like pure vandalism to me."

Dad and I exchanged a look. A mini-tornado named Raeford Overton was my thought. I could tell Dad had the same idea.

Calvin looked from Dad to me to Vince. "We'll have to do it all over again. At least we've got the survey points plotted on the computer. We know where the markers go, but we'll have to restake 'em. Never seen anything like this before," he repeated.

I beckoned Dad aside, lowering my voice. "I know what you're thinking Dad. But there is one other possibility. The Night Riders. Eddie's old pranking group. It's just the kind of stunt they'd pull."

"Eddie? You think Eddie might be involved?" Dad looked skeptical.

"No. I don't. But there's a tiny chance…see, he told me he could never work on Tuesday nights…that he has another obligation. He insisted he's done with the Night Riders, though. And they could've done it without Eddie."

"Tuesday night, eh? Today is Wednesday. Yes, well, I guess we'd better check it out. See if the Night Riders meet Tuesdays." Dad shook his head and looked at me. "Sad to say, it would be better if it were the Night Riders than…"

"Tornado Raef," I finished. A force to be reckoned with, for sure. If we only knew how.

For a while we stood watching the surveyors work, unloading new stakes from the truck and referring to a computer print-out. What a colossal waste of time and effort. We'd have to find a way to keep it from happening again. I looked at my father. "Any ideas?"

"Actually, I do have something in mind. Let's say your instincts are correct—that Eddie has quit the Night Riders—that he and they are completely innocent of any wrong-doing here."

"Okay. Let's say that. What's your idea?"

"Why not see if we can get Eddie to agree to a stakeout?" Dad chuckled. "A stakeout to keep the stakes in. Let him spend the night at the cottage and maintain lookout."

"Brilliant idea! We tell him somebody's ripped up the stakes—he'll know nothing about Raef—a completely objective view. And even if he is still somehow connected to the Night Riders, he'd have to halt any further action on their part as a means of self-preservation." I offered a high five. "As I said, brilliant!"

"Of course, the plan compromises Eddie's personal safety. I mean, is it fair to stick him out here alone at night completely unaware of…of what might happen…in terms of…"

"A mean-spirited spirit?" I felt my grin fading. "You're right, Dad. But if we tell Eddie to take his gun along—just in case…"

"And that dog I've seen following him around the barn. He could take Barney along for protection."

"I have no idea what effect a dog—or a gun— would have on a ghost, but at least Eddie would consider himself safe, and we won't feel so guilty about setting him up." I always harbored a soft spot for my cousin.

"You ask him, Ashby. I have a feeling Eddie will do anything for you. The guy's obviously crazy about you."

"Consider it done. I'll ask him to camp out at the cottage tonight. But, in all fairness, I think I'll let Eddie know we've seen some—shall we call it—paranormal action. Let's see what happens."

We both turned to look at the surveyors scurrying around. "Can we help?" Dad called to Vince and Calvin. "If it's just grunt labor, I can pound in a stake as well as the next guy."

"Me, too," I chimed in.

"I'm afraid not. The county supervisor wouldn't look so kindly on that. But thanks for offering." Vince continued to work at his task.

Calvin looked at his partner, then at us. "Tell y'what. There shouldn't be any objection to your scouting out the rest of the property—further out—you know. Where we haven't checked yet. Maybe the damage is contained to this area." He indicated the circle of destruction. "If we're lucky."

"No problem. I'll go down by the creek, if you'll check toward the cedar grove, Dad."

Mounting our horses, we took off in opposite directions. "See you in a bit," I called back to the surveyors.

All along the winding creek bed the stakes had been vandalized similarly to those close to the cottage. However, the farther I got from the vicinity of the cottage, the more the stakes appeared untouched. Circling back, I pondered over the situation. What would Dad find? And what did it all mean?

"Whoa." Dad pulled in the reins. We had arrived back at the cottage at almost the same moment. "How's it look, Ashby?"

"The stakes are fine once they track away from the creek. How about you?"

"Out of sight of the cottage, the stakes remain intact."

"So, the damage is confined to the cottage and its immediate surroundings." I dismounted from Sasha. "The guys will be glad to hear that. Cuts down on their work."

Dad chewed his lip in thought. "Any conclusions, dear daughter?"

"Yeah. I'd say so. But first, what do you think?"

"Whoever destroyed the survey stakes was only concerned about the cottage and the yard where it touches the creek."

"Only concerned about the cottage being destroyed or altered. It's like he's saying, 'You are not going to tear down this building. You are not going to sell off this land if I can help it.'"

"Raeford Overton." We spoke in unison.

"And Eddie gets a chance to be the hero."

"Or not," Dad finished my statement. "Now, I think we need to get back inside the cottage. Maybe we've missed something important." He gave me a questioning look. "You know, a real caring father would never lead his daughter into the slaughter like this. I saw what happened last time we entered this black hole. My every instinct tells me, get Ashby out of the way of this deranged spirit, or whatever it is. And here I am, saying *we* need to get back inside." He paused. "Look, why don't I go in—look around—report back to you."

"No dice. It's my battle. I can't stand on the sidelines and ask you or anybody else to do the dirty work." I thought for a moment. "I admit, I'm feeling guilty as all get-out about bringing Eddie in."

We went over every inch of the cottage with care. Dad was surprised to see Jeff and Nick's *casa* in the loft. "So Raeford hasn't tried to run the kids off?" He looked around at the books, chairs and tables.

"He's made himself known, according to Jeff. But other than noises and smells, it seems he hasn't shown any more overt opposition."

"More evidence that he's singled out you for his aggression."

"It's like the spirit knows I'm the one who's instrumental in changing things—the cottage, the estate land, whatever it is he doesn't want touched. Up until now, and I'm talking since the days Miss Emma and Grandmother Lenore were kids, the ghost has been able to scare away any interest in the cottage." I took a while to collect my thoughts. "You know, Dad, I think he's desperate. That's why he's doing all the bullying—slapping me, pushing me down the stairs, trying to strangle me. If he gets me out of the way, his world can maintain status quo. Does that make sense?"

My father gave me a curious look. "You're the one with experience in the occult, Ashby." He threw up his hands. "I'm clueless. I feel like I'm missing a huge chunk of the puzzle. I mean, how do you deal with this…this unknown, unreal world? I don't even know where to start to try to understand."

"It's all about the *who,* the *why* and the *what.* If our ghost is, indeed, Raeford Overton, why is he fixated on the cottage? Because it was his home? Possibly. Because something happened here—something that kept him from crossing over into the afterlife? Also possible. But what? If Raef died in the cottage without resolving something of paramount importance to him or to someone close to him—well, then we might have probable cause. The key is finding answers to the three *w*'s: who, why and what."

"I have another *w* for you. Where? Where do we look for the answers?" Dad shook his head.

"There's got to be a clue somewhere. Something well-hidden. Something Raeford Overton does not want anyone to find."

"So what are we missing? I feel like there's nothing left to explore." Dad shook his head again in frustration.

"You know, I'd almost forgotten about this. Jeff and Nick discovered a small hole in the foundation. They pushed in a pebble, and it took a long time to land. There must be something under that side of the house. Maybe just a crawl space—maybe something bigger—deeper."

At that moment, a wave of foul vapors blew into my face, and I braced for another attack from the netherworld. My heart pounded out the seconds as I held my breath, but nothing happened.

Dad pulled in his chin as the smell reached him. "Whoa!"

"There's something rotten in Denmark," I said with an exhale.

Dad held his nose. "Do I remember correctly— *Hamlet*—Act I, Scene one—the ghost of Hamlet's father appears."

I fanned my face. "Not bad for a chem major."

Everything went black.

****

I awoke to find myself lying on a blanket beside the surveyors' truck, looking up into three worried faces. Dad, Vince and Calvin bent over me with expressions somewhere between panic and hope.

Dad was the first to speak. "Ashby! Are you all right? You're pale as a pearl, child."

"Whew!" Vince breathed. "What in the world happened in there?"

I started to sit up when a searing pain shot through the base of my skull. "Ouch!" I reached back to touch the tender spot.

Calvin jumped up. "Ice—I've got an ice pack in my lunch cooler." He scrambled inside the truck and pulled out the blue plastic rectangle. "Here. Try this." He wrapped it in a towel.

I reached for the ice pack and applied it gingerly to the back of my head. "O-o-o-h. That hurts."

Dad wrinkled his brow. "We need to get you to the doctor. I'll ride back to the house, get Luke's truck. It will take a while, but you can rest here."

"What hit her?" Vince looked to Dad for answers.

"It seemed to come from behind, so I can't be sure. One minute we were talking, and the next she crumpled to the floor—like a crushed soda can."

"You didn't see anything—hear anything? She just blacked out for no reason?" Calvin looked confused. "She prone to fainting spells or something?"

"Not that I know of." Dad turned to me. "What was it, Ashby? What hit you? Let me see the sore spot." Bending, he felt with gentle fingers until I squirmed with discomfort. "Well, at least there's no blood."

He stood, hands on hips. "You haven't said a word, dear. Can you help us here? We don't know what to think."

"Hamlet," I squeezed through tight lips. "The ghost of Hamlet's father." With an iron fist I added to myself.

Vince and Calvin shot a "she's-lost-it" look at each other.

"Never mind." Dad appeared to speak to no one in particular. "I understand." He walked toward his horse.

"Mr. Overton, if you can take her horse, I'll drive her back." Vince flashed his keys.

Still holding the ice pack in one hand, I stood and leaned against the truck. "I'm okay. Just a little woozy. Give me a minute."

Vince retrieved a bottle of water from the truck and opened it, handing it to me. "Drink this. It'll help clear your head."

I sipped the water delicately as the three men watched. "Just a little woozy," I repeated.

****

By afternoon I felt recovered enough to head out to the paddock, having talked Dad out of the doctor's appointment. The whole place was a bustling hive of activity. Carlos' assistant, Julio, was busy with riding lessons in the yard—a new group of five kids ranging in age from about ten to teens on ponies going through the paces of riding basics. Julio showed the kids how to hold the reins, urging them to turn the horses' heads gently, no heavy-handed pulling. The notorious bully, Winn Davies, bit down on his tongue with concentration. His father would have appreciated the generous stream of sweat coursing down his face. Good for Julio. Make him work like everyone else. "Close your leg. Heel down—rhythm," Julio called out. "No slumping! Remember your impulsion." Obviously, we'd succeeded in bumping up our pony class—from the ads and new website—or from Monica's "power golf" tactics—who could tell?

The usual order of events is that the kids who take lessons end up talking their parents into buying a horse, which has to be boarded somewhere—so why not at Overhome? Then more lessons as the kids advance to horse shows and competitions. All a good way to build up our business.

In the paddock, Carlos led Adonis, Mrs. Davies' horse, on a lunge-line—four feet of chain through his halter. He's getting the buck out of Adonis, I thought. I'd seen Carlos do this with high-strung horses many times, and he was a master at it.

While I wondered if the Davies had any idea how lucky they were to get the Overhome treatment, I walked smack into Mrs. D herself acting out her role as

Barn Queen like a pro.

"I asked you a question, but I didn't hear an answer." She glared at Eddie, her nostrils flared unattractively. "Did you or did you not use the hoof pick on Adonis today?"

"I already told ya—I'm doin' my work as usual. I don't need t'be reminded."

"Adonis is very susceptible to hoof problems. Have you brushed him? I insist he be brushed regularly."

Eddie stoically ignored her while she followed him around harping and questioning his every move. Even though I sympathized with his having to deal with a BQ, I thought it was probably good for Eddie. Maybe it would take him down a peg or two, as he *was* becoming a bit smug about his well-run barn. I felt a twinge of guilt at what I planned to ask Eddie as soon as I could get him alone. Was placing him on recon at the cottage unfair? Ruefully, I rubbed the lump still throbbing on the back of my neck.

All the while, Nick and Jeff kept to their tasks, filling water buckets, cleaning stalls, petting the horses and talking to them at every opportunity and sneaking peppermints under the horses' greedy lips.

At long last, Sam brought Adonis in for grooming. She carried a groom box containing a body curry, comb, and hard, medium and soft brushes, a towel and the much-discussed hoof pick. She and Eddie got busy on the gorgeous gelding. Eddie worked him over while Sam calmed him with her incessant baby talk. Even Mrs. Davies was impressed enough to shut her trap for a while.

Leaving Sam to finish up, aided by Jeff and Nick, Eddie stepped back and headed for his office. This was my chance to set out our plan. I admit I was nervous as cat on a rolling pin.

"Eddie, I want to talk to you."

"I hope it don't have nothin' t'do with that woman," he jerked his head in Mrs. Davies' direction. "I've had a belly-full of her today."

"You're handling her beautifully. I congratulate you on your patience."

He smiled then, and the familiar lovelorn look softened his features. "Sorry, Ashby. What's up?"

"Umm, we've had a spot of trouble on the land parcel we're planning to sell. Somebody's removed the surveying sticks—broken them up—tossed them all over the place."

Eddie held up his hands in protest. "I don't know nothin' about that. Honest."

"Well, it could be the Night Riders. But we have no way of knowing, Eddie. That's where you come in." I gave him an encouraging look. "We—Dad and I—we want you to spend the night out there at the old cottage. Watch out for anything strange—trespassers or vandals. Whatever. You could take your gun. And Barney, if you like."

Eddie studied me for a while before answering. "You figgerin' I know about the Night Riders and could deal with 'em if they's at fault? 'Cuz I rode with them once upon a time?" He bit his lip in thought before coming to a conclusion. "I'll do it fer you, Ashby. Only fer you."

I swallowed hard. "There's one other thing you need to know. I…we…Dad and Luke and I…well, we think there may be some paranormal action involved." When Eddie looked blank, I hastened to clarify.

"Spirits, Eddie. A ghost."

"I don't believe in haints," Eddie declared bluntly. "My ma, she's alla time goin' on about haints in th' old house whur I grew up. Well, I flat-out don't believe it."

"Okay. I just wanted you to be forewarned. But, we can't afford another act of vandalism on the survey stakes—or anywhere else, for that matter. It's very important. We're counting on you, Eddie."

"I'll take my pup tent an' my sleepin' bag. Build me a campfire. Sleep with my pistol at my side." He shot me a confident look. "But fergit Barney. He wouldn't hurt a fly. I'll take my new wolf dog along. He'd scare th' bejesus outa anybody."

I'd had some prior experience with Eddie's wolf dog breed—indeed terrifying to humans. But would the half-wild animal have any effect on spirits? "It's completely isolated out there, you know."

"Consider it done," Eddie said. "An' if it's them Night Riders, yer right. I know jest how t'handle 'em."

I'll bet you do, I thought. "Then it's settled. Thanks, Eddie." I walked around the desk and gave him a peck on the cheek. "I can't think of anyone better suited for this job."

Eddie glowed. "If y'ever decide to dump Luke, you'll give me a chance, won't ya, Ashby?"

"You're already the best cousin a girl could hope for." I patted a light touch on his arm.

Chapter 14

We made ourselves comfortable in the library. Luke and I snuggled close on the loveseat, absorbing each other's precious presence. Gathered around in a casual circle were Mom, Dad, Jeff and Miss Emma. All eyes rested on Hal, seated at a table littered with papers and books, his laptop and notepads. Monica sat beside him.

Looking around the room, Hal cleared his throat and began. "First, I want to thank all of you for allowing me to research your family history. I consider it a privilege and an honor. Most of all, it's been more fun than any other project I can recall." Blushing, he made eye contact with Monica when he got to the "fun" part. She smiled as though she harbored a lovely secret—a Mona Lisa smile, for sure.

He looked at me. "Ashby, I have to tell you, the Overton women's diaries were absolutely crucial. Without them—well—there would be a lot more holes in the story." He pointed to several ancient volumes, one of which I recognized as Angelina Elisabeth Overton's diary, which I had read my first summer at Overhome.

"There's much to tell. I hope everyone is interested. I suggest we put ourselves back in time—about one hundred seventy-five years—right here at Overhome Estate—a thriving plantation. Close your

149

eyes. Picture the Big House flanked by extensive grounds, scattered with out-buildings—a smoke house for curing hams, tobacco barns, tiny wooden slave quarters lining the fields, ice house, outdoor lavatory, barns and stables and workshops. Fields of corn, beans, sweet potatoes and other food crops, and tobacco, of course. Way off in the distance, beyond your sight, is the furnace with its own universe of out-buildings. Can you picture it all? Everybody there?"

Well, he had me, for sure. I was a sucker for period drama. I envisioned young girls in hoop skirts, their slim, competent fingers plying embroidery needles as they sat demurely on the shady porch. The mistress bending gracefully over her writing desk in the parlor, issuing invitations for a lavish upcoming party. In the fields the slave women with their bright head scarves and the men in straw hats, hunched over their tasks, as barefoot youngsters romped over field and stream.

Hal continued. "Ashby, you told me that you remember reading nothing about Raeford Overton in Angelina's diary."

I nodded. "She wrote about her older brothers—both killed in the Civil War. But nothing about another brother."

"Well, here's what I found. Angelina was such a comprehensive writer. There's an earlier volume of her diary covering the 1840s and afterwards."

"Right! I remember seeing the volume, but it was barely readable, owing to the faded ink and curly-cue writing. Tell me, Hal. Is Raeford mentioned in Angelina's earlier diary?"

He touched the cover gently. "I've taken the liberty of transcribing many of Angelina's entries—especially the ones where she talks about her youngest brother, Raeford Burwell Overton. I'd like to share some with you now, if you'll bear with me."

Everyone murmured agreement, waiting as Hal rifled through some notes. "Let's begin here, see what Angelina at the age of twelve has to say about the birth of Raeford." He cleared his throat and began reading."

At first I must admit I was angry with Mother for producing yet another brother. I had so wanted a sister to share my life with— my hopes and dreams—whispered confidences in our room. Hair ribbons and silk frocks. Parties and beaus. But poor, dear Mother. This baby like to killed her—such a difficult confinement and a long, painful delivery. Mother turned over the diary writing to me for she felt too weak and tired to tend to it properly. "You're quite the writer, Angelina," she said. "You record our life at Overhome whilst I concentrate my energy on surviving!" and so I must report that the squalling red infant is not so kind on the eyes, but we all fell instantly in love with his feisty determination to survive. Raeford Burwell he is to be called. Father's choice, though surely the little lad's name will become simply "Raef." Even though he cries constantly, I love to hold the precious, tiny bundle. Mother says I have a calming effect on the baby. Robert and Johbe feel he cannot grow up fast enough for them—as though they needed another playmate! As Mother's milk has dried up, we are grateful for a wet nurse. Sukey, one of the slaves who gave birth a short while ago, has taken over the baby's nursing needs. I hope this young, healthy gal may strengthen our frail little brother—that her milk carries full measure of her stamina as well as nourishment. I fear we will all spoil little Raeford, knowing this will surely be our last sibling ever, due to Mother's fragile health and long recovery. I, myself, am enchanted.

Hal looked up from his transcription. "So, Raeford Burwell Overton was born in 1840, as Angelina surmised, the last of the Overton children begat by Hannah and Burwell Overton."

I sat up. "Well, that explains the silver baby cup." I looked at Jeff, who nodded. "It must have been Raeford's—the date was 1840. But, Hal, I'm sure others are wondering just as I am. Raeford Overton—youngest son, beloved by all, favored by Angelina and named for his father—how could Raeford disappear from the family archives?" I thought for a moment. "And why would his baby cup be in the cottage for Jeff and Nick to find?"

"As you suggest, it's quite a story. Listen to some excerpts from Angelina's diary, written in 1848, when Raeford is eight years old." Turning some pages, he resumed.

What's to be done with young Raef? He refuses to listen to Mother—even to Father, who silences the rest of us with a mere look. Tho' I know only disobedient slaves are reprimanded with the crop, I often wonder if a thorough thrashing would do Raef some good. He runs off without finishing his lessons, sasses Mammy about any moral teachings she tries to impart and throws a tantrum over performing the simplest chores. His temper grows fiercer daily. Long gone are the days when he would listen to advice from his only sister who adores him.

Hal pushed his glasses higher up on his nose. "Here's a diary entry from the summer of that same year. We meet Angelina's Aunt Rachel. " He bent to his notes again.

Aunt Rachel, Father's youngest sister, loves to tell the story about meeting William Stover, a distant cousin, at a social in Page County up in the Shenandoah Valley—how he was the handsomest fellow in the room and how she longed for him to invite her to dance the Virginia reel with him. William Stover did, indeed, invite Rachel to dance. He became a regular visitor at Overhome and eventually they married, then moved to Luray, a wee town in Page County to live on a small plantation, where Rachel had to work hard as mistress of the house with fewer slaves. Yet, she always seemed happy and fulfilled, with a brood of children born one after the other for five straight years. Her eldest, Jeb, began spending the summers at Overhome when he turned six.

Hal raised his eyes to us. "Rachel Overton Stover would become an important component in Raeford's life. So would her son Jeb. And so would Page County in Virginia's Shenandoah Valley, the location of the famous Civil War Valley Campaign, where both Jeb and Raef would fight for the Confederate side." He looked at his notes again. "Let me continue with Angelina's diary."

I know that Mother and Father hope that Cousin Jeb will have a softening effect on Raef as he lives at Overhome for the summer. The cousins are almost exactly the same age—two weeks apart. The boys climb trees, fish in the pond, swim at the water hole, ride bareback and play games. I am happy that my family plans to host Jeb every summer for as long as possible.

Jeb is a dear—everything Raeford is not. It breaks my heart! Though they share a cousinly-kinship, their souls differ beyond imagination. Watching him and Raef play with the slave children is a study in contrasts. Raef bosses them, lords it over them with rules of his own making when none are necessary. Jeb welcomes the participation of our young slaves. It does seem that Jeb's sunny nature appears to alter Raeford's attitude and calm his temper. I dread the end of the season when Jeb returns to Luray and Ruffian Raef rules the roost again.

As Hal read, Miss Emma's rapt expression hinted at some powerful remembering. She'd surely have some pertinent comments to share before the end of the day. The others were evidently as engrossed in the saga as I was—even Jeff—who sat on the edge of his chair, his attention riveted on Hal.

Flipping through a handful of pages, Hal addressed us again. "This first volume of Angelina's diary refers to Raeford's eleventh birthday. Unfortunately, to his big sister's regret, Raef has become ever more surly and out of control, calming down only when cousin Jeb arrives for their summers together at Overhome. Though the older brothers have tried to act as role models and Angelina herself has made gallant efforts to 'civilize' young Raef, the parents have, evidently, given up all attempts to discipline him. Sent off to military school, he lasts only a few months before being expelled."

Hal adjusted his glasses. "We're coming to the end of the first volume. By 1851, Angelina makes fewer and fewer references to Raeford, though there does seem to be a shift in his behavior. Not necessarily a good shift, mind you. In adolescence, the tantrums and sassing subside, Angelina writes, but Raeford becomes quietly sneaky, lying about his whereabouts during frequent absences. Bullying the slaves when he thinks nobody can observe his actions. He's suspected when money goes missing or valuable items are 'lost.' He always blames the slaves when this happens."

Dad shifted in his chair. "Sounds like a real bad seed."

Hal nodded agreement. "In 1857, when Raeford is seventeen, he goes off to Washington College, along with his cousin Jeb. College life seems to fit him, though when he comes home on breaks, his father complains that Raef learned only how to drink and gamble while away at school. Jeb, meanwhile, is a real scholar, into his studies and making excellent grades. Needless to say, while Jeb remains at Washington College and graduates, Raef is kicked out and sent home after two years."

Mom looked thoughtful. "What with Civil War

stirrings in the air, I can imagine there was plenty of strife in the Overton household at this point. I suppose today we'd call it a dysfunctional family."

Hal handed a sheaf of papers to Monica. "Would you like to share this part? It's the climax of the action." He zeroed in on Mom. "Dysfunction reaches the breaking point, you might say."

Monica picked up the manuscript and read.

At last Raef has committed the unpardonable act. He has maimed a slave—a productive male his own age—in fact Sukey's son Abram. Sukey who nursed Raef when he was an infant. Why Abram? Raef claims Abram stole from him. Raef retaliated by grabbing the axe from Abram's hand as he worked on a woodpile—beating him with the blunt end. Now Abram is useless to us—his right arm broken beyond repair and a leg so badly mangled that he can scarcely walk. When Father forcefully pulled Raef away from Abram, a packet of jewels fell from my brother's waistcoat. Mother's jewels—her pearls and the precious cameo brooch willed to her by her grandmother. Raef confessed that he had stolen the jewelry to pay off his gambling debts. Father was furious, Mother resigned. Raef is to be banished from Overhome and expunged from any inheritance. He has gone to live with Aunt Rachel and Uncle William Stover in Luray. We have been instructed never to speak of my poor, dear little brother again.

Monica raised her eyes from the transcription.

"Angelina's post script offers a tidbit of psychological insight from an older sister. Listen to this."

> *Raef is obsessed with the fact that he was nourished on a slave's breast milk. He has felt contaminated ever since he found out, he once confided in me. It's as if he has black blood running in his veins. He blames all of his own failings on that "sad fact," and he blames Mother most of all for causing it to happen. "Don't you see why I am a lying, thieving, lazy wretch?" he said. "Those miserable traits were infused in me, along with that slave's vile milk." How I longed to tell him I wished he had acquired the courage, strength, hope and stoic resolve of noble Sukey and, yes, her son Abram. They are, in many ways, far better human beings than he. Still, I shall miss my once-sweet baby boy. Raeford has told me I am the only one in the family who loves him— he calls me his "angel." I have cried so many tears to think I am not allowed to say or write his name ever again. I shall think of him and pray for him daily. May God watch over Raeford.*

There was a moment of silence in the room before Miss Emma found her voice. "Yes. Lenore and I read that diary many years ago. We actually wept at poor, spoiled, flawed Raeford's plight. And we understood the whispered references to the 'Black Sheep' the family wanted to hush up. We knew it must be Raeford Overton. He was considered a waste of humanity!"

Luke tapped my shoulder. "What say we take a little break? Get something to drink. I could use a strong dose of sweet tea, myself." We stood.

"Need some help?" Mom rose from her chair.

"We're good," I said. "Be back in a jiff."

Luke and I made our way to the kitchen. "I wonder how Eddie did out at the cottage last night. I can't wait to talk to him. Do you think Raef showed up?"

Luke gave me a droll look. "You know, babe, you have one messed-up family. It wouldn't be so bad if they'd just die and leave—instead of hanging around for years and years. What am I gettin' myself into here?"

I punched him in the ribs. "Oh, great. That's all I need. Listen, buddy, you're not getting out of marrying me with that excuse." We walked through the dining room on our way to the kitchen. Ever sensitive, I glanced at the chandelier. "Look, Luke. It's tinkling. He's here. Raef's here! I'll bet he's listening in, since he's the main character in Hal's story."

"Pay attention, Raeford Overton," Luke barked out, startling me. "Get over it! What would Angelina, your angel, think of your behavior?"

The crystal teardrops rattled, then stopped. We waited a minute. Another minute. I braced for the freezing, foul air, but it did not materialize. The chandelier remained steady and silent. "I think you touched a sensitive chord," I whispered.

"Whatever works." Luke also spoke in a hushed tone. "Whatever works."

Loud noises erupted from the yard outside the kitchen window. "What in the world?" I ran to look out. Eddie, pistol in hand, ran zigzag between the house and barn, yelling like one possessed as he chased after his wolf dog, firing an occasional shot into the air. The dog howled and snarled and barked as if it were having a rabies attack, running in circles and dashes, eluding his owner.

Luke and I hurried out the back door. "Eddie! Eddie! Stop! Hold your fire!" Luke sped up in an effort to head him off while I jogged behind trying to catch up. "No shooting! Put down the gun, Eddie! Drop it!"

Slowing to a trot, Eddie dropped the pistol to the ground and turned a contorted face onto us. "Sorry. I shouldn't of shot it off. I know that. I was excited—chasin' Wolfdog. He's gone nuts on me. Jes' like he done at the cottage last night. Somethin's got to him, all right. Beats me what it is."

Luke and I looked at each other, then at the half-breed animal which had finally slowed to an exhausted lope. The others from the library headed in our direction. The stable workers also watched from the fringe—Carlos and Julio from their training stations and Sam who had been working in the stable. Thankfully, there were no students on the grounds.

"Tell us, Eddie. What happened out there at the cottage last night?" I waffled between sternness and sympathy.

Eddie's miserable pet came slinking back to his side with his tail between his legs. "Can't say's I know rightly. I pitched my tent and had a good campfire roarin' when I fell asleep in my sleepin' bag. Hours later I woke when I heard a noise in th' yard. I hopped up, grabbed my pistol. Wolfdog's hackles was standin' up like a horse brush, and he was growlin' real low in his throat—like he does when he's huntin'."

Eddie looked baffled. "Me? I never saw nothin'. There wasn't no Night Riders, neither. But Wolfdog—

159

he sure sensed somethin' an' he took after it. Run right into a tree, then stood there looking back an' forth and up an' down, howling like the wolf part of him does when he gets excited. Like I said, I never saw nothin', but, whatever it was—my dog scared it away." He shook his head, then flared his nostrils. "It stunk somethin' turrible. Maybe a skunk or a polecat. Wolfdog still smells bad from it. After a while I jes' went back to my sleepin' bag and me an' Wolfdog was fine fer th' rest of th' night." He scratched his head. "Jes' now—I was puttin' my pistol away in th' office an' Wolfdog—well—he started in agin."

By now Dad, Mom, Monica, Hal and Miss Emma, along with Jeff, had caught up with us. Luke addressed Eddie. "The surveying sticks—they're okay?"

He shrugged. "I didn't see no damage. Checked 'em out agin this mornin' before I left."

Dad wanted clarification. "So, Eddie, you say you did not see the Night Riders and you did not fire the pistol last night when your dog sensed something—alerted you?"

"No Night Riders. No shots fired."

"Might I suggest you lock up the firearm, then? Obviously, it's not necessary. And it could be dangerous. It's a good thing there were no students or horse owners around to hear the gun go off just now. We could be scaring away a lot of business." Dad looked at the stable employees gathered around the periphery.

Eddie appeared chagrined. "Okay. I'll lock my pistol up in my desk drawer. In th' office there." He pointed toward the barn. "Looks like I c'n trust Wolfdog t'be my weapon."

Luke and Dad and I exchanged looks. "Secret weapon," Luke said tersely. "Like I said: Whatever works."

"I have to get ready for my afternoon class." Hal looked at his watch. "But there's more to the story. Can we meet again? Oh, and Ashby, you really need to look into the preservation of those diaries. Possibly donate them to a Virginia museum or archive where they can be treasured for what they are: a valuable historical source."

Miss Emma's sharp eyes had not missed a thing. "Had another visit, did we?" she asked no one in particular. She looked pointedly at Eddie's wolf dog. "Lenore and I could have used that animal. Though we did not know the 'identity' of the spirit in the cottage, Lenore was convinced he was a bully who wanted to scare us. 'We should find a way to scare *him*,' Lenore said, more than once. Lenore was such a spunky girl."

Hal and Monica looked at each other, and my aunt seemed puzzled at Miss Emma's brief speech as well as the ruckus with Eddie and his wolf-dog. She turned to the old woman

"You say there's a spirit in the cottage?"

Miss Emma did not answer Monica's question. "Lenore was fearless. It would take more than a ghost to scare her."

"Ghost?" Monica threw a questioning look at Hal, who cocked his head, and lifted his brows as if to say, "Don't ask me what's going on here."

Eddie pressed his lips into a hard line, clucked at Wolfdog and headed back to the barn. "I don't believe in haints," he mumbled under his breath.

Chapter 15

July Fourth at Moore Mountain Lake was not to be taken lightly. Anyone who owned a boat would be out on the water to watch the fireworks—just not the same as sitting on the grass or slouching on the bleachers or watching from a dock. Anchoring in a sea of boaters on the slick, dark waters of Moore Mountain Lake created an esprit de corps unlike any other—one big watery picnic in an atmosphere made festive by patriotic music which blasted from aquatic radios and CD players. When the fireworks began, it was outdoor theater on the lake, complete with 3-D and Surround-Sound, as the fireworks replicated images from sky to water and reverberated sound off the mountain in a booming ricochet. Even the air smelled expectant, heightened with a nocturnal lake breeze that blew back the hair and cooled the cheek.

Luke captained our boat; I sat in the co-pilot seat across from him. Monica and Hal, Jeff and Nick and Mom and Dad filled in the bow and stern seats, maxing out our capacity. Chowing down on chips and fruit and icy cold drinks from the cooler, we awaited the annual fireworks display eagerly. Knowing this was Nick's first experience with fireworks by water, Jeff bubbled over with enthusiasm, explaining how everything worked. Dad and Mom, too, chattered excitedly. Monica, with her usual aplomb, was dressed in what I can only describe as "casual-elegance." White linen slacks, red tank top and a blue and white-striped big shirt graced her slender figure. Hal could not take his eyes off her.

"I feel like the matriarch here. We're parenting a boat full of excited children." I gestured toward the back of the boat with my head.

"Except for Monica." Luke responded with a whisper. "She looks poised as a model. For a flag store."

I suppressed a giggle. "A flag Hal would like to unfurl, I'll bet."

"Who says he won't? Though, I've gotta admit. Hal's about as different from Hunter as they get."

"Who knows? Maybe that's what Monica has been waiting for."

"Here goes!" Jeff shouted, as the show began. "See, Nick. They always start with fountains. It's reflected on the water. You hear the boom. And then the echo. It's gonna sound like a battlefield out here."

Nick was mesmerized, as were Mom and Dad. I sneaked a peek at Hal and Monica. Ostensibly engaged in the colorful drama overhead, they kept looking back at one another, and I saw Hal's arm encircle Monica's shoulders.

"Remember our first July Fourth by boat?" I reached over and touched Luke's hand. "Five years ago. My first summer at Overhome."

"Where you wanted to sing 'Yankee Doodle,' and I was all about waving the Rebel flag and singing 'Dixie'? Oh yeah, that was unforgettable."

"You know what I mean! Where we stole in a few kisses back there on the stern seats. And afterwards…"

Luke moved into the co-pilot's seat with me, then, pulled me onto his lap, causing me to squeal in protest. "Luke! There's a boatful of people watching us! A lakeful of people!"

Luke turned and waved. "Don't mind us! Just keep your eye on the sky." Then he kissed my cheek.

"You are a bad boy." I nuzzled against his shoulder.

"That's why you love me, dear Ashby." Luke tightened his arms around me. "Now, watch the fireworks. We get these folks home, then we'll create some sparks of our own." A giant glittering silver spray ignited first the sky, then the surface of the lake.

"Oooh. Aaah," Luke and I breathed in one voice.

By the time it was over, my head rang and my eyes felt as googly as the spirals in the sky. Anchor lights firmly in place, we slowly churned our way back home while Jeff and Nick led us in a slightly off-key rendition of "The Battle Hymn of the Republic." Strains of "Glory, glory halleluiah" followed in our wake all the way back to our dock.

While Jeff and Nick raced to beat each other up the steps to the house, Hal and Monica took their time, pausing at each landing to look up and admire the random stragglers—late-blooming, sparkly blossoms lighting up the sky. Dad and Mom lingered as we raised the boat in the lift.

Mom looked over the clutter on the dock. "Dad and I will be happy to help you secure the boat and bring up the supplies."

Luke was quick to answer. "Tell ya what—take up the cooler and beach towels, Mrs. Overton. Ashby and I can deal with the boat."

Mom gave Luke an amused look, confirming my suspicion that she and Dad were well aware of Luke's and my cohabiting arrangement. "Fine, Luke. But, my soon-to-be son-in-law, do call me something other than 'Mrs. Overton.' Please."

"Mom?" Luke's voice was tentative. "I haven't called anyone Mom for a very long time."

"That will be perfect, then. From now on, I'll be 'Mom' to both you and Ashby. It feels just right." She lifted the towels as Dad took on the cooler.

Luke's smile melted my heart; I could tell it felt just right to him, too. Orphaned at the age of ten, when his parents died in a plane crash, Luke was raised by his grandfather Abe.

"That officially makes me 'Dad,' then, doesn't it?" My father wore a big grin.

Watching them head up the stairs, I wiped a tear from my eye. Could anyone ask for more wonderful parents? By the time I looked back to Luke, he was well on his way to stripping off his clothes.

"Last one in gets nibbled by a fish!" He splashed off the dock with a cannonball.

I peeled off my own duds and dived in.

"Watch out!" Luke swam toward me. "Here comes a big fish, and he's in a nibbling mood. Been waiting for skinny-dippers all day."

****

"What a beautiful animal." I stood admiring Tiffany Norton's large, sinewy cinnamon-colored Thoroughbred with a blaze and four white socks.

"Isn't he though?" Carole, Tiffany's mother said. The two were dressed in jeans and tee shirts and worn-looking work boots.

Sam and Eddie watched them from the corners of their eyes, with evident curiosity.

"Could you please get me the brushes and grooming tools?" Carole looked first at Eddie and then Sam. "I'd like to take a go at Stormy here."

Sam headed for the tack room and returned with a box of implements.

"Oh, good." Tiffany picked up a curry brush. "Once you're done with the hoof pick, I'd like to curry him, Mom."

The two women set about their tasks, humming and chatting and petting Stormy all the while. Eddie, especially, and Sam, too, appeared to be chalking up the difference between the Norton ladies and Mrs. Davies, our BQ. I certainly was.

"We've a gelding on the way from Northern Virginia." Tiffany included Sam and Eddie, as well as me, in her look. "Your barn is so clean and orderly—I'd like to board all of our horses here if there's room."

"We've heard such good things about your trainers, too," Carole said. "And I've recommended your riding school to several horse owners I know here at the lake."

"Carlos and Julio are top-notch. We're lucky to have them working for us at Overhome. Why, look, here they are—just finishing up with a group lesson." Carlos and several young students moved into the paddock.

Winn Davies dismounted somewhat awkwardly, but at least he wasn't wearing the negative mask I was used to seeing.

"You are getting it, *mi amigo*," Carlos told him. "That fine line between what you want and what the horse can deliver. But there is much work to do."

Jeff and Nick appeared at the barn door. "Papa, Jeff and I want to ride our horses. Okay with you?"

Carlos zeroed in on Nick. "Have you finish your reading assignment, Nick?" and when Nick nodded, he waved them on. "Be back in time to help with next lesson. Two hour, *no mas*."

"Great!" Jeff grabbed two helmets from the tack room and headed for the pasture where Sunshine awaited. "Saddle up, Nick!" He tossed a helmet to his friend, then, he saw me. "Ashby, do you have time to ride out to our *casa*...the cottage?" He looked so eager I found his invitation hard to resist.

"You guys go ahead. I'll catch up with you shortly." I instantly regretted my response—there was way too much to do to be taking a break. I turned to the Nortons. "Thanks for entrusting us with Stormy. I can't wait to meet your other horses."

Jeff and Nick trotted out of the pasture and moved smoothly into a gallop. The race was on. The look on Winn Davies' face, as he watched, was one of pure, slack-jawed awe. Was he thinking that wiry little Nick—son of immigrants—target for his own bullying—was a master rider?

"Adonis is upset," came the irascible squawk of our Barn Queen as she barged in from Eddie's office, overdressed as usual. "Why haven't you turned him out to the paddock? Why…" She stopped when she saw Tiffany and Carole working on Stormy. "You're Carole Norton. And Tiffany. I've seen you at the club. What…What are you doing in that horse stall?"

Tiffany looked blankly at Mrs. Davies. "I'm— we're grooming my horse." She returned to her task.

"Sorry." Carole barely looked up. "I don't believe

we've met."

"I'm Belinda Davies. My husband Winnfield and I belong to your country club. I've seen you folks in the clubhouse dining room." She moved her hand tentatively, perhaps considering whether to offer a handshake, then changed her mind and dropped the hand to her side. No sense allowing horse smells to dirty her manicure. She looked at her son. "Well, I certainly hope you're learning something useful at long last, Winn," she snapped. I watched the ugly mask cover Winn's face once again. "As much as we're paying for these lessons…"

With a disgusted grunt, Winn turned his back on his mother and headed out of the barn.

"I look forward to seeing you at the club," Belinda Davies called over her shoulder to the Nortons as she followed her son's retreating figure.

"Not if I can help it," Carole said cheerfully, just quietly enough that only Tiffany and I could hear.

****

I saddled Sasha and prepared to make my way cross-country to the cottage. It wouldn't do to let the youngsters go it alone. Though it was obvious that Raef Overton had it in for me, who knew what an angry spirit like him might do if given the opportunity. That I'd promised both Dad and Luke I wouldn't go there without one of them flitted through my mind. Well, Luke was back at Tech, and Dad was nowhere to be seen. Too late. I should have quashed the whole thing when Jeff first proposed it. I decided at the last minute to grab a hammer from the office toolbox. Not much of a weapon, I knew, but better than nothing. I clucked Sasha into a canter. Got to catch up with the boys.

"Let's go, Sasha!"

I found them in the loft-clubhouse they call their *casa*, looking puzzled. Jeff picked up a saucer and peered closely at it, then at Nick. "Candle's burned down to the nub. Just a puddle of wax left."

"This one, too. And this one." Nick held a saucer in each hand. "Looks like every candle we left up here has been burned out."

"And the books." Jeff pointed to the bookshelf. "They're out of order. *Huckleberry Finn* is mixed in with the horse books, and I just added those three volumes of Harry Potter books. I put them in order on the shelf. One, two, three. Look here. Three, then one, then two."

"There's comic books scattered everywhere." Nick scanned the littered floor. "Somebody's been in our *casa*, all right. What a mess."

Jeff leaned over and picked up a small object from the floor. "What's this?" He turned it this way and that, peering intently.

Nick plucked the object from Jeff's palm. "Looks like an Indian arrowhead. A real one—not one of those fakes you can buy off the Internet or something."

"Well, where'd it come from?" Jeff's freckles bunched together. "Look, Ashby. What d'ya make of this?"

I turned the small, flint triangle in my fingers, rubbing the sharp tip. "Nick's right, Jeff. This looks like the real deal." I handed it back to him. "Somebody's left it here for you to find. I suspect it's the ghost—and I believe its actions say something interesting."

The boys looked at me with identical expressions that said, *Do tell. We're stumped.*

"It seems to me that this entity has tried its best to scare everyone away from this cottage. In fact, it…he has been trying the same tactics for a very long time. When she was a child, Miss Emma encountered similar things…"

"No way!" Jeff exhaled with a whoosh. "Miss Emma?"

"*Fantasmas*, Jeff. They can hang around a long time, you know." Nick nodded solemnly.

"To continue, guys. The spirit tried to scare you and me and Miss Emma and probably many others over the years—tried to run people off the property with bad smells, freezing air and scary demands—'*Go away. He's dead.*' That's the standard line he's been uttering for decades." I hesitated, not sure whether to tell them more. "Let me just say he's been somewhat more aggressive with me—tried to knock me down the stairs and hit me in the back of the head. And—well—other things, too." I paused. "Remember the crashing chandelier?"

"So why would he mess with our candles and books? Read our comics?" Jeff mused out loud. "Leave us a gift?"

"Maybe he has given up trying to scare us." Nick laughed. "Maybe he wants to join our club!"

Jeff howled. "Honorary member! *Fantasmas* of the *casa*."

"Not so fast, Jeff. Nick may be on to something. I've wondered why your *casa* here has seemed to be largely untouched. Why the ghost has not harmed you the way he's tried to get at me. This spirit is a mean and ugly one, but he's not into equal opportunity. When he realized he couldn't scare you guys away, he decided to see what you were about in the loft here—check out your books and comics—light your candles and watch them burn. Whatever it is, he's trying to keep people away from, it's not in the loft. It's not about your clubhouse. And it may have nothing to do with you." I looked to the boys for a response. As for the gift of the arrowhead—all I could think of was Boo Radley in *To Kill a Mockingbird* leaving gifts in the tree for Jem and Scout.

Jeff had been fiddling with the arrowhead as I talked. Ambling back to the burned-down candles, suddenly, he cried out. "Whoa! Nick! Ashby! Look here." He picked up the now-polished silver baby cup and turned it over in his hand. A tiny object fell into his palm. "It's a key. A little key."

Moving to Jeff's side, Nick and I each took a turn fingering the old-fashioned metal key, which was about an inch and a half long and solid-feeling despite its size. Both boys looked to me for an answer, but I could only shrug my shoulders and wag my head.

"Where did this come from? It sure wasn't in the cup last time we were here." Jeff lifted his eyes to Nick. "Remember—we dumped out the coins we'd left in the cup—getting together our dough for a movie."

"The *fantasmas*," Nick said with assurance.

Jeff pulled out a key chain from his pocket. "I'm gonna attach the key to my lucky rabbit's foot key chain. So if we ever figure out what it goes to, I'll be ready to unlock it."

"Lucky rabbit's foot?" Nick scoffed. "What's that all about?"

Jeff gave an embarrassed laugh. "My dad gave it to me. A long time ago. I've always kept it with me,

171

since…since he died. For luck, you know."

Nick gave his friend a sympathetic look, but said nothing.

"Works for me, Jeff." I loved my cousin for his resourcefulness, and I, too, felt a pang of regret for his loss of a father at such a young age.

For a while we were silent. "So…what's he want?" Jeff stroked the rabbit's foot thoughtfully.

I waved my hammer in the air. "Don't know. I think we need to look further. One place we haven't explored is the hole in the foundation you and Nick found."

Jeff's freckles seemed to expand between his widening eyes. "The one we put pebbles into!"

Nick looked at the hammer, then at me, then at Jeff. "Do you think we can open it up with that hammer?"

At the last minute, Jeff thought to snag the flashlight hanging on a nail. "Might need this." He headed for the stairs.

We pushed a dozen pebbles through the coin-sized hole, counting the four to five seconds until we could hear them hit ground inside, making it seem bigger and deeper than a crawl space. We took turns wielding the hammer over the hole but managed to enlarge it only enough to shine in a thin beam from the flashlight. The black interior swallowed the narrow beam of light so effectively that we could see nothing beyond a couple of inches into the interior.

"Gotta make this hole bigger." Jeff picked up the hammer. "It could be…"

The hammer flew out of his hand, ripped away by an unseen force, so quickly Jeff had not had time to react before the flashlight assumed a life of its own and wrenched itself free of my fingers. Then the blast of freezing air blew us back to the wall of the house.

"Whew!" I sucked in my breath. "Looks like we've caught someone's attention."

Jeff retrieved the flashlight from the yard. "Case is cracked. Bulb shattered."

"Wonder where the hammer went?" Nick searched the ground nearby. "Oh, here it is. In two pieces." He displayed the broken parts. "Not much good for anything now."

"We're coming back." I spoke firmly. "We'll bring reinforcements—tools, muscles. We're not finished here." I turned toward the pebble hole and raised my voice. "Are you listening, Raeford Overton?"

The boys watched with big eyes as a fog of foul air encased me from top to bottom, then evaporated into the air.

"Jeez, Ashby. That was crazy! You think it's the force…the ghost of the guy Hal was telling us about? The one the family shunned? Raeford…Raef Overton?"

"Our *fantasmas*," Nick breathed.

For a moment I was too stunned to speak and too afraid of foul air to take any soothing yoga breaths. Finally, I gathered my wits about me. "I'd bet my life on it. Raeford Overton. Now, we'd better skedaddle. Carlos said you two need to get back to work and we're running short of time."

As we prepared to mount our horses, a truck with the county seal on its side rattled up to the property. Two men stepped out. "Miss Overton? We're from the health department. Setting up for the soil tests."

"Oh, yes. Fine." I tried to collect myself and make

my voice steady when the rest of me was wobbly as a drunk on a treadmill. "What is it you need to do?"

"Stake out the perimeter—prepare for percolation holes to be dug." One man flipped through a spiral notebook. "We have an order here from a Mr. Overton."

"That's my father. He's the developer. I'm sure it's OK to go ahead. I'll let him know you're here. I take it you're starting to work now?"

"We're ready to prepare the sites." He moved to the truck bed and began removing tools. "Should be done by day's end."

As we headed home, one thought pushed at the outer edges of my brain. Wouldn't you know today is a Tuesday. We can't count on Eddie for night watch at the cottage. Damn.

Dear Diary:

One step forward, two steps back. The health department workers returned to the cottage on Wednesday to find all the stakes marking the soil sites had been removed. Well, DUH. I knew I should have done something proactive to prevent Raef's wrath, but the timing was a bummer. With Eddie and his trusty Wolfdog camping out Wednesday night, the second round of stakes stayed put. Next step: perc holes to be dug and filled with water. Must make sure this does not occur on a Tuesday—Eddie's one day of rest. Rest? Who knows what he does on his sacred Tuesday night.

On a brighter note, Luke's coming home for at least a twenty-four hour stay. The M&M

Express has planned our wedding reception down to the last table setting, my gown is ready for pickup, and Luke has ordered his own wedding garb. Please, God, may nothing prevent the wedding from going on as planned. No spirits invited. As for the citizenship studies, Mom has been grooming the Vasquez parents for their test, and Mariana is positively glowing at the prospect of their taking it before summer's end. I can't imagine how Mom also works in tutoring Nick with all that's going on, but she does and his reading is improving slowly but steadily. Mariana told me Nick is asking for an electronic reader so that he can download some books for pleasure reading. Awesome!

While Dad is doing his best to act as a developer for our fifty-acre tract, he's dealing with problems beyond the ordinary, to say the least. Still, we all press on. The real estate deal simply has to work. Dad plans to apprise Paul Gordon, our Realtor, of the latest site destruction. Not sure just how much he'll reveal about our fantasmas. *What's to be done with the resident spirit who is "dead set" against our housing project? It's the thought that keeps me awake night after night. How do you kill a ghost?*

Chapter 16

We watched with growing curiosity as Hal dragged a large cardboard box into the library. "Jeff, would you help me out here? I need an assistant."

"Sure!" Jeff leaped from his chair and moved to the table where Hal had situated the box.

"I'll bet you're all wondering, 'Are those Hal's notes? I hope not! We'll be here all day!'"

Jeff stood, looking at the mystery box, barely able to keep from opening it up and digging in. I could see it in his busy freckles. Mom and Dad and Miss Emma also stared at the receptacle with attention. Monica looked smug, so I figured she knew what lay inside.

"Well, these are not notes—or records." Hal pried open the box and reached in, pulling out a hat with a big feather plume. "This, my friends, is a replica of a hat worn by a Confederate Cavalry officer." He plunged into the box again and brought out a heavy cape, unfurling it for all to see. "And this is a cape, which, along with knee boots and fancy spurs, made up the glamorous outfit of the early Confederate troops on horseback." He handed the items to Jeff. "Would you be so kind, Sir Cavalier, as to don the hat and cape whilst I locate your saber?"

Jeff draped the cape over his shoulders and plunked the plumed hat on his head, turning for us to admire, a huge grin on his face. "No kidding! How do I look?"

Hal handed a sheathed saber to Jeff, who waved it menacingly.

"G-a-a-r! Avast, matey," Jeff growled, then, laughed. "Oh, that's not right. That's for pirates."

"Not so far off, Jeff. Southern cavalry thrived on destroying enemy communications and supplies—burning bridges and stores, ripping out telegraph lines and raiding behind the lines—all in an attempt to keep the enemy from attacking. Pirates on horseback."

"Hal, I presume this is all about Raeford Overton's joining the cavalry during the Civil War," Luke said. "Nice props—they do lend authenticity."

"Props they are. Borrowed from the theater department at the college where I teach. But pretty good replicas, actually."

"Well, I'm all about drama, myself. What a great way to illustrate the situation for us." My respect for Hal was growing by the minute.

"So, I'm Raeford Overton, I've joined the cavalry and I dress up, hop on my horse and I'm off to battle, waving my saber and hacking away at the enemy?" Jeff sliced the air with the weapon.

"Something like that. Now, Cavalryman Raeford Overton, you and your first cousin Jeb Stover have signed on with the 7th Virginia. For two years, your companions on horseback will dominate the Union cavalry. Your troops are disruptive and you have knocked many a Union commander off balance."

Jeff swung the saber again, as if to knock his invisible enemy off balance.

"That's the spirit!"

"What about my horse?" Jeff asked.

"You had to bring your own steed, though you received compensation for its upkeep. If your horse was killed or injured or became sick, you would have sixty days to find a replacement at your own expense and return with a new horse. Otherwise, you'd be forced out of the cavalry and into the infantry, which was considered an insult."

"So, my cousin Jeb and I would take our horses along for battle. I like that idea! I'd take Sunshine with me, and I'd never get homesick."

Jeff's comment made everyone smile.

"Military scientists consider the cavalry to be the 'eyes' of the army'—exploring enemy territory."

"The cavalry sounds elite. What do we know about Raef Overton's and Jeb Stover's individual service?" Luke asked.

"We know both cousins served with General 'Stonewall' Jackson in the Shenandoah Valley Campaign of 1862. The battle of Gettysburg, in which the VA 7th participated, was in 1863, but after that, things get murky. We can follow Jeb fairly well, but Raeford? Not so much."

"Raeford Overton deserted, didn't he?" It was the quiet voice of Miss Emma.

Monica started. "How did you know that, Miss Emma?"

"I just now made the connection. Lenore and I overheard the Overton relatives bemoaning the fact that there was a deserter in the family. One who had dared to abandon the 'Cause.' Raeford Burwell Overton." She assumed a sheepish look. "Actually, we were eavesdropping. Lenore and I were experts. It was at a particularly dour family reunion of some sort. We found ways to amuse ourselves, you know."

"Then Raef came home—to Overhome," Hal seemed to be talking to himself. "To live in the cottage."

I nodded. "So, that's why Burwell and Hannah Overton wouldn't allow Raef to come back to the Big House. Why they relegated him to the overseer's cottage." It was a statement, not a question. It made sense to me, at last.

"Yes, Ashby. You're right. They must have been so ashamed of him—or possibly fearful of the consequences of harboring a deserter in their home— whatever. At any rate, they never turned him in and Raeford lived in the overseer's cottage from some time in 1863 until he died years later." Hal rubbed his hands together. "The pieces are coming together."

"Still doesn't explain his return as a spirit—his determination to chase away intruders from the cottage." Luke looked at Hal and then Monica. "I realize it's hard to accept that Overhome has a history, if you will, of ghosts. For a long time, I've struggled to understand it myself."

"Hal, Monica—I know you've read about our family ghost in the diaries. She was not a figment of ancestral imaginations," I said. "Though she's no longer roaming among the living, Rosabelle appeared to me when I arrived at Overhome five years ago."

Monica looked thoughtful. "Did Hunter know?"

I shook my head slowly, giving a little shrug as if to say, "I'm not sure," when, in reality, I knew very well that Uncle Hunter had all but invited the spirit to appear.

Deliberately, Luke moved on. "And now we're

confronted with Raeford's spirit—at least we think it's him. He's following Ashby. Attacking her. What's his game?" Luke frowned. "Hal?"

Hal cocked his head. He cast a quick glance at my aunt, thinking, no doubt: *It's your family's story and who am I to refute it?* "All I can do is add to the mystery. Monica and I have been unable to find any record of Raeford Overton's burial site. Not here on the grounds. Not at the Baptist Church, relocated with the other Overton family graves when the lake was built and the cemeteries flooded."

"What about Jeb Stover?" Mom asked. "I assume he's buried in Luray with all the other Stovers?"

"Well, that's another question. From what we can tell, Cousin Jeb made it through the war—or just about. We are fairly sure he was on his way to Appomattox where Lee eventually signed the surrender."

"But the trail stops there," Monica put in. "And no. There is no Jeb Stover or Joshua Stover or any other Stover who fits the time frame in the Page County cemetery where the other Stovers are interred. The old genealogist corroborates that."

"Jeb Stover is essentially considered MIA," Hal said.

"Rats." Jeff removed the hat and cape. "One deserter and one MIA. I guess they couldn't all be heroes."

Hal patted Jeff's shoulder. "By all accounts, Jeb Stover was an outstanding cavalryman—the pride of Page County. The family considers it a true tragedy that his remains were never recovered. And, Jeff, MIA is not to be equated with desertion."

"I know. It's still an unfinished story, though."

"That's what makes history so fascinating." Hal donned the plumed hat, then, swept it off with a bow. "A bow to history."

Though I could not see beyond the library, I was fairly sure there was a crystal chandelier rattling against itself in the old dining room. Raeford Overton venting his frustration yet again.

****

Dad caught my eye in the rearview mirror. "Nice of you to invite your mom and me along, Ashby. It's been a while since we had a double date."

"We appreciate your being the designated driver," Luke answered from the back seat. "These wine tastings can be intoxicating, or so I've heard. Never been to one myself." He poked my ribs. "We had a few beer bashes at Tech, you know, but nothing quite so swishy as a wine tasting."

"Well, it's a first for me, too. I've been to the Moore Mountain Wine Fest a couple times, but never an actual tasting at a winery. A bonus event for my latest article on local arts and artists for *Blue Ridge Heritage*. Plus, we'll see if we want to serve their wine at our wedding."

Luke chuckled. "There you go, multi-tasking again."

"Is wine-making considered an art?" Mom questioned.

"I guess we'll find out. We're set up for a tour, as well as a tasting. I'll work in the artistic element when I write the article." I snuggled closer to Luke. "Just glad you're here. For your own enlightenment," I whispered in his ear.

Luke kissed my cheek and nuzzled my neck.

"Anything we do together is an art."

"Well, you three can indulge all you want at the wine-tasting," Dad commented. "I'm more in line with Luke's beer bash, I'm afraid. I find wine a thin alternative."

Winding around the verdant countryside, we topped a ridge and Dad slowed, then turned into a gated driveway with the white, wrought-iron curlicue sign that looked as if it were made of snowflakes: "White Rock Winery." Bumping along a meandering, gravel driveway, at length we stopped and stepped out onto a breezy overlook. The four of us took in the panorama: Row upon row of lush green grape vines entwined the fences. Prolific rose bushes rambled without direction, reaching across the furrows. Bumble bees and butterflies and birds flitted and fluttered over the grassy lawns. The winery itself, a large white house, with a sweeping porch overlooking the vineyard, perched high above the pastoral setting as if it meant to both observe and protect the rich flora below. We breathed in the fragrant air and feasted on the natural beauty before us.

"Welcome, welcome!" Our hosts ushered us inside. A youthful-looking couple of self-proclaimed "empty-nesters," Alisha and Lewis Alexander, exuded warmth and Southern hospitality—both brightly eager to share their winery as if we were their very first visitors ever. "We call this the verandah." Alisha narrated as we ambled through the huge screened porch we'd spotted from the outside. "The guests love to watch the sun descend over the vineyard while they sip wine and enjoy live music during our sunset tastings."

"We'll use the tasting room for you folks today." Alisha indicated a room off the entrance to the verandah, light-filled, airy and modern with blonde hard-wood floors, white walls and polished wooden bar and tables. Racks of bright-labeled wine bottles lined the walls and bar shelves. "But first, Lewis will take you on our deluxe tour." She smiled, and I knew that all their winery tours could be considered "deluxe," not just the one for us today.

"Follow me." Lewis waved a hand and we followed him downstairs until we reached the guts of the operation. The large, cool area felt homey, with low ceilings and indirect lighting—spanking clean, and, unlike "commercial operations," as Lewis put it, a place where the Alexanders could take their wine-making slow and easy. Five-foot tall aluminum tanks, each holding 230 gallons of wine stood spaced around the concrete walls.

"We start picking in August and finish in October. We're family owned and operated, so all our kids come home to help during harvest. Friends and neighbors, too. We're currently producing 1100 cases yearly."

"How do you pick?" Mom had been following Lewis' talk closely.

"Incredible as it may seem in this day and age, we hand-pick every grape that goes into our wines. Then we lug them inside in those plastic containers—thirty to thirty-five pounds per lug." Lewis pointed out the huge stack of crates near the door that led out to the vineyard. "We bring them to the stemmers and crushers. For red wine the result is called the *must*. I'm going to purge the *must* from my tank to my barrel and add yeast to start the fermentation process. The sugars break down to alcohol in ten to fourteen days, causing the temperature to rise."

Susan Coryell

"Who says you never use chemistry after you take the class?" Dad beamed.

Lewis laughed. "We have to be careful about the temperature—too high and it spoils the wine—too low and it stops the process—called *sticking*. And you're absolutely right, sir. Chemistry and chemical instruments are key here. In fact, today wine-making requires an increased amount of scientific knowledge. I am an oenologist—oenology is the science of wine. Before we even started up the vineyard, Alisha and I consulted Virginia Tech to evaluate and test the site and soil for suitability."

Dad looked pleased. "How do you know when it's ready to drink?"

"The wine tells you. By taste, smell and sight. We use a wine thief." He held up what appeared to be a long turkey baster. "You stick the wine thief into the hole here in the barrel and pull up the wine." He demonstrated. "The barrel, by the way, creates a vacuum which pulls in air from the outside into the wine."

"More science," Dad observed. "A bit of physics, there, eh?"

Lewis nodded. "The wood barrels are toasted on the inside. Different degrees of toast give the wine inside a distinctive flavor. And, during the aging process, there are different ways to affect the taste and smell of the wine in each barrel."

"I can see why wine-making is considered an art." I was already framing my article in my mind. "Would you say that the vintner puts his own personality on his product?"

"Absolutely! And that's what gives White Rock its

character—what every wine-maker hopes for—a recognizable character the wine lover can appreciate."

"An art," Dad said, "*and* a science."

I had been writing notes at warp speed. I shook out my wrist and flexed my cramped fingers. "What's next?"

"Ready for some tasting?" Lewis rubbed his hands together eagerly.

"You don't have to ask me twice." Luke took my arm. "I am ready to move on from beer."

"Ready to move UP from beer!" Lewis led us back up the steps to the tasting room.

We were on our way home. "I vote for Moonglow,' I said. "White Merlot. Smooth and rich, refreshingly light on the tongue. With a hint of granny apples."

Luke slung an arm around my shoulder. "Scarlet Sunrise is my choice. A sweet blend of Cabernet, Merlot and Traminette with earthy aromas—an explosion of flavors with a hint of cherry and smoke." He kissed his fingers and lifted them to the air. "I read that on their brochure," he admitted.

"I love the natural-sounding names they've come up with." Mom turned to look at us from the front seat. "And I vote for Velvet Sky—semi-sweet with a velvety mouth. We could write the labels ourselves!"

"Personally, I'm waiting for a local brewery start-up so I can sample the beer." Dad gave a sidelong look at my mother.

"You are incorrigible!" Mom thumped his shoulder. "Who ever heard of a beer snob?"

"And you are all tipsy," Dad rejoined.

I leaned up and tapped Dad's shoulder lightly. "Drive on, oh designated one."

Luke pulled me over for a long, winey kiss. "Ummmm. I call this a velvety mouth."

"When you two finish, I have something to run by you," Dad said. "Hate to say it, but it may sober you up."

"Oh, dear. Not now," Mom protested. "Can't it wait, Madison? We're all feeling so mellow."

"Who knows when we'll get the four of us together again? A little soft edge might even help you hear me out."

I sat up, disentangling myself from Luke's embrace. "What is it, Dad? Something to do with the property?"

"I told you I intended to clue in Paul Gordon about our problems with the survey stakes. I got a completely unexpected response, I must say."

He had our undivided attention.

"Seems Paul's wife, Sheila Gordon, is a charter member of the local Historical Society. When she heard about the overseer's cottage from Paul, she was immediately interested. Wants to meet with us—give us a proposal or something."

"Is that good or bad?" Mom asked. "Something to be concerned about?"

"Don't know. But there's more." Dad eyed Luke and me in the rear-view mirror.

Luke and I were leaning forward at this point. "What, Dad?"

"When I told Paul about the survey stakes being destroyed—about Eddie's night watch and his wolf dog's reaction, Paul didn't blink an eye. 'Sounds like a matter for Phoebe. Phoebe Swift, Sheila's sister. She's a medium, you know. Well-respected around here. You might want to consult Phoebe.'"

For a moment there was silence in the car, as we were all deep in thought. I was the first to speak. "Paul thinks we should consult a medium? About Raef?"

"Paul knows none of the details. I merely described the destruction scene and Eddie's experience. He took it from there."

"Whew!" Luke exhaled. "A medium. Never considered that before."

I pressed my lips together in thought. "What harm could it do? We're not talking an exorcism here. Just someone to act as an intermediary—call up the spirits, see what's going on there. Right?"

"This is a bit out of my comfort zone." Mom shook her head.

"I have no experience either with mediums or the paranormal or anything like Raeford Overton, if that's, indeed, whom we're dealing with here. But I get the feeling it's not all that unusual for Paul—or Phoebe, for that matter," Dad said.

"There's a lot of history in these parts," Luke mused. "Maybe Paul's used to dealing with…with spirits who don't want to let go of the past, or something." He looked at me. "What's your take, Ashby?"

"Let's talk to Sheila and the Historical Society. Engage Phoebe. We have to move forward on this project, and we've reached a real stalemate."

Luke looked skeptical. "It's your call, Ashby."

"Good luck." Mom looked at Dad, then, turned to me. "And be careful, Ashby. It seems we're dealing with a force we know little or nothing about. Your father tells me I'm not to worry—but how can a mother avoid it? I just wonder if this whole idea is something we need to abandon."

Mom and I had not actually discussed the danger element, and I truly didn't know how much Dad had told her about my experiences with Raef. I spoke gently. "You know, Mom, we've resurrected Raef's spirit, so to speak, and now we have to deal with it. Abandoning our plan for development—ignoring the opposition in hopes it will go away—it won't solve the problem."

"It's all way too scary for me." My mother's voice was almost a whisper. "Possibly stirring up violent spirits? So totally out of our realm."

"Precisely why I think we need to give this Phoebe Swift a go at it, Mom. If she's truly a medium, Raeford Overton is definitely within *her* realm."

****

Dear Diary:

While we were touring White Rock, our wayward spirit was busy at work. All of the dug holes surrounding the cottage were filled with sand—nullifying their purpose, which is to test the soil for a suitable septic system. In broad daylight, Diary. It's as if the spirit knows Eddie will be standing surveillance at night, running interference with his wolf dog, so he elected to do the deed while we were gone during the day. Well, this clinches it. We have to do something or we'll never be able to move the property, sell the lots, save Overhome. This is one mean and ornery hold-over who not only has it in for me, but who is single-handedly keeping us from doing what has to be done: selling that land. Damn, damn, damn.

Okay. I've made up my mind. I'm calling Sheila Gordon about the Historical Society and I'm inviting Phoebe Swift to come to Overhome. The sooner the better, but I want Luke to be present. For sure, I need his steady shoulder and steely demeanor to bolster me up—help me decide how to proceed. I think I need a large dose of that smooth, rich, refreshing White Rock Velvet Sky to steady my nerves.

Chapter 17

Monica leaned forward and spoke in a low tone. "Helen, Ashby, thank you for agreeing to come with me for lunch today."

"A lovely idea," Mom said. "And this is a very nice restaurant."

We looked around appreciatively, taking in the light-filled room decorated with nautical blue and white tables and cloths, each seating area partitioned off with thick ropes. Oversized picture windows revealed land and seascapes: docks, pilings, boats, and wide-open lake waters. In fact, we had come by boat ourselves—an easy trip from Overhome.

"Yes. The Lake Landing was a favorite for Hunter and me—for special occasions." Monica sighed. "Which leads me to the topic for discussion. I value your opinions, both of you, Helen and Ashby. You are so...so steeped in family dynamics, so knowledgeable. You represent the functional family at its best."

I caught my mother's eye, wondering what my aunt was leading up to.

Mom looked briefly at the menu, then, placed it on the table. "Well, I never gave the functional family, as you call it, much thought, Monica. Madison and I—we fell in love with Ashby the minute we saw her. We were unable to have children, and it seemed so—so natural. Perfect. She was our little girl to love and rear as best we could."

Monica reached for Mom's hand. "That was my main reason for inviting Ashby to Overhome that summer so long ago. Coming from a completely dysfunctional family myself, I was floundering with no practical experience in building positive family dynamics. I knew how close you and Madison were to your daughter—how well she had grown and matured. My hope was that she would bring that sense of family to us. Show us how to bond." She let go of Mom's hand and reached for mine. "Ashby, you were invaluable. You became so much more than a mere companion to Jefferson—more like a big sister, obviously championing his free spirit while guiding him in all the right directions. You showed Hunter, and especially me, how to be a family, solidly connected with our son."

I did not know how to tell Monica that I never saw myself quite the same way she did. I was crazy about Jeff, but honestly, I always felt I had nothing whatsoever to do with drawing the three of them together in some kind of family unit. I'm not sure that ever happened the way Monica saw it.

"So," Monica spoke while flagging down a waitress. "I am calling up some badly-needed advice from you two. I am truly in a quandary."

After ordering sweet tea all around, Monica returned to her theme. "When Hunter died so suddenly, I felt we never had a real chance to try out our newly-found family unit or to build on what we had learned. I am afraid I was in such a daze…I numbly followed whatever course life took." She looked at me. "Ashby, again you came to the rescue. You were essential in getting me…and Jefferson back on track. In a way, I was forced to double my efforts at being his mother. How could I have done that without you to prop me up? And Luke! Ashby, hang on to Luke. When you have children of your own, why, he'll already know how to be a good father. He was such a positive role model for Jefferson, especially after his father's death."

The waitress placed our iced tea on the table and took our orders. For a while we sipped in silence. At length, Monica spoke. "I must say, you both look positively baffled."

"Out with it, Monica." Mom seemed to have anticipated what was coming; she seemed to barely contain her merriment.

I, myself, was not so sure. "You've certainly piqued our curiosity, Monica."

My aunt patted her lips delicately with her linen napkin and sighed. "It's Hal, of course. Surely you have guessed." She looked at Mom and then at me. "Hal has proposed marriage."

"Ha! I thought so! That's wonderful, Monica." Mom raised her glass as if toasting my aunt. "Now— you want our input about…about…?"

"Let me give you a little background. Perhaps that will help." Monica pressed her lips together, then, began. "Hal has never married. He spent the last decade caring for his parents who were in bad health. When they passed away, he began to work on a graduate degree in earnest. With his job as historian for a small museum and his teaching position, he never had much time to date or even think about meeting someone. Then…then…"

"Then he met you. Your work on Overhome's

history put you in constant proximity. Your relationship grew. We all could see a closeness developing." I smiled. "We were all glad, too."

"How do you feel about Hal, Monica?" Mom's blunt question was softened by her concerned look and kind voice. "You say he's proposed. Are you willing to marry again?"

Monica lowered her eyes briefly, before answering. "It took a while for me to realize it, but I do love him. Hal is so very different from Hunter—not nearly as handsome." She gave a wry look. "Not remotely as self-confident."

Not as controlling, I could have added.

"But he is kind and focused and intelligent. Gentle—so completely honest about his feelings for me. I know, for sure, Hal loves me."

"So let me get this straight," Mom ticked off her fingers. "Hal loves you; you love him, he's proposed marriage. No problems there." She spread her hands as if to say, "DUH!"

"Oh, I wish it were that easy, Helen. I no longer have the luxury of satisfying only myself. And I could never accept Hal's proposal until…"

"It's Jeff, right? You're worried about how Jeff will take it—a stepfather." I knew what was bothering my aunt.

Monica nodded. "As I told you, after Hunter's death, I worked doubly hard to be a good mother to Jefferson. And we have become close—closer than ever. I am not sure now is the time to…"

"To rock the boat," Mom finished.

For a few moments we looked at each other in sympathetic silence. Mom was first to speak. "Where are you and Hal considering making your home? Will you and Jeff move from Overhome? Relocate to his place, perhaps, or get something new?"

"We have discussed that. Even though Hal inherited his parents' home—spacious and updated enough for a family, I think Hal would be amenable to moving in with us at Overhome. But he is ambivalent— feels it is an intrusion. He says a 'clean break,' as he calls it, might be better." My usually so poised aunt seemed to be completely lost. "I...I do not know what to think."

I sat up straight as the waitress brought our salads and fussed about our table, seeing that we had everything we needed. When she left, I spoke as clearly and honestly as I could. "Monica, have you and Hal considered that it might be a much easier transition for Jeff if the three of you stayed on at Overhome? Jeff has his horse, his friend Nick, his father-figure, Luke, and his big sister-cousin, me. He's lived here all twelve of his years of life. And he loves Overhome."

"Well, yes. I know that. Hal knows that, too. But, Ashby, you and Luke will be just starting out your married lives. I cannot imagine that having another newly-wed couple under the same roof would be ideal or even workable."

"Nonsense. Put that worry aside right this minute, Monica. This house is always to be a home for you and for Jeff and for anybody else you love enough to bring in as family."

Mom gave one brief but decisive nod. "Good for you, Ashby. Your thinking is straight and it's right."

Monica wiped her tears with her napkin. "Oh dear. I hoped you would feel that way. And thank you for your corroboration, Helen. But there is another worry." She replaced her napkin in her lap. "Hal has no idea how to get close to Jefferson. He has had no experience with young children. While approving Jefferson's energy and intelligence, he is at a loss as to how to interact on one level as an understanding outsider and on another as a father."

"Spending time with Jeff might do the trick," Mom suggested. "It's amazing how close Nick and I have come this summer just with my tutoring him for an hour each day."

"Let's face it, Jeff is full of life, loves to have fun. He's curious and cheerful—I'd never had much experience with kids when I first met Jeff, and he brought out the kid in me in a trice." I'd always felt there was something special about my cousin that defined his relationships with others.

"It is true that, while Hal and I have spent many hours together, the three of us have not had much of a chance to interact—much less Hal and Jefferson on their own. Can you suggest some activities they could do together?" Monica reached for her glass. "I just do not know where to begin."

"I understand Hot Shots has a great mini golf course and arcade. And there's always Port Plaza—all kinds of kid-friendly things to do there—even a simulated rock-climbing wall," I said.

Mom offered a suggestion. "Invite Nick to go along—whatever you do. That could ease any awkward moments."

"Give Hal riding lessons!" Monica and Mom both blinked at me with surprise as I blurted this out.

My mother was first to regain her voice. "Not a bad

idea, Monica. Jeff lives and breathes horses."

"How do you think Luke and I got so close—when we started out so far apart! It was horses—Luke's patient riding lessons—hitting the trail together. I'm glad you agree, Mom." I turned to my aunt. "What do you think, Monica?"

"Well. I...I must say I had not thought of that. But if Hal can embrace the idea with any enthusiasm...it just might help him find a starting place with Jefferson." Her face brightened for the first time, then fell. "Though, Hal could never reach Hunter's riding level. It would be an unfair comparison."

"Let the horse decide." I paraphrased Carlos' advice. "Horseback riding can be a magical thing. What do you say, Monica? Broach the idea with Hal—let him take it from there. We have a top-notch riding school right under our nose, you know."

As we puttered out of the dock at the restaurant and I rolled the boat into open water heading home, I could not help but feel good about our lunch date with Monica. Sure, there would be bumps. There would be challenges, but what better place to start a new life than Overhome? It had worked for me.

****

Sheila Gordon sat in our library chair, sipping iced tea as Dad and I talked with her.

"The Historical Society is all about preserving and collecting the history in this part of Virginia. We operate a history museum and research library, and we have over 350 members all around the world."

A neatly-dressed, slightly plump woman with a pleasant expression and ready smile, Sheila was obviously heart and soul into her work with the society.

"The minute Paul told me about the proposed sale of your property containing a pre-Civil War historic structure, I knew I would have to see it for myself. Worm my way in somehow. Your invitation to meet today has saved me that embarrassment, Ashby." A warm smile lit up her bespectacled eyes. I appreciated her candor.

"Well, we've had a spot of trouble with our historic structure." I squirmed at my understatement.

"So Paul tells me. And I can't say I'm surprised. You see, we have layer upon layer of history to dig through here in Southern Virginia. Native American settlements, Revolutionary War encampments, Civil War homes. Of course, the society is all about preserving historic buildings and sites—just as we are about erecting historical markers, unearthing lost cemeteries—do you like the play on words?" She laughed merrily. "We manage all sorts of records— marriage, birth and death certificates, wills, deeds and other court documents. All the things you'd expect of a group such as ours."

We inclined our heads without speaking and Sheila went on. "Often we find that certain, shall we say, *entities* have remained trapped in a layer of history— stuck in time. Nobody knows how or why such a phenomenon occurs, and many, of course, do not believe it is possible, despite the evidence. As for your 'spot of trouble,' based on what Paul has told me, I'm wondering if you're thinking there's some paranormal resistance to your real estate plan."

Dad looked at me before speaking to Sheila. "I told Paul about the problems with the surveying stakes and the perc holes. I alluded to some of the odd experiences we've had in the cottage—the foul smell, the acts of aggression against Ashby and the voice telling everyone to 'go away.'" Dad's gaze moved from me to Sheila. "Paul was actually there when the entity, as you call it, attacked Ashby, though both he and I were unaware of it at the time. Paul has drawn his own conclusions; I can't say we disagree, though I am a bit surprised the Historical Society holds any credence in the paranormal."

Sheila looked amused. "Did you realize that our Historical Society conducts annual ghost tours? Using antique buses to get around, we tour all sorts of historical sites rumored to be haunted. Now, I'm thinking, we all feel that trouble spot you mentioned might have something to do with a spirit—perhaps one that does not want to let go of its 'home.'" She reached for her tea and took a sip. "Not every member of the society is on that same ancient bus, so to speak. But I don't see anyone suggesting we shut down the annual ghost tours, either. They're very popular—always sold out, in fact. We like to do them around Halloween. We call that particular tour our *Ghost-Escape*."

"Holding off for a moment on the 'layer-of-history' idea, what sort of plan might the Historical Society put in place with the old cottage?" Dad asked.

"Ideally, we'd love to see it restored and preserved and open to the public at times. The cottage represents so many aspects of our local history. Ultimately, we'd like to see it on the National Registry of Historic Sites in America."

"What would that entail on our part?" I was becoming a bit uncomfortable with the direction the conversation seemed to be taking.

"First—don't tear it down. Second, let our historians do the research. Then we can look into funding for the restoration project."

Though he must have shared my reservations, Dad, apparently, wanted Sheila to know we were not opposed to her suggestions. "Hal Reynolds has already done extensive research on the cottage."

Sheila brightened. "Dr. Hal Reynolds? Of course, I know him—well—I know *of* him at any rate. He's top-notch in the field of historic restoration. That's a stroke of luck."

"We'll have to talk to Paul about keeping the cottage intact." Dad included me in his statement. "Make sure it doesn't devalue the sale property or anything."

Sheila took another sip of tea, patted her lips with her napkin and smiled. "Quite the contrary, Madison, Ashby. A well-done restoration on a property is a huge draw for many home-owners. I think Paul would be the first to tell you that."

"But...there's still the problem of our resident spirit, Sheila," I said. "I can't imagine anyone would be willing to deal with such antisocial behavior at any phase of the project. Layer of history or not. As you know, we've already had numerous, shall we say, unpleasant encounters."

"That's where Phoebe comes in. If anyone can sort it out, my sister can." She raised her eyebrows. "I believe Paul told you, Phoebe is a medium."

"Ashby and Luke and I have discussed using a medium. We're ready to give it a try." Dad looked to me for corroboration.

"Here's Phoebe's card." Sheila dug down into her

purse and produced the medium's calling card—a simple white background embossed with the words *Phoebe Swift, Spiritual Guide* and contact information. I was glad there were no skulls or hexagrams or other creepy symbols in evidence. Just a slash of wavy black lines in one corner—a musical score without the notes. "Please give Phoebe a call. I believe she can lead you to some answers."

We stood and thanked Sheila and ushered her to the door. "I'm getting in touch with Phoebe right away." I tucked the medium's card into my pocket. "Let me get a hold of Luke—find out when he'll be home. If Phoebe can meet with us, we'll see what she suggests."

"I hope this works out for you—and for the Historical Society. It's a win-win situation, believe me. And, if it's okay with you, next time Paul works the site, I'll come along with him to have a good look at the historic building."

We watched her climb into her car and drive away. "Are you prepared for meeting the medium, Ashby?"

I sighed deeply. "Can't say I am, but what alternative do we have at this point? Look at the bright side—it will be an experience none of us has had before."

"Agreed. Let's pledge to keep an open mind."

"Scouts honor. Now, let me give Phoebe a call."

As if on cue, my phone gave a beep, which turned out to be a text from Luke: *CU in Loveboat penthouse 2nite.* I chuckled and turned to Dad. "What do you know. Perfect timing. Luke's coming home tonight. I'm going to see if Phoebe Swift can meet us tomorrow."

"Tomorrow it is. I'll tell your mom."

"And Miss Emma," we both said at the same time.

****

"So the horse's tongue continues to loll out of his mouth—like a panting dog. The owner is beside himself." We sat in the bow cushions of our penthouse suite, Luke's arms encircling me.

"Dr. Luke to the rescue!"

"Well, that was a no-brainer. I examine the horse's mouth, and, sure enough, there's a nasty raw sore under his tongue—bitten by a bit."

"You'd think that would be the first thing a horse owner would look for." I snuggled in closer.

"In the old days when people lived with their horses and worked them on the farms, they picked up on such things. Not so much now, I'm afraid."

"Tell me more, Luke. I love these vet stories of yours." I also loved his warm touch and dreamy smell. I closed my eyes and fell into the zone, listening to his voice.

"Another case that didn't require a detective. Sweeney, blind in his left eye, develops neck problems—so sore he can barely move his head. I notice the owner has Sweeney housed in the last stall in his barn. Poor Sweeney is always craning his neck to see the other horses, social creatures that they are. So, I suggest Sweeney be moved to a stall directly across from the other horses where he can communicate straight on with his one good eye."

"And…?"

"End of Sweeney's aching neck," Luke snorted. "One more?"

"As many more as you've got," I murmured against his shoulder. "Luke, do you think an observer might consider us a bit crazy—hanging suspended high above the dock in the dark, in the bow of a boat telling horse stories?"

"*Crazy*? Who cares? Though, I must say, I look forward to the day we can lounge around in a real bed. On the ground," he pulled me in for a long, slow kiss.

I sat up. "Okay. Let's hear another horse story."

"Ever see one of those miniature ponies?"

"They're cute little creatures."

"Not as little as some folks think. Lilli, short for Lilliputian, develops a shoulder injury. The owner calls me, and I notice Lilli going in circles. Round and round—which is further irritating the injury. 'Look,' I say to the owner, 'this stall you have Lilli in is too small. You need to move her out into the hall where she can walk straight. That shoulder injury will clear up a whole lot faster.'"

"Did he move little Lilli?"

"Yep. And next time I checked on her, Lilli's shoulder was A-OK. Just goes to show: Common sense is all that's required sometimes."

"Horse sense! Speaking of which, I called Phoebe Swift, medium. She's meeting us tomorrow afternoon."

"Interesting segue there, Ashby. From 'horse sense' to 'medium.' How the mind works. Some might call it crazy."

I stuck out my tongue. "Call it whatever you want. Just plan to be there, please. I want witnesses. Many witnesses, lest I be considered crazy enough to believe in calling up the spirits of the dead."

"Touché! My horse sense tells me it's time to settle down on the stern cushions for some serious love-making. I don't want to hear any neighs, either."

"I say yay, not nay, and that was a terrible pun." I stood and made my way to the back of the boat.

Chapter 18

Phoebe Swift defied her own name. Phoebe *Slow and Deliberate* would have been a better fit. She began with a quiet, prayer-like chant directed at the spirit world. "We circle ourselves in the light of protection; we benevolently seek the best for all concerned. We come with open hearts and minds to understand. To hear your words. To seek the best. We entreat you to communicate with us so that we can support and help you."

We sat in the semi-dark silence of the library for what seemed like hours, though it was probably closer to twenty minutes. Phoebe, head tilted back, sat granite-still with eyes closed, hands stretched forward, palms up above the table. Her long, silver-streaked red ringlets dangled around her neck like a faded feather boa. Her parted lips, moving in silent recitation, revealed a gap in her front teeth. All I could think of was the Wife of Bath from Chaucer's *Canterbury Tales*, whose toothy gap supposedly indicated a licentious nature. This is what happens to a sane mind forced to focus too hard and long on the completely abstract. Were the others as stultified by this meditation as I was? Though Phoebe had asked all of us to close our eyes along with her, I sneaked a peek at my parents and Miss Emma and then caught Luke, who was simultaneously glancing under his lashes at me. Oh dear. We'd never engage the spirits at this rate. I quickly closed my eyes and tried to clear my mind.

"We are here in love. Pure love. Nothing more." At long last, Phoebe broke the silence, her husky voice, low and even, a mesmerizing monotone. "We seek the best for all concerned." (Long pause.) "We represent positive energy." (Pause.) "We come in love."

A cool breeze ruffled my hair and I opened my eyes in alarm. Nobody else seemed affected—all sat in a trance-like stillness, eyes closed. Did I detect a dark shadow on the far wall? Perhaps not—maybe the shadow of a bird flying by the window. I closed my eyes again, waiting.

"We come to understand. We thank you for letting us know of your presence. We ask for signs so that we may hear—may know what it is that disturbs you. As a part of the Overton family, we embrace you and we come, always, in pure love."

I sneaked a peek just as the lamp on the desk flickered once. Twice.

"*No love*," Phoebe said. But it wasn't her voice anymore. A shaking, raspy-deep growl. Again my eyes flew open. I stared first at Phoebe, then at the others, who also had opened their eyes to stare.

Phoebe's hand fell awkwardly to the table in front of her with a thud as if she'd fallen asleep and lost control over it. She twitched, then, settled to her former pose, all without opening her eyes. "*No. No. No love*!" This time the enunciation was tortured, snarling, wailing as if on the verge of angry tears as it piped from her throat in the same gravel-tone as before.

"We are here to help." Phoebe's own voice again. "We come in love."

Once more the breeze fluttered about my face, then the sudden plop of a book falling from the shelf to the floor at my feet. Jumping half out of my chair, I wanted to cry out, but Phoebe had asked us all to refrain from speaking. I pressed my lips together, took some yoga breaths, and waited, one eye on the book shelf. Everybody else appeared as unsettled as me. I had the odd sensation that the room was now, somehow, more vacant than when we had all entered it—a hollow, empty feeling, as if I, and I alone, sat here, waiting.

After another silence, Phoebe spoke again. This time the tone was light—a whisper-breath of a voice—a new and different vocal sound altogether—and definitely not Phoebe's. "*Help. Please help.*"

"We are here to help," Phoebe answered in her throaty monotone. "I see you."

Every eye opened at that. A swirling, glowing, ever-moving wave of light, blending into a single human-like shape, then blurring and expanding again, flitted about the walls and ceiling, touching down to the floor, before morphing again into a human form. A sound emerged, but I could not distinguish words. It sounded like, "*Ahnnnnnllll.*"

Phoebe picked up on it. "Angel? You say you're an angel?" She raised her hands as though to touch the entity. The humanoid form hovered, glowing—diminishing—glowing again like a flashing beacon warning of a hazard ahead. Monotone abandoned, Phoebe pleaded, "Speak, Angel. Speak to me. Please. I entreat you."

Holding my breath until I could stand it no longer, I exhaled loudly. Except for Phoebe—and the angel, perhaps—nobody had uttered a word. Then it hit me and I could not contain the rush of words. "Angel…Raeford's angel? Angelina! Angelina Overton!"

With that, the energy dissipated instantly. Phoebe slowly lowered her hands. She looked at me as if she had forgotten I was present—that anyone else was present. "What did you say, Ashby?" She shook her head slightly and the curls bounced around her ears.

I was speechless. It had all happened so fast—in the blink of an eye. "Sorry. I—I guess I broke the…the spell. You told us not to talk, but I couldn't control myself."

"Yes, well that does happen. But what was it you said? 'Angelina?' Did I hear that right?"

"Angelina Overton," Miss Emma murmured. "She lived at Overhome before and during the Civil War. Raeford Overton was her baby brother. He called her 'my angel,' and she loved him as no one else in the family did."

Phoebe puzzled over this information before responding. "So it may have been Angelina, not an angel, per se." Her eyes lit on Miss Emma. "She asked for our help."

"Yes, that would be my guess."

"Mine, too. Thus, my outburst, which evidently sent Raef's angel scuttling off in a flash." I felt I should apologize.

"Oh, no worry," Phoebe soothed. "We made contact. That's the important thing. A bit of a contrast, though. The first entity seemed bitter, unhappy and un-resigned. 'No love. No, no, no love.' The second—Angel, or Angelina—a different story altogether."

"The bitter one. Raeford Overton?" Dad appeared

to be thinking out loud. "Brother and sister—as unresolved after death as before?"

"What do you make of it, Phoebe?" Mom asked. "What have we learned here?"

Luke and I nudged each other. All eyes were on Phoebe.

"I'm only beginning to get a feel for the situation." Phoebe looked thoughtful. "Violence, hatred, ill-will— these are negative energies which can stagnate and pollute the air, the land, the people who inhabit such an environment. Conversely, love, joy, peace can lighten and lift—shifting the bad and evil to radiate with a higher vibration, which causes change. Positive, flowing goodness, which attracts more goodness."

"So…what we need to do…" Luke pursed his lips in thought. "We try to change the whole dynamic—one that started out hundreds of years ago?" He raised his eyebrows quizzically. "We can do that?"

"We *have* to do that. I've felt it for a long time, but had no idea how to go about effecting such a change." I looked at Phoebe, searching for an answer. "I still haven't a clue."

"Think about the terror of being trapped between two worlds. I know nothing about either of these two entities we may have identified—Raeford, if that's who it is, complains of 'no love' and Angelina who emerges with the light, a benevolent spirit, asking for help. I can only surmise. Did Raeford suffer abuse during his earthly life? Was he attacked, often?" Phoebe looked from one to the other of us for answers.

I felt, in some way, I knew Raeford better than the others. "According to Angelina's diary, it was Raeford who attacked others—abused them. Ultimately, he was banished from the family, shunned for most of his adult life as a result of his uncontrolled anger."

"He maimed a slave, falsely accusing him of theft," Dad said.

"Nursed by a slave, Raeford felt her milk had infected him—infused him with inferior qualities he imagined slaves to have," Mom added. "He certainly seems to have had a terrible attitude as a young man."

"Angelina still loved him," Miss Emma contributed. "She refused to banish him from her thoughts and prayers."

Phoebe rocked back in her chair, putting her fingers to her temples. "Let me think on this." Silent, we waited several moments for her to continue. One by one, she looked each of us in the eye. "That's certainly a load of negative energy the Raeford spirit is carrying. If there is 'no love,' what is there? Judgment from others: *I am less. I am wrong. I am bad*." She let her gaze fall on each of us again. "Can you see how this entity might feel it was *he* who was attacked and abused? Judged a failure all his life by those who should have loved him, no matter what?"

"It's a new perspective for me." Luke's eyebrows contracted in thought. "We've all figured Raeford for a badass, plain and simple." He looked to Phoebe for help. "What's the next step?"

Again, Phoebe took her time answering. "We must place ourselves in the historic building. The cottage, Sheila called it. We may find more to work with there."

"Tomorrow?" Luke knew he'd be leaving after that—going back to Tech for who knows how long until he could return to Overhome.

Phoebe pulled out a small notebook and looked at

it. "Afraid I have a full schedule for the next several days. But if you're up for it, I could meet you tomorrow night. Now, timing can be crucial. The veil between worlds thins out some time around three o'clock. That's three A.M. I recommend we shoot for that. Otherwise, it will have to be next week."

"I can't be sure I'll be here next week." Luke shook his head. "But—three a.m.? That's awfully late—the middle of the night. There's no electricity in the cottage, you know."

Dad tapped Mom's shoulder, as if asking for permission. "Count me in. We'll set an alarm—sound a wakeup call for all who are interested. We'll caravan out there—take plenty of flashlights."

"I'll go along." Mom focused on Miss Emma. "Are you up for it, Miss Emma? It's asking a lot—could be awfully tiring, you know."

"An adventure." Miss Emma smiled. "Just what my old bones need, eh? My bones and I—we don't really care much about the time of day."

"We'll take that for a yes, Aunt Emma." Luke put his arm around the elderly lady. "You can always beg off if you change your mind."

Monica had been silent through the entire channeling session. Even aware that Overhome housed spirits, she must have been shocked by this bizarre experience.

"How about you, Monica? Will you go out to the cottage tomorrow night with us?" I had no idea how she would respond.

Monica puffed out her cheeks, then, exhaled. "I—I—have been w—wondering about one thing and one thing only." She looked at me wide-eyed. "H—How to

210

d—d—describe all of this to Hal."

I remembered that Monica stammered sometimes when she was agitated.

"You could invite him to come to the cottage for the next channeling," Luke said.

She got a grip on herself, and spoke without stuttering. "I will think about it. We'll be seeing each other tonight. And we have been talking about this…problem spirit. I will try to describe what we have experienced here and I'll ask him if he wants to join in on the next session. Though it might be a real burden, what with his work load." She thought for a moment. "But I do not believe I, myself, can handle any more of it." She put her hand over her eyes as if to block out the experience.

Phoebe flashed her gap-toothed grin. "I'll see whoever wishes to be involved tomorrow night, then. Say we meet here at 2:30—travel to the cottage as a group." She stood, folding her appointment book into her tote bag. "I think we'll make some headway just by placing ourselves physically in the midst of a complex combination of issues."

Before we walked out of the library to see Phoebe off, I bent to pick up the book that had fallen from the shelf to my feet. *Cold Mountain*—a story about a Confederate deserter who was pursued by bounty hunters all the way home. Coincidence? Who knew? I placed it back on the shelf. One more thing to consider.

Luke and I headed automatically for the horses. I was feeling rattled, ragged-out. "Oh, man, that was nerve-wracking. I'm literally shaking; I'll bet my blood pressure is scary."

"And I'm in a sweat." Luke pulled his damp shirt

away from his chest. "Let's ride this out of our system. Calm ourselves down."

"My thought exactly. I just feel that I—well, I need grounding. Going to nature is the one thing that will bring me back to physical and mental stability."

We found both of our horses in the paddock. I approached Sasha automatically, without thinking. My horse always greeted me eagerly, with a whinny of approval. But this time Sasha danced around, his ears laid back flat against his neck, with no move toward me whatsoever. "What is it, boy? What's wrong?"

Snorting, Sasha planted his feet firmly and refused to budge. "Come, Sasha. Come, boy. It's all right."

"Luke, are you watching this? I can't imagine what's up with Sasha." At my words, my horse had started slowly in my direction, but he was nervous as a gnat, I could tell.

Luke shared my puzzlement. "Whatever it is, Dickens has a touch of it, too." I watched his horse react much as Sasha had, skittish, keyed up. Unusual behavior for both of these usually compliant creatures. "Do you think they feel it? The horses? Are they sensing our edginess—reacting to it? Is that possible?" He blinked. "I'm the vet, for Pete's sake, but I've never seen the likes of this."

"You know, Sasha acted this way the first time I encountered Raef—at the cottage. I think you're right. Our horses sense some weird vibe—an evil aura." *Something wicked this way comes,* popped into my head. That ominous line from Macbeth. "Let's get out on the trail—out in the wind and sun. Shake this off."

By now, we had both drawn our horses in so that we could get our saddles out of the tack room. Though they'd calmed down considerably, they were jumpy and a bit wild-eyed. Luke reached for his saddle. "Let's get out of here. The sooner the better," he said grimly.

****

We had a brisk canter across the fields, then a leisurely ride along the trail. Stopping by the stream, we tethered our horses and settled on the bank. Luke leaned against a big oak, and I curled up against him comfortably. We indulged in a few warm kisses before easing into conversation. "Well, I'm back to normal—so's my horse. How about you, babe?" Luke massaged my shoulders.

"So beautiful. Take this moment for what it is—a bubbling brook, a shady resting place, you and me. Nirvana," I heaved a deep sigh.

"Let's never get so busy that we don't take time to appreciate all of this." Luke stroked my cheek. "I see us—an old married couple, resting our weary bones on this bank, admiring the stream, holding hands…"

I chuckled at the image. "I can picture it. And, I must say, you're as handsome as ever, even with white hair." I patted his hand. "But—in the here and now—it seems there's always so much to do. To worry about. To fix."

"All I know is I'm the luckiest guy in Virginia. Heck, in the world. The universe. Because I'm marrying my dream girl, my sweet babe." He pulled me to him, pressing his lips to mine."

"Mmmmm. Where'd you learn to kiss like that?"

Luke set me gently upright. "Ashby, we have to talk over something. I wasn't going to tell you until I have more details, but I want your input now."

"Okay. I'm listening." I leaned back into his

shoulder and waited.

"It's Doc Forest. He's made me an offer, and I'm not sure what to think about it."

"What kind of offer?" I was growing increasingly curious.

"His practice is not far from Overhome, you know. He's kept me busy most of the summer with my tracking duties—really the only way I've been able to get home as often as I have since he lives so close—what? Forty minutes away on a slow drive behind a lumber truck." Luke swallowed hard. "He wants me to go work with him starting this fall."

"Work with him? At his place? What about your plans to set up practice here?"

"Don't know. It might be a way to get a start. He's hinted that he's considering retirement in the near future—maybe turning his practice over to me. I'm really torn—he's pressing me for an answer."

"Well, this is certainly unexpected. But, it may be a good thing. Like you say—a way to establish your own practice. Work Doc Forest's patients as well as your own at Overhome." I plucked a blade of grass and smoothed it between my fingers. "Could you handle it all?"

"Did I just say let's never get too busy to enjoy each other—Overhome and all it represents?"

"And in the next breath we talk about double duties for Luke Murley, rooky vet." I leaned into him. "Go with your gut, Luke. I'll support whatever decision you make."

Luke's arm tightened around me. "Thanks, babe. I'll fill you in on the details when I know more myself. Now I guess we'd better get back to the barn. Take care of our horses before dark."

As we reached the farm, we encountered Jeff and Nick mounted on their horses inside the riding ring. "Hey, Ashby. Luke!" Jeff hailed us, waving. "Nick and I have been practicing jumps. Wanna watch?"

"Sure thing." Luke propped a foot on the corral gate. "Show us what you've got."

One at a time, the boys maneuvered running jumps over the schooling fences, their steeds arching gracefully and effortlessly above the raised white planks, over and over again. I'd seen Olympic equestrians not much more skilled. Grinning widely, they reined in beside us.

"Smooth!" Luke offered a high five to one boy, then, the other. "You both nailed it. Even with the rails at top height. Excellent form!"

"Beautiful, guys. We should videotape it—put you on YouTube or something." I was impressed by their level of competence at such an early age.

"Carlos says we can do some teaching." Jeff's eyes shone with excitement. "With the pony class."

Nick flashed a nervous grin. "Oh boy—that means I'd have to teach Winn Davies."

"Now, that ought to be interesting," Luke said. "You mean Winn-the-Loser bully? You gonna show him how to be a gentleman?"

"My dad doesn't know how Winn treated me at school." Nick ducked his head shyly. "I never told him."

A thought surfaced. "Jeff, while Nick is taking on that challenge, how'd you like one of your own?"

Jeff's freckles appeared to multiply over his nose as he lifted his brows inquiringly. "What, Ashby?"

"How'd you like to teach Hal to ride?"

Jeff thought for a moment. "Hal's an adult...I'm a kid."

"As Shakespeare might say, 'Aye, there's the rub.'" How quickly children could get to the very heart of the matter.

"But he's nice," Nick said. "A whole lot nicer than Winn Davies."

"He's a nice adult," Jeff agreed. "That's true." He looked at me. "Do you think Hal would want me to teach him?"

Why did I always open my mouth prematurely? "Tell you what, Jeff. Why don't I be the go-between. See how Hal feels about it. As long as you're okay with teaching a...a nice adult."

Jeff's freckles settled back to normal, and he smiled. "I'll check with Carlos. If it's okay with him, it's okay by me."

Luke and I dismounted and led our horses to the barn. "Whoa—are we spinning webs of intrigue? How to take down a bully—how to break in a stepdad? Who says farm life is dull?" Luke patted my behind with a playful smile.

"Just wait until tomorrow night. I have the feeling we'll be wishing for *dull* after Phoebe gets through with us." I gave a slight shudder. "Creepy!"

"Phoebe and a couple of long-dead Overtons. And who knows what—or who—else." Luke was no longer smiling.

****

Dear Diary:

Luke told Miss Emma she could always beg off going to the cottage with Phoebe and the rest of us. What about me? Can I beg off? I cannot imagine anything scarier than sitting around in that decrepit, isolated cottage conjuring up volatile, unpredictable spirits of the dead. Oh, did I mention we'll be in the dark? Make that dead dark. But I suppose it has to be done. If there is a way to change the dynamics set in motion more than a century ago, a way to use the spirit world to set the scenario for positive action here and now, well, we have to give it a try, right? How else to make any progress whatsoever on the Overton property sale?

Phoebe seems to feel we're making headway. Though it's something she understands a lot better than the rest of us, I have to admit—I got it. It was infinitely clear to me that Angelina Overton was with us, responding to Phoebe's call. Making herself known to me. Yes, to me! But this next foray into the spirit world, actually calling on the spirits in the cottage—I just don't know if I'm ready for it—and my mind is actively conjuring up worst-case scenarios. Yet, I know I can take comfort in the crowd. Surrounded by those who love me—love each other—with enough love, we could possibly be a match for the meanest and vilest of spooks. This thought must sustain me. In the meantime, I wonder where I might get my hands on a bullet-proof vest. Body armor? A steel crash helmet at the very least. I can't get around the fact that this ghost-guy, Raeford Overton, is fixated on me. I should feel so honored. Hah. Hoping this is not my last entry, Diary. Wish me luck.

Chapter 19

Fog had settled over the fields, blocking out any hope of moon or star shine. Luke, Miss Emma and I followed in Luke's pickup as Dad, Mom and Phoebe led the way in a Jeep borrowed from Paul Gordon. Hal had decided not to join us, possibly a bow to Monica's reluctance to endure another chilling episode. More likely, because he had an early-morning class to teach.

At times the mist was so thick we could barely discern the taillights ahead of us. It was like trying to follow a candle covered in gauze. There is nothing darker than a foggy night in the country, devoid of street lamps and traffic and houses. Jolting and bumping over the jagged terrain, I put an arm around Miss Emma.

"Sorry, Miss Emma. This is awfully rough. Are you all right? Do you want to stop and rest?"

"Oh, glory, no. Don't stop. I'm afraid we'd be forever lost on the moor without our guiding light ahead." She motioned toward the bleary Jeep taillights.

"Like in *The Hound of the Baskervilles*. Sherlock Holmes, with the twisting, churning mists settling in, obscuring things that ought not be hidden."

"You can't scare me, Ashby dear. I'm far too old and I've seen way too much. Shall I recite a few lines of Poe for you?"

I squeezed her thin shoulder. "Miss Emma, you are

precious." I kissed her on the cheek. "And I'm so glad you decided to come along tonight. Neither Luke nor I know what to expect after yesterday's session with Phoebe Swift."

"It's bound to be altogether different." Luke leaned closer to the opaque windshield. "This fog alone changes the mood, don't you think? Sort of shrouds us in mystery. And, let's face it—we're in the middle of nowhere in the middle of the night." He shivered and I was not entirely sure it was put-on. I felt my own cold, trembling arms.

We pulled into the clearing and trooped cautiously over the rotting porch to the door, no longer boarded up. Dad shone his flashlight on the steps, then, handed it to me while he helped first Mom and then Miss Emma into the cottage. Luke and Phoebe had preceded us, and they stood waiting to usher everyone inside. As Dad and I made our way over the ramshackle threshold, I pantomimed whether to shut us in. He nodded, and I reached to secure the creaking, warped door. The rusty hinges scraped ominously, echoing into the hollow of the front room.

Phoebe and Luke set out folding chairs and a camp table they'd brought in from the Jeep, and Phoebe lit a candle and fired up some incense in a ceramic jar, which she set on the table. Nobody said a word; in the eerie silence, I tried to open my five senses while relaxing my mind in hopes that a sixth sense would find its way to me. I put myself in a state I'd learned in yoga class, concentrating on mindfulness, staying in the moment, blocking out all other thoughts. The air smelled only faintly rotten, stale and oddly warm— almost stifling. Even after adjusting to the dim interior, my sight was somewhat limited, so that I was surprised when I realized that Phoebe had not sat down like the rest of us. She made her way slowly, from wall to wall, speaking in a low, musical voice some kind of prayer or chant. I heard only snippets of her monologue— "…support the spirit angst about life…our intent is to hear you…love…love…love…"

We watched the circular illumination of her flashlight advance in sync with her form as she murmured her way around the perimeter of the room. She wore a long, flowing skirt whose horizontal bands of color melted mysteriously into one another when she moved. My nostrils began to burn with the aroma of the sandalwood incense which had completely erased the slight, lingering rotten smell I associated with Raeford's spirit.

"There. That should do." Phoebe seated herself behind the table on which the candle stood, casting its feeble, mellow light on her features. With her back to the fireplace, facing our semicircle, she shut her eyes. Breathing in through her nose and out through pursed lips, she spoke to us: "Let's all be receptive now, banish any fears. Let this space be a place for communicating our collective desire to understand. Think about our higher purpose for coming here. Remember, always, that we come in love."

For many moments we sat in silence. Had the chair been more comfortable, I might have dozed off, but I concentrated on staying mindful. Just when I began to think this was all futile, Phoebe spoke, and I knew she was not addressing us, but the spirit world. "Feel the love. We are here to help you resolve the issues, disperse the veil of negativity stagnating inside these walls. We welcome your needs. We seek to know: Why are you here?"

Again, a long, silent wait. This time I could feel my head drooping and I wondered how the others were doing—especially Miss Emma.

THUNK! The door swung open with a force sufficient to shake the walls, rousing everyone in the room except for Phoebe. Even though we knew we were to sit quietly and follow Phoebe's lead, we created a lot of small noise with our shuffling and murmuring. Still, Phoebe's eyes remained closed, and the rapt expression on her face never wavered. The candle light burnished her reddish curls with a surreal glow.

Without warning, Phoebe emitted a shriek…blood-curdling and violent, to be followed by another and another scream.

We were all leaning forward now, frozen, suspended between fear and wonderment, when a last screech pierced the stagnant air and Phoebe collapsed onto the table, knocking the candle to the floor.

Luke, closest to her, scrambled for the still-burning taper. He held it close to Phoebe's form, which was folded over the table like a collapsed bellows. After several moments of unbearable suspense, Phoebe raised her head slowly and glanced around. Even in the dim candle light her face was ghostly pale. She seemed to be confused, unaware of her surroundings.

"Rocks. Boulders," she said faintly. "Heavy, heavy stones. Such cruelty. Such pain." She closed her eyes, then, opened them slowly. "I see a wall. A stone wall. A wall of pain and suffering." She paused. "And I hear the crack of a whip. Crying. Men, women, children."

Not a one of us broke in. I am sure I was holding

my breath; perhaps we all were as we awaited Phoebe's next move.

It was a long time coming. Gradually the color returned to her cheeks. When she opened her eyes, they showed a weary, heavy-lidded exhaustion, as she addressed us. "Much sorrow has filled this space. Pain. Death—unexpected death. Merciless force. Cruelty beyond imagination."

"Raeford Overton?" My voice shook. "Was it Raef, Phoebe?"

Miss Emma stirred from her seat, speaking in a gentle, kind tone. "Phoebe, we can tell you are spent— that whatever it is you've experienced or seen with your special sense has completely done you in. But you must stay strong. We need to know. You are the only one who can tell us about it. What was it, Phoebe? What happened here tonight?"

Phoebe shook her head. "So powerful. So evil."

"You mentioned a stone wall—a wall of pain and suffering." Miss Emma was not through with Phoebe. "Could that be the stone wall here at Overhome? The stone wall built by slaves—the wall that stretches from the house to the gazebo?"

Phoebe flinched, inhaled, blowing air gently from her mouth. Closing her eyes, she spoke. "I saw many human images—piling up stones. Women and children as well as men. Hauling them in hods. Hefting them onto wagons. Heavy loads of stones. Too heavy. All to the sound of the cracking whip. The wall. Yes, the wall of pain." She paused—appearing to gather strength for what she would say next. With her eyes still shut, she continued, her voice strained with emotion. "Smells of sweat and blood and the hot leather of a cracking whip mixed into the pungent stench of human waste. Mewling cries, like abandoned kittens in a desperate search for a mother cat. Rancid air. Limping, crawling bodies reaching out hands of supplication to a power-figure lashing his whip. Blood splattering into the air with every stroke of the whip."

As Phoebe spoke, I had the uncanny sensation of stepping outside myself. All of my senses were on edge. Suddenly, I was there with Phoebe: I saw, heard, smelled, felt and tasted the horror of the scene. Shrinking from the sensory onslaught, I thrust my arms out in front of me as if to push it all away. I tried to cover my eyes, then pressed my fingers into my ears, but it was so real, so shocking, I could not shut it out. With huge effort, I tightened my eyes until they ached and shook my head so hard my teeth rattled. The scene slowly receded from my senses. Returning gradually to reality, I blinked as the dim walls of the cottage placed me in the present.

"Ashby?" Phoebe wore a worried expression on her face. "Are you with us?"

I looked questioningly at her and then the others. "What…what happened?"

"You were out of it." Luke reached for my hand. "Whimpering, groaning, waving your arms. Tears rolled down your cheeks. Now, your forehead is covered in sweat." Gently he wiped my face with a tissue.

My voice shook as I tried to explain. "I asked Phoebe if the vision was about Raef, but I don't think it was—although he, of course, lived through slave times. What Phoebe experienced—what I just tuned into—it had to be about the slaves themselves. The callous overseer. The whip—the blood. The effort of moving piles of stones too heavy for human hands. I was there—like it was happening here and now, and it was horrible."

Miss Emma spoke into the silence that followed my outburst. "The dismantling of the furnace? The overseer—the slaves moving stones from the furnace foundations to build our wall?"

Momentarily, a vision of the whip-lasher's demonic face flashed before my eyes. "He was so cruel," I murmured.

Dad gave me a sympathetic look, then, spoke to Phoebe. "Hal told us about the furnace. The remains of the furnace foundations lie just outside this cottage."

"It seems you both saw a vision of slavery in action. How is that possible?" Luke looked confused.

I reasoned out loud. "What if there was already an aura—an evil aura—one that permeated this cottage long before Raeford Overton ever set foot inside?" I hesitated, searching for the right words. "You know, I could feel the mood—cold, dark, mean, twisted. I smelled the desperation and heard the crack of the whip and the pitiful cries for mercy." I looked at the medium. "I glimpsed the entire scene just as you described it, Phoebe. Could that aura have affected Raef as he lived here? Warped his soul or something?"

Phoebe perked up. "Could be, Ashby. The Historical Society calls it 'layers of history,' you know. Where evil has existed and spirits have not found rest for some reason." She took a deep breath. "I'm ready to go in again. Can you bear with me for another try?" She gave me a piercing look before she closed her eyes again, and I knew she realized I had experienced her vision as vividly as she had.

We all nodded. I was as worried about Phoebe as she was about me. The first go-round had obviously sapped her strength. Was she up to it? Was I? The medium settled herself, taking time to close her eyes and point her chin toward the ceiling. Continuing that nose and mouth breathing and holding out her hands, at last she began to speak in her smoky monotone: "To anyone trapped between the worlds. We are here to help; we want the best for all concerned." Through a long silence, we waited and waited and waited.

The atmosphere of the room altered noticeably. The stultifying air cleared away like a cloud lifting off the mountains. A hint of incense wafted over us, a wave of purified breath. The heaviness peeled away as if the barometer had instantly plunged. I opened my eyes and sat up straight, straining through the gloom to see if others had noticed the sudden shift in the atmosphere.

Phoebe began to chant anew: "Pure, loving joy and peace. Benevolence for all."

Aware of something hovering over me, I tilted back my chin like Phoebe's. Instantly, I felt a puff of air on my cheeks. Watching now, my eyes drawn to the fireplace wall behind Phoebe, I sensed rather than saw a shape, a dark shadow expanding and contracting, moving without apparent direction over the old stones in an oddly caressing motion.

"Who are you?" breathed Phoebe. "Reveal yourself. We have come to help you."

A moaning sigh emerged from Phoebe's lips. A hollow, muffled male voice chanted what sounded like, "*St-stonnne. Stonnnes.*"

The stones again. More about the slaves building

the wall? The utterances were quite different from the shrieking and screaming Phoebe and I had heard before; it was obviously a single, deep voice, a new voice, and it was not Phoebe's. The shadow continued to feather the fireplace wall.

"We can help remove the darkness," Phoebe vocalized in her ever-patient tone. "We are the light."

At that, the spirit intoned again. "*Beneath*," it said quite clearly. "*Beneath the stones*."

"How can we help you? Who are you?" It was Phoebe, the medium speaking, but there was no answer. The shadow on the fireplace disappeared in a snap. A spark popped from the fireplace opening and I smelled smoke. Then, a gust of air blew directly in my face, but it was not a threatening force—rather a gentle stroke— like a mother caressing her child's cheeks. Nothing like the cold, stinking presence of Raeford's ghost—and I knew the spirit was gone.

Phoebe's shoulders slumped, and she sat without speaking for a few moments. Then sitting up straight she addressed us all. "I saw an image—a vision. It was a man dressed in some sort of uniform—I couldn't tell exactly what kind, or even what color. He carried a weapon—a gun. He wanted me to understand—tried to say something. Tried to tell me his name, but I couldn't quite make it out. I believe it started with a *G*—or possibly a *J*. I could feel his urgency." Phoebe shook her head slowly, a puzzled look on her face.

"I heard him," I told Phoebe. "I didn't see him, but I heard him say, 'Beneath the stones.'"

"I heard it, too," Mom said. Dad and Luke concurred, chiming in together, "Me, too."

"Well, it's pretty obvious to me." Miss Emma's

227

wavy old voice carried in the dark room. "Phoebe saw him and we heard him. We've experienced the spirit of Jeb Stover, Confederate Cavalry hero, and he's with us all right. He's beneath the stones."

If anybody could intuit the identity of a historic Overton figure, it would be Miss Emma Coleville, who had lived with the knowledge and nuances of that heritage all her life.

"Jeb Stover? Starts with a *J.* Okay—I can see that, maybe—but, the stone wall?" Luke said. "The wall the slaves built?"

"Perhaps not." Phoebe's look was enigmatic. "I believe our collective energy—right here—within these walls—is what brought this spirit out. More likely the stones he's referring to are here in the cottage."

All eyes gravitated to the stone fireplace behind Phoebe.

Dad spoke to Miss Emma. "Why Jeb Stover?"

"Jeb spent every summer at Overhome as a child. When Raeford was banished from Overhome, he went to live with Jeb and his family. And when war broke out, they both joined the same cavalry unit. That's a close Overton-Stover bond as I see it. Jeb Stover would have every right to haunt this cottage that Raeford Overton inhabited."

It left us all with a new thought: Whatever is going on with the spirit world in the cottage, Jeb Stover's ghost could be involved. Along with a whole lot of everlastingly mournful and desperate slaves.

"Did you see the spark? It came from the fireplace. I smelled smoke," I said.

Luke nodded. "At first, I thought the smoke was caused by the candle falling over—that something caught fire—a dead leaf or something." He tapped his finger on the table, touched the candle. "But it was something else, wasn't it?" He looked around the room for an answer.

Phoebe briefly closed her eyes, then opened them. "There is one other thing. I cannot explain it— something I saw in the moment the smoke puffed. An image—a split-second flash of silver or chrome— possibly gold. Round, flat objects—smooth and shiny."

We stared at Phoebe. Though the others were surely baffled and nobody spoke, I, too, had caught the flash along with the smoke puff. Round and flat, yes. But not chrome or gold. I saw silver. Definitely silver. I decided to keep it to myself for the time being. I wanted to think it over.

"We're done here." Phoebe stood. "They've left us—Jeb, if that's who it is, the slaves, all of the spirits have gone. We can leave now. If you'll load up the chairs, I'll sweep the walls with sage. Just to be sure. The sage clears out the spirits; we don't need them lingering after a channeling, doing who knows what."

As we filed out into the night air, I immediately noticed a change. The fog had lifted. The sky was alive with stars and a sickle moon hung on the horizon. I'm afraid Sir Arthur Conan Doyle, author of Sherlock Holmes, would not have approved. But one thought lingered: Where was Raef Overton? And why had his spirit not shown up tonight in this, his self-appointed territory?

****

Dear Diary:

Well, now I'm really confused. Phoebe is a wonder. She's unleashed a plethora of spirits. Yesterday, Angelina Overton emerged. It seems she wants to help Raeford, her black-sheep brother. Are she and Raeford both stuck between worlds? And, tonight, we all harbored thoughts of our own, I'm sure. First, many tortured spirits, probably slaves, appear to be trapped in the cottage. Then, I agree with Miss Emma that we have experienced yet another troubled entity from the spirit world: Jeb Stover, Raeford's cousin and boon childhood companion. Two words describe his quandary: "stones" and "beneath." While subject to various interpretations, I have my own theory.

Again, I wonder why all of Phoebe's efforts failed to unearth Raef's spirit. Raef, who so willingly attacks me whenever he gets the chance. Would it have anything to do with that collective "love, peace and joy" Phoebe insists we bring along to the channeling sessions? Does the barrier of love hold off Raef's wave of hatred?

One thing I have determined, however, is to clue Jeff in on Phoebe's channelings. Nick, too. Phoebe said from the beginning that she will not permit children to be present during a session, but she said nothing about telling them what's happened at one. I still think Raef Overton, or perhaps it's Jeb Stover, has formed some kind of bond with the boys. It needs to be explored and, thus, we need the lads' insight. I'm remembering the arrowhead and the tumbled comics and books. The tiny key left in the silver cup. Is someone from the other world trying to tell us something? We must be vigilant!

Here's something to chew on, Diary: I actively experienced a grim moment in Southern slavery. The spirits did not so much speak to me as evolve within and around me. How do I explain this? It was quite clear. Real. Perhaps the five years I've lived here have enabled the otherworld, so prevalent, to seep into my psyche so that when stimulated, that spirit world emerges spontaneously. I am confused and puzzled, but this new sense is empowering.

One more thing: Jeb is still with me. Now that Phoebe has conjured him up, for some reason he's apparently attached himself to me. Evidently, Jeb escaped Phoebe's sage scrub at the end of our session. I feel his presence. I sense him near, hovering and buzzing—a feathering shadow. He wants something. He wants something of me. I cannot rest until I know what it is.

All I want to think about now is that in a few weeks Luke and I will become husband and wife. We'll live together at Overhome, face our problems together, rejoice in the joy of our union, our love, our companionship— "for as long as we both shall live."

****

We had a grand celebration in the dining room. Carlos and Mariana had both acquired U.S. citizenship, and they were jubilant. Nick sat proudly between them at the head of the table with the rest of us gathered round.

Monica was in her element. She'd coerced me into helping her with a decorating frenzy of red-white-and-blue. Candles, placemats and napkins for the table, balloons, and bunting pinned to the walls. A scattering of gold stars from one end of the table to the other and a small American flag for every place setting. Patriotic music, marches, anthems, rousing songs by John Philip Sousa played in the background. A crinkled paper red-white-and-blue ornament hung suspended from the chandelier.

Mom and Dad had collaborated to prepare a delicious meal, to which Miss Emma contributed her awesome chocolate chip cookies. Chilled bottles of White Rock wine adorned the buffet, which sported its own patriotic runner. I swear, Monica even came up with shimmering blue champagne flutes she claimed to have found at a flea market in the Valley of Virginia.

Seated around the table were special guests. Sam, our caretaker, sat beside Julio, Carlos' assistant. Next to Julio was his niece, Bonita, who happened to be working on her own citizenship journey. Wearing an expression of pure pleasure, Eddie sat close to Bonita, and I became suspicious they were holding hands under the table. Had I been replaced as his object of affection? Sitting quietly, with her long, shining black hair, ebony eyes and smooth olive complexion, Bonita was both pretty and poised. Miss Emma reigned at the foot of the table, taking in everything, her faded blue eyes reflecting brightly in the candle light.

Carlos stood. "*Señora* Helen. We could not have done this without you." Mariana nodded her approval and everyone clapped.

"Not true, Carlos. You both did all the work, the studying, the practice tests. I simply suggested organization for your efforts."

"Tell us some of the questions, Papa." Nick glowed. "I want to see if I know the answers."

Jeff looked on with interest. "Me, too."

Everyone waited expectantly.

"Okay. For what is Susan B. Anthony known?" Carlos remained standing.

"Women's rights!" Nick called out.

"Women's vote!" Jeff shouted.

"What is supreme law of the land?" This from Mariana.

"The Constitution!" Nick and Jeff shouted at the same time.

"Name one native American tribe," Carlos said. "And spell it correctly, *por favor*."

"C-h-e-y-e-n-n-e," Eddie responded, looking pleased with himself.

"Name one of the first three American Presidents." Mariana looked around the table for an answer.

"George Washington," Nick sang out.

"John Adams." Jeff waved his little flag at Nick. "We did pretty good, buddy."

Sitting down, Carlos finished with, "I had to write 'Nothing matters more than peace.' Again, spelling counts!"

"Both your parents answered one hundred percent correctly on the written quiz." Mom spoke with a hint of pride in her voice.

"The test was easy." Mariana's voice was soft. "But I found the personal face-to-face interview to be…I think the word is intimidation."

Carlos nodded agreement. "It is like you are on trial the moment you enter the room—being watched for how you pronounce as well as what you know."

"They want you to be of good moral character," Mariana added. "Lots of questions about how we feel about United States of America."

"Then we took oath of allegiance to the U.S. before we received our certificate of naturalization." Carlos proudly held up a framed certificate. "I cannot wait for next election, so I can vote."

Jeff sat between Monica and Hal, who observed the event with happy interest. "It's wonderful to see the acculturation process first hand." Hal looked serious. "We take so much for granted."

"It is blessing to be in the family of this great nation." Mariana's eyes glistened with tears.

"And you add so much to this great nation," Hal said. "Diversity, culture, work ethic, family ties. Without our new citizens we would eventually grow stale and too set in our ways. We must always welcome our naturalized citizens with open arms."

Jeff had been listening to Hal's speech. "Ya know…" He swept his arm to indicate the three Vasquez family members. "Nick and Carlos and Mariana—have sure added a lot to our horse farm and our riding school. I'm even learning some Spanish."

We all smiled at that. "Diversification. Nothing more enriching for any culture—but especially for a horse farm." Hal took in the whole scene as a history lesson.

"Now, let's dive into this fried chicken, baked beans and corn on the cob," Mom urged. "The all-American meal, for sure."

"Let me guess," I sniffed the air. "Besides Miss Emma's cookies, would there be apple pie for dessert?"

"*Me gusta*." Carlos waved his own little American flag before picking up his knife and fork. "I am proud to be American."

I watched as Jeff and Hal talked to each other through the meal. I didn't catch all of their words, but it seemed Hal was proposing a trip to the Museum of the Confederacy in Appomattox. What a neat field trip that would be—a perfect way for Hal the historian to bond with Jeff, his future stepson. Jeff had just the sort of creative and curious mind that could blend fact with everyday observations. I was almost jealous of the opportunity, but felt sure my cousin would be generous about sharing what he and Hal learned at the museum. We'd have one of our good old heart-to-heart talks afterwards. My love for Jeff overflowed; I had a whole new concept of family to think over.

How my sense of family had expanded over the past five years! Once it was just Mom, Dad and me. We three and my peers and friends and school chums made up my little world. Now? Holy cow! My world had grown into a universe, with a winsome cousin, a beautiful aunt who would marry a distinguished historian, a loving grandmother image in Miss Emma, along with an international cast of characters working my beloved horses. And Luke, my love. However, I could have done without those ancient Overton entities hovering in the wings—If ever there were a case for too much family, I'd say they qualified.

Susan Coryell

Chapter 20

Following a spirited canter, Jeff and I slowed to a walk. Letting Sasha and Sunshine crop the grass, we ambled astride our horses along the wooded riding trail, talking. The day was mild and the air clear of humidity. Tree branches arched above us, their leaves rustling gently. Squirrels leaped from limb to limb like gymnasts, and birds called to one another with distinctive chirps. It was the perfect Virginia summer day to be outdoors and riding horses and talking companionably with my voluble cousin. How I'd missed these cozy talks with Jeff. I loved the way he poured it all out—always willing to talk about his own shortcomings or mistakes and never sugar-coating the ugliest details, reporting everything with optimistic enthusiasm. Such honesty! But the summer's activities had taken precedence over all else; we simply had not had the luxury of time we used to. Then again, Nick had absorbed most of Jeff's leisure moments. A good thing, for sure.

"So how did your trip to Appomattox go?" I tried to sound nonchalant, but I was curious to see how much bonding, if any, had taken place between my cousin and his future stepdad.

"Hal took me to the Museum of the Confederacy. Nick was supposed to go with us, but he came down with a sore throat and had to stay home."

"That's too bad. Do you think Nick would have enjoyed the trip?"

"Well—maybe not as much as me. But I've told him all about it—everything I could remember." Jeff brightened. "History is really interesting, Ashby."

A good start for a father-son relationship when the father lives and breathes history.

We dismounted and moved to a spot on the bank of the creek, which bubbled merrily on its way. "What did you find so interesting?"

"Did you know Virginia was right in the middle of the action during the Civil War? Richmond was the capital and Jefferson Davis, the president of the Confederacy, lived there. Robert E. Lee surrendered at Appomattox Courthouse." Jeff plopped down to the ground. "We saw where that happened." Picking up a rock, he tossed it into the creek and watched the splash with interest. "And there were tons of battles all over the state. Now I want to go see some of the battlefields. And there's reenactments around here sometimes. Hal says we should definitely take one of those in."

I lowered myself to the ground beside my cousin. "I could spend weeks in a good museum myself, but I don't know about an actual battlefield. Maybe too creepy—thinking about all those soldiers killed in action. One minute they're alive, charging the enemy with their guns and sabers, and the next…"

Jeff eyed me critically. "Yeah. I thought about that too, but I liked the weapons best. Man, you should see those swords. Remember when Hal brought in the stuff from his theater department? Well, the *real* swords, in the museum, are so cool. They could cut a guy into pieces so quick." He made some slicing gestures, and I pretended to shiver.

"And the pistols. Huge. Heavy. Y'know, they could only get off six shots before reloading. Defending yourself while reloading was key. There was this army Colt revolver captured from a Union cavalryman and it was engraved with *May, 1843*, from the Mexican War or something. We got to pick it up. I never touched a gun before." Jeff threw a few more rocks into the creek. "Did you know the Confederate soldiers had to buy their own uniforms and equipment?"

"Nope. There's a Civil War factoid that's new to me. Looks like you learned a lot. Did Hal offer a running commentary while you toured?" I could practically hear that enthusiastic teacher's voice supplying detail after detail.

"He pointed out stuff I probably would've missed. You know—like what the typical soldier carried with him—not just weapons and cartridges. They each had a knapsack, haversack, cartridge box, cap powder and a canteen or two." Jeff counted off the items on his fingers. "And personal stuff too—like Bible and prayer book and, oh! Did you know most soldiers took along a *housewife*."

I'm sure I looked blank. "A housewife?"

"That's a sewing kit! For repairing bullet holes and rips in their uniforms." Jeff cackled. "Who'd think a soldier would take a housewife to war?"

"I am impressed. You saw a lot, you learned a lot, and you remember a lot, too."

"You know what I remember best, Ashby?" My cousin shifted and caught my eye. "Something Hal said when we were looking at the cavalry photos."

"Must be important if you remember it best."

"Hal told me he's been fascinated by the Civil War forever, but he always admired the cavalry soldiers most. Even when he was a kid—younger than me—he thought going to war on a horse was cool. 'A gallant soldier astride a beautiful steed, galloping headlong into battle,' or something like that, he said. It got me to thinking, and I asked him if he wanted to learn to ride."

"Just like that?"

"Know what, Ashby?" Jeff's freckles sprang to life, doing a little cha-cha over his nose. "He said, 'I'd like that better than anything else I can think of right now.' And you know what else?" Jeff did not pause for my answer, charging ahead. "He said he wants *me to* teach him. How cool is that?"

"When you and I talked about that, I remember you said, 'He's an adult—I'm a kid.'"

"Hal doesn't care about that. What do you think?"

"I think it must be great karma—meant to be." I couldn't resist hugging my sweet cousin. "And you'll be a grand teacher. I remember how much you helped me when I was learning to ride, young as you were then."

We sat in silence for a few minutes. I don't know what Jeff was thinking, but I was busy framing how I'd tell him about Phoebe Swift and her churning up the spirits. I took a deep breath and plunged in, going over every detail from start to finish, from Phoebe's channeling in our library to the séance in the middle of the night in the cottage. When I was done, Jeff gave me a hard look, sending his freckles into a pile over the bridge of his nose.

"Thanks for telling me. Nick and I already knew a *fantasmas* was in our clubhouse. And we kinda thought he was watching us—you know—to see how we would react to his…his…"

"His overtures?"

"His voice. His smell. The time we think he left us the arrowhead and key and maybe even read our books. But we sure didn't know all that history behind him." Jeff looked thoughtful. "Do you think…could there be more than one ghost? One mean and one nice, maybe?"

"We don't know. Just be aware, Jeff, you can never be sure when it comes to the spirit world. For sure a spook is at its most spiteful when I'm around, but you never know—it could turn on you and Nick without warning." I picked up a pebble and threw it into the creek. "You know as soon as Luke gets home, let's look into that tiny hole you and Nick found in the cottage foundation. See what's there—or not there."

"Remember what happened last time we tried? Wham!" Jeff smacked his fist into his hand. "Hammer flew off one way and flashlight the other—all in pieces." There went Jeff's freckles again. "Man! Now that's something to write about when we get back to school. You know, 'What did you do for your summer vacation?' Well, see, there's this haunted cottage and when we explored it, we found…"

We both rocked back and laughed at the idea. "I'm afraid nobody would believe it, Jeff, though you and Nick might each get an A for creative writing. Now, I think we'd better shove off. There's much to do." I looked at my cousin. "Did you and Hal set a date for his first riding lesson?"

"Hal has one more trip to the Valley of Virginia—researching some family records. After that, we'll schedule some riding lessons."

I wondered what else Hal hoped to learn—the man was already a walking encyclopedia when it came to Overhome and its history.

As we trotted home, my thoughts turned to my cousin's advancing maturity. I knew he was only twelve, but it wouldn't be long before he'd shoot up to his full height, fill out, start shaving, and begin thinking about not just horses but also girls. Jeff was going to be a very fine young man; still, I hoped he wouldn't leave behind all his charming little-boy traits. Would he even want to go riding with his old cousin? It was a bittersweet thought.

We walked our horses to the paddock before heading for the barn, but stopped when we heard some commotion inside. "Whoa, Jeff. What's going on here?" We moved inside.

Jeff shrugged. "Isn't that Winn's mother?"

Belinda Davies was squaring off with Eddie. She jabbed her finger squarely in his face. "It's come to my attention that my son is being taught by a child."

"Not my call," Eddie said with surprising oomph. "Y' don't like it—talk t' Carlos." Eddie knew good and well Carlos would stand his ground with quiet patience no matter what Belinda Davies threw out. And she knew Carlos had her number: She was a whiner with no grounds for complaint.

"I'll take my Adonis and my business elsewhere," Belinda screeched.

A head popped up over one of the stalls and Tiffany Norton, who had been bending over, out of sight while grooming her horse, spoke. "Oh, that would leave an opening for a friend of mine. Buffy's wanted to board her horse here for the longest time. You know her, Mrs. Davies. She's a member of our club."

Belinda hesitated, hands on hips, rigid as a rod. "All right. I'll leave Adonis, then. But I want Winn to have his lessons with Carlos, not that—that *boy.*"

Just then, Winn's father appeared. Acknowledging Jeff and me, he strode past us into the barn where his wife and Eddie stood firm in their grip of contention. Tacitly ignoring his fuming wife, he spoke directly to Eddie. "I have to say I couldn't be more pleased with the change in my son. Winn actually has some color in his cheeks." He glared at Belinda, as if daring her to contradict him. "You know, I've tried for years to get him outside. Made him join the soccer team. Baseball. Football." He emphasized "soccer," "baseball" and "football" with a thrust of his prominent chin. "Nothing worked. The kid wimped out of every team. All he wanted to do was sit inside with his damned electronic gadgets. But now? Winn lives for these riding lessons. If he's on the computer, it's because he's looking up information about horses, not playing those ridiculous games. We'll be buying a horse for him as soon as we find the right match." He glowered with a deprecating glance at his wife. "And we'll board the animal here, if there's space."

At that point Winn himself burst through the door from the paddock. Nick followed close behind. "Dad! You'll never guess what I learned today! Nick's teaching me to canter!" Winn's face dripped sweat, which he wiped with a quick gesture after throwing off his helmet. I had never seen such excitement on that jaded face before.

"You don't say," his father replied with obvious approval, reaching to shake Nick's hand. "Good work, young man. You're doing a hell of a job here."

I couldn't take my eyes off Nick who glowed with his accomplishments. "Thanks, Mr. Davies." Nick ducked his head shyly, then, tilted it toward Winn, whose cheeks were bright red. "Winn has learned a lot."

More than either of his parents would ever know.

While Mrs. Davies stomped out, tossing her head, Winn and his father took their time, petting the horses and talking to them. When, at last, they, too, left, Tiffany emerged from her horse's stall, a big grin plastered over her face.

"Y' know we got plenty of space fer yer friend's horse." Eddie patted the door of an empty stall.

"I know that, Eddie, but Belinda Davies doesn't."

Wanting to hug my old friend, I watched Jeff glide to Nick's side. "Got a lot to tell you." He spoke in an undertone. "About our *fantasmas.* They hired a medium…You're not gonna believe it."

Tiffany finished her chores, brushed her hands on her pants, and walked with me out of the barn. "The Davies are about the most obnoxious couple I've ever met. She jabs her finger and he jabs his chin. Mr. and Mrs. Jabber, I call them. She's forever poking at the waiters, pro shop employees, even the poor lifeguards at the pool. Nobody at the club can stand them. No one else would treat our wonderful staff like that."

"I'm amazed that Eddie has managed not to blow his top with her. And Carlos and Nick—they're a wonder, aren't they? You know, my Uncle Hunter used to say, 'Horseback riding is good for the soul.' Well, I could add to that: Horseback riding is good for taking the bully out of the boy."

Tiffany laughed. "You could be right. Oh, Ashby, by the way. Buffy Harrington really is interested in boarding her horse here. She should be giving you a call soon. Mom and I have been talking to her and she's eager to pay you a visit."

"Thanks for spreading the word. We could use the business."

"Let's do lunch. Are you free tomorrow? Noon at the club? My treat."

"I'd like that a lot. Sometimes I do need to get away from here. Just promise me one thing, Tiffany."

"Don't worry. If the Jabbers show up in the club dining room, we'll take our lunch elsewhere."

As I left the barn, I felt, once again, the presence of Jeb Stover's chilly spirit hanging overhead. His breath ruffled my hair, his whisper nudged my ear. "*Beneath the stones*," he reminded me.

****

We arrived at the cottage fully armed with crowbars, sledge hammers, shovels, picks and other heavy tools. I don't know who was more excited, Hal or the boys and me. We were practically giddy with expectation. Dad and Luke were more stoic, but none of us had any idea where our explorations would lead us.

As we studied how best to break through the foundation to open up the "pebble hole," as we were now calling Jeff and Nick's discovery, I looked around for Hal, who had moved to the front of the house.

"Hey, everybody," we heard Hal's call. "Come here. I just found something interesting."

Leaving the tools beside the pebble hole, we trooped around to the front. Hal knelt beside the remnants of the old porch that stretched from the front door to the side of the house. He stood up. "If you get down on your knees and look up behind this porch floor, you'll see something unusual."

Luke and Dad, the boys and I lowered ourselves to ground level and scrutinized the stone foundation that lay beneath and behind the porch. Jeff was first to spy it. "A board! A long strip of wood in the stone. Right, Hal?"

Hal looked pleased as we took turns peering under the porch, searching for the horizontal piece. "Well-hidden for many years behind this porch floor," Hal said. "Was the porch constructed purposefully in order to obscure the header? That's what I think it is. A header above a door."

"A door leading to…" Luke began. "A room under the house?"

"That would be my guess. Or, it could be just a crawl space. Help me tear out this porch." Gathering up the tools, the men whacked away at the rotting wood, and the kids and I piled up the splintered timbers out of the way. It did not take long to reveal what must, indeed, be a header over a long-unused door.

"Let's dig it out," Luke said. Wielding a pickaxe, he cleared out a good-sized swatch of hard-packed dirt underneath the former porch. "Take a look at this, guys. We've got a row of stones on each side, perpendicular to the header. Looks like a stairwell." He swung the heavy tool again and again, until we heard a different sound—a solid crack, and we saw sparks fly. "Uh oh. There's rock under the dirt. I'm gonna need some help."

Dad and Hal grabbed shovel and grubbing hoe. Dirt flew in a frenzy of excavation. The men stopped periodically to let the boys and me remove layer after layer of big rocks and smaller debris. Before long, we'd excavated enough to reveal a door-sized opening flanked by stone walls. "It's a stairwell, all right." Hal wiped sweat from his brow. "Let's keep digging."

We worked together, and by turns, having to rest and drink bottle after bottle of water, we cleared away a ton of rocks and rubble—all packed into what turned out to be eight steep, narrow, stone stairs. The rocky walls seemed to close in the farther down the stairs went, until we were faced with a blank limestone wall, solid as a vault.

Dad groaned. "Let's take a breather. Hal, do you think we've done all this excavating merely to unearth a staircase leading to a wall? A dead end?"

"I think someone was very careful to obscure what's below these stairs." Hal removed his gloves and gulped down an entire bottle of water in a few glugs. "That wall is there to hide something. There's more to this, Madison. Believe me."

Poe's "A Cask of Amontillado," with its underground burial trap, flashed across my mind.

Renewed after a brief rest, Hal looked over the tools and selected a digging bar. "We want to do this next step carefully. We don't know how thick this wall is or what may lie behind it." He picked up the tool and tapped just enough to break the mortar, using the top end of the bar. Once loosened, he pulled the chunks out by hand and handed them off to the boys to pile up on the side. "Lucky for us—it's only a few inches thick."

Working from the top down, Hal removed enough of the wall to call for a flashlight. Beaming it down and peering in, he took his time before pulling back. "It looks cavernous down there. We haven't reached bottom yet."

Each man took a turn and less than an hour later, enough of the wall was down so that we could step over it, but we elected to keep working until about only a foot of wall was left standing—just to be safe.

Jeff was first to exclaim, "Let's go in! We can climb over what's left of the wall."

While we agreed with Jeff, we stood as if paralyzed, not knowing what to expect and half dreading what we might find. We proceeded slowly.

After a flat landing, five more steep stone stairs lay before us. Cautiously, we descended, feeling a coolness rise up as we moved downward. At the bottom, we all shone our flashlights to discover what appeared to be a good-sized room, with a domed ceiling and a dirt floor.

We stood like explorers on the margin of a subterranean cave. It must be the same feeling the discoverers of King Tut's tomb had experienced. My heart was racing, and when I reached for Luke's hand, I found his fingers clammy. "This is unbelievable," Luke said.

"Spooky," Jeff breathed, while Nick mumbled something under his breath.

The air was dank and musty, and the interior was black as outer space.

Picking up flashlights in both hands, Jeff and Nick pushed in front of us. "These lights are pretty strong." Jeff's voice rose with excitement. "Want Nick and me to go first?"

"Be careful," Dad warned. "You don't want to stumble. Don't hurt yourselves, boys."

With barely contained caution the two boys shone

Susan Coryell

their lights from the doorway into the cave-like darkness beyond. Jeff moved an inch at a time before calling out, "Come on. It's huge. Floor's flat—dirt. It's just a big, empty room."

We filed in, flashlights tight in our grips, shining shafts of surprisingly dim light sucked up by the dense darkness. "Whew! It's cold in here." The atmosphere was so unnatural—so unfamiliar and odd that I could be on the moon—or some other place never experienced by most human beings. I had to rub the goose bumps from my arms and blink rapidly to assure myself I was awake and not engulfed in some surreal dream. I noticed a wooden niche in the wall to the right. I Illuminated the space with my flashlight. "What's this?" It looked like an empty picture frame recessed into the stone wall.

Nobody had an answer to my question.

"Watch out!" Jeff brushed frantically at his face and shoulders. "Phew! Major cobwebs."

Hal, silent till now, had been studying the composition of the walls, holding his flashlight within inches of the surface and rubbing his fingers over them. "These walls are limestone. Just like the rooms above us, dressed up with the same clay and wheat plaster." He lifted his light to the ceiling. "Look, the whole room is domed—would you say about nine feet high at the apex?" He scrolled the roof above us with his light. It looked, indeed, like a big igloo.

Even in the dim atmosphere, I could see Hal's shining eyes. "Folks, we have here a real Flurkuckenhaus cellar." Realizing nobody had a clue about his reference, he continued, sounding a bit chagrined. "Sorry. I've been researching this building

248

style ever since Monica and I began looking into the history of the cottage. The first time I saw the interior I suspected it was modeled after that old German design."

The stone arc overhead was unique—almost startling—like pictures I'd seen of Roman grottoes in my high school Latin book. Or the catacombs, maybe. Completely alien in terms of ancient Southern architecture.

At length, Hal was ready to move on, captivated as he was by the arched ceiling. "Let's continue." He focused his flashlight on the boys. "Lead the way, guys."

In stronger light, I could imagine them scrambling to push ahead of one another in search of adventure. Limited in the dimness as they were, they still managed to scour the area thoroughly about a foot at a time, until Jeff called out, "Look! Up there!" He shone his light near the top of the arch on the far wall, then, turned it off. "See that itty-bitty stream of light? I bet that's the hole in the foundation—the one we threw pebbles in." The boys stared at the small, but steady beam above our heads.

Nick bent to the floor directly beneath and scooped up something in his hand. "Yep. Here's the pebbles we threw in." He and Jeff exchanged a look of satisfaction.

"More niches," I observed with my flashlight against the side walls. "Do you think these were shelves, Hal?"

Before he could answer, Nick cried out. "Oh! Look at all this stuff here." The boys stood facing the entry side of the room where a large niche was recessed into the stone wall. The bottom ledge held several objects.

"What's this?" Jeff edged nearer, pointing a finger at the small, shallow cups on the niche shelf. "Looks like old blobs of wax. Must've been candle holders." He picked one up and handed it to Hal, who nodded agreement.

Nick flashed his light onto a dark urn-shaped vase also placed on the wooden ledge of the niche. "What's this?"

While we eyed his find, Hal focused his light on the floor beneath the niche, illuminating a heap of rubble. "A pile of rocks." He steadied his beam on the collection from different angles. "This is not random; there's a pattern." He was quiet again. "I believe it's a…it's a cairn! A memorial. Let's not touch it until we can do more exploration."

We stared for many minutes. Hal was right about the pattern—a rough pyramid-shape formed by layers of even, flat stones—all told, eight to ten inches in height.

Nick had discovered another puzzling object placed in the niche. With his light he pointed out a rusting metal curio standing about a foot tall near the center of the shelf.

Jeff joined his friend. "Looks like a big X."

Tilting his head to one side, then the other, Nick studied the object, then, looked at Hal for permission to touch it. Hal nodded, and, hesitantly, Nick reached for it. Rust crumbled from the surface as he raised it to eye level. "Look! It's a cross." He adjusted the arms from an X to a T shape, then, quickly crossed himself.

By now we were all engaged. We gathered around, each touching the rusty, flaking icon. Hal appeared deep in thought.

"A cross," I murmured. "Candles. A vase for flowers. This niche—do you suppose it's an altar?"

Nick was the only one to acknowledge my comment with a slight nod. Even in the dim light I could see his lips moving, possibly in silent prayer. Everyone else stood in static wonder. Luke moved to my side.

"And a cairn." I peered around me, trying to judge my companions' reactions. "Sure looks like an altar to me."

"I agree," Luke said. "The question is—what's it doing here, of all places?"

"Notice"—Hal shone his flashlight onto the floor—"flagstones." He flared his light around the stone-covered rectangular space that stretched from the cairn some six or seven feet in length and maybe four feet wide before it stopped abruptly. "This is the only place in the entire room with a stone floor." He moved the light back and forth, back and forth over the flagstone patch under the altar, assuming that's what it was. Then, he bent down and touched the floor. "Whatever this memorial is about—whoever it was built in recognition of—I think we may find our answers somewhere between these flagstones and that cairn."

With a drift of frigid air, I braced myself for the smell of rotten eggs. But it never emerged. Instead, a humming drone filled my ears, pulsing inside my head, accelerating in intensity until I felt my ears pop. Dizzy, I reached out a hand to Luke's shoulder to steady myself. "Did you hear that, Luke?"

Luke's eyebrows shot up. "What?" He gave me a startled look. "Hear what?"

251

My eyes swept the others. Nobody else seemed to have noticed. So it was me, the medium, once again; I knew who it was. Not Angelina and not a troubled slave, and it most certainly was not Raeford. None of his nasty signs—no pushing, slapping—no bad odors. The humming in my ears started up anew. The signal that alerted me to the presence of an entity that had been pursuing me for days, buzzing, whispering, fluttering in and out of my consciousness. I knew who it was, all right.

"We come in love." I raised my eyes to the domed ceiling. "We're here to help. We benevolently seek the best for all concerned."

My compatriots stared at me, frozen. For many minutes nothing happened. Then a slight noise drew our attention to the niche. I shone my light on the cross and watched it fall, as if in slow motion, onto one side before tumbling to the stones on the floor with a clatter. This was not King Tut's tomb, but it was a tomb, nevertheless. I had an idea who was buried beneath the cairn. And I couldn't help but think of the familiar phrase. "Go away. He's dead." No, I did not hear it. I simply knew that we were on the verge of discovering who was dead. And who wanted us to go away because of that.

"Shall we go out and retrieve the shovels?" Luke asked.

Chapter 21

Everyone was unsettled about our discovery in the underground room. I called our family meeting in the library so that we could move ahead in every possible way. Though he'd hoped to attend, Luke had texted me that he and Doc Forrest were dealing with a difficult breach birth. A prized mare. Even if he made it home, he'd probably miss the meeting. I promised to keep in touch and dish the details of the meeting when we got together. Monica had invited Hal, and he planned to dash in, a little late, after teaching his evening class.

I called the meeting to order. "Dad, I'd like you to share whatever you've learned. What's our next move?"

"Delighted, Ashby." Dad looked around the room, making eye contact with each of us individually. "With the idea that we'll preserve the cottage and perhaps be endorsed by the Historical Society, we'll rope off the cottage and immediate grounds surrounding it and leave it alone in terms of development. At least for the time being. That way, we hope to go ahead with the rest of the property without...um...interference."

"Leaving the cottage alone might take care of the sabotage. But won't we eventually have to deal with our problems—you know—with spirits inhabiting the cottage? The entities seem pretty tightly entrenched. And they have been there for a long, long time," I said.

"Plus, they're scary as hell!" Miss Emma grimaced. "I think it's a solid idea, Madison. From what you've told me about the Historical Society, our cottage would be a shoe-in for their Halloween ghost-hunt, eh?" Her bright eyes danced with the idea. "We'd be the highlight of the tour."

Dad chuckled. "Love your input, Miss Emma, but Ashby's probably right. At some point we'll have to deal with our 'infestation.' I don't know what else to call it. By leaving the cottage as is, we could hope that Raef, at least, would leave us alone—for now."

"So what's the procedure?" Mom asked. "What's next?"

"The engineers are working on the roads and storm sewers—doing water run-off studies as we speak. Progress we can bank on."

I heaved a sigh of relief. "So, the project looks like a go. Right, Dad?"

"I'd certainly say so." He looked at Miss Emma. "Getting back to your house of horrors point, Miss Emma, I've done some research on exhumations."

This caught Jeff's attention and he sat up in his chair. "Research, Uncle Madison? You mean…how to dig up a body?"

"Yes, Jeff. That's exactly what I mean."

"I've applied for a license with the county at the registrar's office. They're authorized to issue a disinterment permit. I couched it as a request to relocate the body, if we find one, to a family cemetery."

"Sounds like there may be some red tape involved." Mom looked a bit unnerved at the prospect.

"Once buried, a corpse becomes the property of the law and all matters of disinterment fall under the jurisdiction of the legal system. In the state of Virginia, exhumation is permitted if certain requirements are met. The court will decide if the act of disinterring the body will serve justice."

"About the red tape…" Mom began.

"Of course, you're right, Helen. Once the legalities are settled, we'll have to have an environmental health officer present during the procedure. We'll have to wear masks and gowns and caps to protect against bacteria escaping into the atmosphere where it could harm us."

"Seems to me this exhumation might result in more of a kick-up from our spirits than anything we've done so far," Miss Emma observed.

"It's a risk we have to take."

"Will I be allowed to go?" Jeff's eyes were big. "Nick?"

"Technically, no, Jeff. No children allowed. But—hold that thought. I have a plan that might get at least one of you in." Dad gave Jeff a sympathetic look. "Just try to be patient."

Jeff sighed, but brightened as Dad continued with his details. "We'll have to provide a casket and move the body, or, rather bones, to the medical examiner's office and eventually to a new burial site. I'm sure Hal's museum will be interested in what we find, that is, assuming that we find *anything*."

As if on cue, Hal appeared at the door to the library. "Hal's museum would certainly be interested! Anything having to do with the cottage is bound to be of interest. It's so old, and there are so few of them left in America."

Hal made his way to Monica's side and sat in the

255

chair beside her. He leaned past her and whispered something to Jeff that made my cousin grin. Sitting back up, Hal addressed the room. "Sorry I'm late."

"We're talking about dedicating the cottage to the Historical Society and also about exhuming a body in the cottage cellar," Monica filled him in. "Madison's taking care of the necessary legalities." She twisted her lips into a half-smile and glanced at Miss Emma. "There's some discussion about ghost tours," she said in an undertone.

Mom spoke warmly, turning our thoughts in a different direction. "Glad you're here, Hal. Your research into the history of the Overton clan has been invaluable. We all appreciate it—more than you can know."

Hal squirmed a bit at the praise. "To me, it's all very exciting. History comes alive when we can touch the artifacts, see them in context, interpret their place in our past from a present perspective. Preserving our heritage is a vital link to all aspects of society—the things that make us who we are."

Monica patted Hal's arm and encircled Jeff's shoulder with her arm, as if to say, *"Isn't this learned man a wonder? And he is ours."*

"But enough of that. I didn't mean to get on my soapbox." Fidgeting with his glasses, Hal gave a self-deprecating smile. "However, I do want to share something I acquired by the most unbelievable luck on my last trip to the Valley."

"Do tell," Miss Emma was first to reply.

Monica pulled back. "Something new?"

"Is about the ghosts?" Jeff exploded.

From his brief case, Hal pulled a container a bit

smaller than a tissue box and spoke to Jeff. "Sometimes I think everyone from the past can, at one time or another, live again through us, once we learn about them—come to know them." He returned his attention to the box. "As I was leaving, making my final farewells with Isaac Stover, our favorite genealogist, the old guy held out this box and said, 'Well, none a'my kids or grandkids cares a whit about the Overton-Stover family heritage. But you—you and your friend, Ms. Overton—I knew you'd be interested in these.' I took the box from him and opened it right then and there—started sorting through folded pages, gingerly, as I could tell they were quite old."

Hal's excitement was palpable. "Isaac informed me they're letters written from the battlefronts of the Civil War—from Jeb Stover to his sister Fanny. Letters from Raeford Overton's first cousin and compatriot—in life and in war."

Original Civil War letters. What could they tell us?

"Authentic. Well-preserved. Except for an occasional word or archaic spelling, I've had no problem reading and understanding them, though they're written in an elaborate cursive. More than a dozen, from anywhere the Virginia 7th Cavalry was stationed—where Jeb Stover and Raeford Overton served." Hal's fingers trembled. "For their historical value, alone, these letters are priceless. But, for the Overton family in search of answers—we'll find a lot to love here. Jeb and his cousin Raef served in the same unit for several years, you know."

We sat in awed silence.

"Would you like for me to read an excerpt for you? Get your salivary glands going?" He grinned.

"Please. Please do," I said.

"I've brought one I transcribed so that I can easily read it to you." He pulled a single sheet of paper from his briefcase. "Just listen to a portion of this letter, written from Camp Harmon, September 4th, 1861. Remember, Jeb Stover was an educated man. Educated and observant, with an eye and an ear for everything around him." Hal began.

My Dear Sister,

You need have no fears but that I will do my duty as a soldier. I know the importance of the errand on which I have come. And should it become my duty to do battle against the enemies of our country, I will cheerfully do my part & I think that my conduct will be such that my family will never have cause to be ashamed of me.

"Jeb's patriotism for the Cause is clear. Now, listen to this next paragraph. It jumped off the page when I first read the letter. I think you'll be interested in Jeb's writing style, Ashby."

It is now night & I am setting in my tent with my knapsack on my knees writing. Our Fifer is passing away the tedious hours by playing on his flute. The soft music flows gently with mournful cadences upon the evening breeze which reminds me of my much loved home & the loved ones I left there. It is well calculated to awake fond memories of the past & carries one in fancy back to the scenes of his childhood. The drum is now beating for the roll call & in half an hour the lights must be put out & everything must be quiet. At 9 o'clock our camp is still. Nothing is to be heard but the chirping of crickets & the measured tread of the sentinels walking their posts.

"Jeb Stover was a poet at heart," I breathed. "His description of the encampment at rest is pure, sensual poetry." As I spoke, I became keenly aware of Jeb's aura hovering, listening along with the rest of us.

"What nostalgia," Mom murmured. "Jeb's thoughts carried him back to childhood—maybe thinking about his summers with Raeford here at Overhome."

Hal continued to read.

We have been expecting to get our pay for some time but have not it yet. Our boys need their pay & tents very badly and if they don't get them soon they will all desert. Three went off yesterday.

"Hmmm. Deserters. Makes you wonder if Jeb worried that Raeford would also run off," Dad said. "A premonition? Or had Raef mentioned the possibility of deserting to Jeb, perhaps?"

Hal glowed. "Folks, this letter is the tip of the iceberg. Our archivist at the museum where I work is busily transcribing the rest of them—making them easily read."

"We saw a fife in the Museum of the Confederacy." Jeff's expression had acquired a dreamy quality. "Maybe it was the same flute the fifer played at Camp Harmon. While Hal was reading—I could see it—I could hear the music. I want to read more of the letters."

Hal and Monica beamed at each other. I, myself,

heard another kind of music. Humming in my ear was the ever-present reminder that Jeb Stover's spirit wanted something of me. I just didn't know exactly what that might be.

"It won't be long, Jeff. We have a small staff at our little museum, but everyone is top-notch at their job. I'll bring the transcribed letters here as soon as I can."

"Cool. I've gotta find Nick. He won't care so much about the letters, maybe, but the ex…the exhu…digging up a body? Oh, man. Cool!"

****

Sound asleep as I was, it took me many minutes to awaken to the repeated pinging sound on my French doors and many more minutes to realize it must be Luke throwing pebbles to arouse me. Slipping from bed, I stumbled to the doors and unlatched them, stepping out onto the balcony. "Hold your fire!" I called out, loud enough for Luke to hear from the ground, but not so loud as to disturb anybody else's sleep, I hoped. "I'm awake already."

Luke tilted back his head and cupped his mouth with his fingers. "Meet me in the Love Boat!"

Struggling into a robe and stubbing my feet into flips, I headed down the stairs and out of the house where more stairs greeted me on the way to the dock. I was out of breath and a bit out of sorts by the time I reached my destination. I am a deep sleeper and a quick and unexpected wake-up call always makes me grouchy.

Luke's enfolding embrace erased my bad mood instantly. "Do you know how much I love you, Ashby?" he murmured into my hair. "Even up from a deep sleep, you're as beautiful as a lake dawn." He gently stroked my hair, pulling wayward strands behind my ears. "I could have slept in Aunt Emma's spare room, but I wanted your sweet body next to mine. Wanted to hold and kiss you and tell you I love you." He pressed his lips firmly to mine, and I melted into a puddle right there on the dock.

"Shall we ascend to the penthouse?" My voice was as weak as my knees.

"By all means. I have already lowered the boat. The concierge is off duty, so you'll have to accept my arm to help you aboard."

I stepped in and moved automatically to the stern cushions, our official love nest. Luke joined me, then, pressed the remote that raised the craft high above the mundane world. Okay, so that's a bit melodramatic, but the boat had certainly provided a secret meeting place that allowed us lovebirds to coo the night away far from the madding crowd. Apologies, Thomas Hardy.

"I expect you want to hear about our family meeting," I ventured.

"Every detail. But later. Right now I just want you, dear. I want your body and soul and mind, selfish brute that I am."

Now who was being melodramatic? But Luke's wishes were fine with me. I was ready for a night of love, even it did begin in early morning. We fell back on the cushions, arms wrapped around one another in an embrace that lasted well into dawn.

We both watched as the sun streaked the lake level with golden-pink slashes of light before we lowered the boat to the dock. "Anything for breakfast in the dock fridge?" Luke stretched and yawned.

Opening the door, I peered inside and poked into

the corners. "Cheese," I held it up to the light, "with only a thin film of mold, day-old bread Jeff likes to use for fish bait." Reaching into the crisper drawer, I drew out two apples and triumphantly displayed them. "Breakfast. Complete except for the coffee."

"Let's spread it out, pull up two stools and enjoy. We can talk uninterrupted. You first." He bit into the apple. "Not bad," he said, turning it in his hand.

"First, let's talk wedding plans." I wiped away the white mold film from the cheddar wedge and broke off pieces for both of us. "I know you've asked your college roommate to stand up with you. And I've asked mine. Danielle's already bought her dress and shoes. We've been emailing all summer long. She lives in Northern Virginia, so we haven't been able to actually connect in person."

"Aneesh lives up there, too where his family has a vet practice. You knew that. And you met Aneesh a couple of times while visiting Tech."

"A peach of a guy. You all got along so well—four years as roommates."

"A brilliant peach, for that matter. Odd an image as that might be." Luke chuckled. "He only graduated third in the class. It always got me how he could read a text once or attend a lecture and, without taking notes, remember every little detail when it came time for exams."

"He's, what? Third generation Indian?"

"The family claims Bangladesh as home, actually, but, to my knowledge, Aneesh has never been there. Occasionally his parents return to reunite with relatives or attend a wedding." Luke sniffed the day-old bread. "I think this bread is more like week-old. I'll stick with apples and cheese."

"Maybe Danielle and Aneesh could carpool here for the wedding," I thought out loud.

"Already ran that idea by him. He's going to contact Danielle—see if they can ride together. Save gas and time." He took another bite from the apple. "Did you know Aneesh and his dad wanted me to join their practice? He twisted my arm a couple of years ago, took me to the big bad North to show it off. They actually have a large-animal branch in Middleburg—horse country. But I would have been expected to work at both the city and country facilities."

"You never told me." I acted hurt.

"No need. One go at that horrific traffic between the two practices and I was all about setting myself up in our beautiful, rural homeland." He gave me a close look. "Do you blame me?"

I laughed. "I was just pulling your leg. I cannot imagine Luke Murley, veterinarian, for all things large, bulky and smelly, dealing with pet poodles."

"You mean I wouldn't fit in?"

"I mean you'd hate it. Even if you were working with horses, I can only imagine dozens of Belinda Davies, barn queens in residence." I shuddered at the thought. "All that road rage translated into barn rage."

"Aneesh and his family seem to thrive there—bragging about the museums and art galleries and theaters. And the clean and efficient subway from Virginia to the District." Luke shrugged. "It's just not for me."

"I'm glad to hear that," I gave him a quick hug. "Because I never want to leave Overhome."

"There's something else you may not know." Luke

tossed down the last of the cheese and chewed for a while. "Ironically enough, it was Aneesh who helped eradicate my 'local' accent. Seems his dad had dealt with the same issue since he was raised in a home where both parents spoke Bengali." Luke contemplated the remains of his apple, then scraped it to the core with his teeth and tossed it into the lake for the fish to finish off. "Every time I'd slip in a *talkin'* or a *walkin'* or a *look yonder*, he'd give me a secret signal and I'd make a mental correction. It didn't take long—only three and a half out of four years!" Luke stood up and stretched. "Aneesh always called me a 'quick study.' Ha!"

I, too, stood, clearing off the scraps. "There's lots to fill you in on, Luke. How much time do you have at Overhome this stop?"

"Leavin', make that *leaving*, this afternoon." Noticing my disappointment, he added, "But I'll be back for a full weekend soon."

"Maybe by then Dad will have all the permits and licenses and court matters resolved."

Luke looked blank. "The what?"

"Let me start at the beginning. The family meeting in the library. No ghosts invited and none showed up. Thank goodness." Just one kibitzer. I kept quiet about the buzz I'd felt from Jeb Stover.

Luke looked at his watch. "We've got a couple of hours as long as nobody discovers us here and needs something." We both made ourselves comfortable on two lounge chairs. "Have at it," Luke said. "Tell me everything."

****

Dear Diary:
 As our wedding date draws nigh, I realize

how lucky I am. There was a moment or two, I admit, when I feared the woo-woo would get in the way of the wed-wed (sorry—couldn't resist, Diary). Why did I never voice my concern to Luke? Because I knew what he would say: "Let's elope. Now." Then, I realized, what is really important here: To be secure in the knowledge that Luke and I will forge a strong marital bond based on love, respect and shared values. In addition, we both cherish horses and our horse farm and we intend to make a success of our various operations here despite some setbacks. Bottom line—regarding the wedding, everyone has been so helpful and kind and understanding— it had to work out. I loved being able to go over the details with Tiffany at lunch. She's impressed with our plans. Even if the weather gods douse us with rain while we say our vows in the gazebo, nothing can alter what Luke and I feel for each other. Please, Fate. I am not tempting you here. Do not take my comment as a challenge!

On another note, while I may have morphed into a medium, everybody else appears to, at least, accept the fact that the spirits of the long-dead are, ironically, "alive" and well at Overhome. I loved Hal's comment about those who have passed on living again when we remember them.

I've completed my last article for Blue Ridge Heritage *on arts and artists of our region. "A Glimpse into the Fine Art of Wood*

Turning," I've entitled the article. I never knew the art existed before I did my research. Moore Mountain Lake hosts a wood turners group which meets to share ideas and techniques.

Our lake turners garner most of their materials from native maple, oak, fruit and nut woods. One experienced artisan I interviewed said he kept his eye on a large old tree that was being removed from a church yard. "What are you going to do with that ambrosia maple?" he asked. When he learned it would be disposed of, he salvaged large chunks for future projects. His work is stunning. One bowl, in particular, is exquisite beyond description—so silky and alive with multi-hued grains that it appears more beautiful with every turn in your fingers.

I must say, I've enjoyed writing this series. I shall miss interviewing artists and following their activities. We do live in an artistically rich part of the country.

Now I turn my attention to our wedding, a completely different art form, eh? Oh, lest I forget. And to an exhumation that may or may not elicit a body. Odd combination of tasks, for sure.

One last thing, diary. Hal casually informed us that he saw Eddie on campus last Tuesday evening. They spoke briefly and Eddie told Hal that he's been taking a Spanish course. Oh boy. Could a lovely lass named Bonita be behind this? If so, I could not be *happier for my good old cousin Eddie. He deserves a love interest that is two-sided.*

Chapter 22

We had gathered in the library again. Holding a stack of folded papers in his hands, Hal looked eager to begin. "I have a plan, but first, a little refresher. Remember that shortly after flunking out of college, Raeford Overton was banned from Overhome for maiming a slave. Raef went to live with Jeb Stover's family in the Shenandoah Valley. Both cousins joined the Virginia 7th Cavalry in 1861."

Hal adjusted his glasses. "Here's where the data runs thin. We know that Raef deserted in 1863 and returned to Overhome, where he took up residence in the overseer's cottage. We can guess that the family had no interest in harboring a deserter and thus denied him a home in the big house. As for Jeb? He served throughout the war, only to disappear from sight some time before Appomattox and the end of the war. There are no burial or discharge records for either man."

Hal stopped. "Sorry. That was rather a lot of info."

"Very concise," Mom offered. "And helpful." We all murmured agreement.

Hal continued. "We feel the cottage is *haunted*, for lack of a better word, with the spirits of either Raeford or Jeb, or, possibly, both. The more we can find to help us understand the lives and the personal characteristics, temperaments and dispositions of these two men, the better." Hal let his gaze fall on each of us, one at a time.

"Earlier, I read you one of Jeb's letters home. Looking at a few others today—well, it's a rare opportunity, a chance to actually get inside the head of Jeb Stover, Civil War hero, and, by association, his own account of Raeford Overton."

"Exciting prospect." Dad rubbed his hands together. "Let's get started."

"These letters are so well-written—so personable—I think you'll get caught up in the flavor of Civil War times and be as fascinated with these cavalrymen as I am." Hal fanned out folded letters in his hands, like a magician holding an over-sized deck of cards. "The letters have all been transcribed and are completely readable. Pick a letter—any letter," he offered, walking from chair to chair. "But don't read it yet."

"We're kinda like detectives—like in the books we read in elementary school—the *Super Sleuths*."

"You're right, Jeff. Now—I want you to read your letter silently and then, when we're all done, just call out anything you've found that can help us understand what made these guys tick. Okay. Start reading."

We bent to our task.

I was the first to volunteer. "This is early in the war. January, 1862."

We have fixed our tents for the winter. We have a floor & good chimney to it, which makes it more comfortable than a cabin, but it is not as commodious. Cousin Raeford has chosen to move out of our tent and into a cabin, though I advised against it.

"This shows Raef and Jeb were separated in their quarters, maybe causing Jeb to lose his good influence over Raef," I said.

"I found something in Jeb's letter written a month later." Mom was next to offer a nugget.

Great suffering & privations and as yet little accomplished. Many of our fellows suffered severely from cold and hunger. Two froze to death on the Potomac whilst we were there. Our men have gone hungry since the teams cannot get through the ice. At night the poor fellows had to shiver around the fires hungry, tired & without, but I am standing it finely. A man can endure a great deal if he can keep cheerful & laugh at misfortune. But poor cousin Raef is disconsolate, viewing the horrors of war and families eaten out of house & home & left in a pitiful condition.

"Things are getting tough for the Confederates," Mom noted. "Jeb feels his own optimism can keep him going, but fears Raeford's diminished spirits will be troublesome."

Dad looked down at his letter. "Here's what I found."

We have had several hard cavalry fights & one of the hardest infantry fights of the war resulting in our being compelled to fall back— two Page County fellows killed. Raeford is absent without leave. Nobody knows anything about him. I suspect he could no longer stomach the slaughter and human devastation of war.

"Deaths of Page County boys—enough to turn Raef into a deserter?" Dad asked.

"My letter says nobody from Luray or Page County

had heard of Raef's return there," Jeff said.

"He must have gone directly to Overhome," I surmised. "Where he became so despondent, rejected, disgusted with himself that he died a bitter and angry man. Which, in turn, made him an angry, hostile spirit. But what does that have to do with the way he's opposed our every move with the cottage?"

We sat in silence, each of us pondering just how much we knew and did not know about our very distant Overton ancestors.

"Well," Mom said after a period of silence, "there's another factor here I've long wondered about. Ashby, you've reminded us that Raeford was bitter and angry. Why would he join up to fight in the first place? Was it a chance to redeem himself? To prove his worth as a human being after being banished from home?"

"Maybe it was the plumed hat!" Jeff's freckles hop-scotched over his nose. "The cape and sword."

Hal picked up on that. "You know, Jeff, you may be on to something there. Dashing daredevils as the cavalry deemed themselves. Perhaps Raef was drawn in by the drama of battle. This has been repeated by young men throughout the history of mankind."

"My opinion? Raeford Overton was already an angry and bitter man—he did not need the war to make him so." My mother's words caused us to fall silent with our thoughts once again.

In the quiet, I became distinctly aware that something very peculiar was going on with me. It had started with Hal's summary and strengthened throughout our sharing of Jeb's letters, beginning at my left ear and gradually running all the way down to my foot, like a moving icicle. I don't know how else to describe it—a chilling stripe. Then, a whisper—a brush of sound—a man's voice, filled with anguish. "*Listen. Listen. Listen.*" Shivering, I looked at the others, but no one appeared to have noticed my discomfort. Somebody wanted my attention—wanted me to listen—to understand. The letters had roused a psychic energy I could not ignore and I knew we were on to something important.

Hal adjusted his glasses. "I held on to this last letter to read myself."

April, 1865.

News of Lee's losses has flown like lightning around camp. Most of the Va 7th has decided not to stay on, but I wanted to carry it out to the bitter end. My commanding officer called me in, praising my "honorable" service and asking me to deliver an important communique to General Lee himself who is on his way to Lynchburg for supplies. I am honored to be chosen for this duty. If I don't live through this, remember I love you all.

"This is the last of Jeb's letters turned over to me by Isaac Stover. The trail ends here; we have no more information to go on."

"Wow," Jeff exhaled loudly.

"Miss Emma," Hal looked at the elderly woman. "We didn't hear anything from you, dear lady."

All eyes turned to Miss Emma, who sat upright and engaged, despite her silence.

Miss Emma cleared her throat. "Now that we've read and heard all of this, discussed our feelings and intuitions—I have but one question." She paused for emphasis. "How soon before we get the clearance for that exhumation, Madison?"

****

Dear Diary:

It's finally set. All of the permits are in place, all of the players are ready to assemble for the big reveal. What do we hope to find from the exhumation of a body or bodies that may or may not be buried in the cottage cellar? We hope to find closure for one or more spirits who have, for whatever reason, not made it to the other side. We hope to de-haunt the historic cottage, preserve it for its intrinsic value, and move on with our plan to develop the back fifty.

Where does Hal stand on the paranormal aspects of our quest? Historians have a broad view of life, I think. Of past and present and how the lines can blur between the two time frames. While he is most interested in the possibility of disinterring a Civil War soldier, he distinctly said, "We feel the cottage is haunted." I know he has not dismissed the notion that the spirit of a long-buried corpse might, itself, be in search of something beyond our ken.

Thanks to Dad's perseverance and knowhow, the real estate project is moving along in a timely manner. An excellent builder has professed interest in buying the entire development for custom homes. Excavations may begin as early as this fall. I still harbor mixed feelings—am I compromising Overhome's historic value, its ancestral significance, its intrinsic beauty, by moving on with the real estate deal? Or is it justified as the only way to preserve Overhome from the dismal economic times?

With Luke's promise to come home for the disinterment, I am girding up my loins for the event. I dare say we all are. Dad has come up with a clever scheme to get Jeff, if not Nick, in on the dig. Since we are all to be gowned, masked and capped, Dad feels Jeff's height will conceal his youth. "Just don't talk," he warned Jeff. That unpredictable squeaky adolescent voice would be a giveaway, for sure. Nick, sorry to say, is so short his figure would be suspect, so he will have to console himself with Jeff's first-hand descriptions.

I confess I am worried that we may find nothing. Or that we will find something so horrific that finding nothing would be preferred. Exciting? Yes. Scary? You bet. Terrifying because, let's face it, Raeford considers ME public enemy number one. I pray for the courage and fortitude I'll need in what may be our only chance to settle over one hundred fifty years of unimaginable strife and suffering.

Chapter 23

We stood around the area roped off by the environmental director, Wilson Rosetti. Dressed in our gowns, caps and masks, we looked like surgeons about to operate on a patient. Nobody outside the family suspected that one of the "surgeons" was a twelve-year-old whose mask sufficiently covered his freckles. The entire area was lit up with battery-operated lamps so that the arched dome of the cottage cellar looked like an operating theater.

After removing the flagstones beneath the niche, Mr. Rosetti graciously conceded that Courtney Britt, Hal's archeologist friend, could take the lead in the disinterment. Hal had invited Courtney to the exhumation because, he said, archaeologists are trained to preserve the integrity of what they dig up, rather than destroy artifacts through too aggressive digging. Their tools include tiny shovels, brushes and sieves; they go about their task with scalpels rather than sledge hammers.

Courtney slowly and deliberately began to dig around the perimeter of the roped area with a miniscule shovel. After several spoonfuls of dirt, Courtney would carefully brush away the debris. She began at the cairn end and worked her way through the approximately seven-foot length of dirt and back again. Dig. Brush. Observe. It was slow and tedious work, but Courtney was taking no chances of disturbing one atom of whatever lay below.

After what seemed hours, her shovel struck something solid on the end opposite the cairn. Every one of us stopped breathing, I am convinced of it. Courtney looked up, her eyes large and luminous over her mask. "Okay. We've found something." She brushed even more delicately than before. "It appears to be...I believe we've discovered..."

Again our collective breath hung suspended. Hal readied his camera. "What do you think, Courtney?"

Courtney bent her head and brushed some more. "It's a fragment. Stiff, thick..." She brushed some more. "Leather." She held aloft in tweezers an indistinguishable piece of material, dark and mottled in color and unevenly shaped. "Probably from a shoe, or more likely, it's boot leather."

The flash of Hal's camera blinked. "Great! Keep digging."

Nodding, Courtney continued working until she had unearthed more fragments, each of which Hal photographed. "Uh oh! Here it is." She beckoned to Mr. Rosetti. "You'll want to see this." Her eyes were serious above her mask. "Bone."

The environmental director moved in closer. "Looks like a leg bone. Can you brush along the top of it? Reveal the whole thing?"

Courtney took her time. She was absolutely not to be hurried—a good thing in terms of Hal's museum, perhaps, but trying as heck for the rest of us. After a long, arduous time, working together, Rosetti and Courtney had removed enough dirt that we could see the outline of a full human skeleton, toes to skull.

I felt a bit woozy. Viewing the ancient bones of a "real live" skeleton—amazing, yes. Spooky would be more like it. *Macabre* best describes the experience. I found myself swallowing rapidly as I fought for control. My stomach lurched. Did others share my unsettled feelings? Hard to tell, what with their faces covered, but I thought Jeff's forehead had paled a shade or two. I'll bet those freckles stood out under his mask. I was glad we'd been so far spared overt ghostly activity, as, heaven knows, we were deep into spirit territory. On the other hand, I heard the continuous familiar whispering in my inner ear, the icicle chill down my side.

"There's the body. You were certainly right about that, Mr. Overton," Wilson Rosetti spoke through his mask. "The question now is whose bones are these and why are they buried here?"

Hal, busy with his camera, had insinuated himself between Courtney and Rosetti by now. "That's what we aim to find out, Mr. Rosetti. There appear to be more fragments in the grave. Looks like the corpse was maybe wrapped in a blanket or sheet or something made of fabric. See?" He indicated what he had observed. "Wait a minute. I see something in the chest cavity." He pointed. "Courtney, Could you use those tweezers of yours to get that little object there?"

Moving in the slowest motion possible, Courtney grasped the small, round object in her tweezers and held it to the light.

"What is it?" I peered over the skeleton, as closely as I dared. "Oh, now I see. Looks like metal. Looks like a…a…"

"A button!" Jeff yelped, forgetting he had been

warned not to speak. He put his hand over his mouth and coughed to cover his nervousness.

"I believe it *is* a button," Hal said. "A button that could reveal something about the identity of the corpse."

Hal glanced at Mr. Rosetti. "All right if I take a closer look?"

With a nod from the environmental director, Hal took the button in his gloved hand, turning it over and over. "It's encrusted with dirt. Courtney, can you use one of your fine brushes on this?"

Courtney removed the layer of grime one grain at a time. At length she held the button up to the light again, then, gave it back to Hal, who examined it and returned it to Courtney. "Interesting. Tarnished, of course, but it looks like brass. Check out the inscription. What do you think, Hal?" She handed it over to Hal again.

Hal frowned, his forehead knitting into lines above his glasses. "I'll be darned. Okay if I pass this around?" he asked Mr. Rosetti.

Rosetti reached for the button himself, looked at it and then passed it to Luke, who passed it to me. I, in turn, scrutinized the small metal object before handing it off to Jeff who passed it to Dad. It was a silent game of button-button—who's got the button.

We all looked at Hal at the same time. "NY?" Dad look confused. "NY is engraved on this button. What could that possibly stand for except New York?"

"Many of the Northern troops distinguished their divisions with their home states imprinted on their buttons. NJ would indicate a unit from New Jersey, for example. This button is most likely one that adorned a Federal uniform. There must be seven more of them inside that grave if they came from a Yankee overcoat." Hal took the button from Dad. "Puzzling, all right. We thought for sure we were going to exhume either Raeford Overton, Confederate deserter or possibly his cousin Jeb Stover, active duty Virginia 7th Cavalry." Hal cocked his head. "What's with a Union uniform?"

"Before we move the bones to the casket," Wilson Rosetti said, "I think we should dig some more around the perimeter of the skeleton."

"Good thinking," Hal agreed quickly. "Courtney, can you use your trowel there?"

Within minutes, the archaeologist had unearthed a rusting rifle, a moldering canteen and three silver coins only slightly tarnished.

Again requesting permission to touch the findings, Hal picked up the rifle. "This is the famous Special Model 1861 musket produced in Springfield, Massachusetts."

"Meaning what?" Luke asked.

"This musket was issued exclusively to Union soldiers. Though Rebel soldiers might lift a Union rifle from the field of battle."

"What about the silver coins?" I remembered a vision I'd had during one of Phoebe's sessions.

Hal reached carefully with his gloved hands, then, rubbed the surface of one. "These coins are Mexican. You know, a large portion of Mexican silver made up the Confederate treasury—the treasury Jefferson Davis loaded up from Richmond and took to Danville for safekeeping shortly before the end of the war."

"Indicating…?" Dad queried.

"Not sure. Much of the Confederate treasury was lost and has never been accounted for." Hal shook his head. "Multiple theories have sprouted over the ages, but we may never know the true story." Hal looked thoughtful. "Could be a Union soldier from a New York regiment managed to capture some of the silver as it was in route to Danville. That doesn't explain how the fellow ended up here with the coins, though, does it?"

Jeff had picked up the canteen, after Hal's nod of approval. "Just like the one in the Museum of the Confederacy," Jeff growled, in an attempt to hide his adolescent voice.

Mr. Rosetti gave Jeff a sharp look, which caused my cousin to clam up for the duration.

Hal took over for him. "Both sides used canteens, of course. Many Southerners were supplied with canteens made in the North. I'm afraid the canteen doesn't tell us much about the corpse's identity." He turned to Courtney. "Do you think there's anything else in this grave?"

"Give me a minute."

Digging with her trowel, brushing, digging again, eventually Courtney pulled out something else that appeared to be leather. Holding it aloft in large tweezers, she raised an eyebrow to Hal.

"Could be the remains of a knapsack." Hal took it into his gloved hands for inspection. "It probably held a Bible, perhaps a comb and brush, maybe even a housewife." He glanced at Jeff. "Again, we may never know. And again, both sides used such carry-alls."

"About time to get these bones on their way," Wilson Rosetti announced. "We'll remove them carefully—keeping them as intact as possible—take them to the coroner. They'll run the DNA and get back to you as soon as we know anything about who this poor fellow was."

Hal snapped photos of the artifacts. "May we take the canteen, coins and button to the museum?" Hal looked at the inspector. "We can do the research—maybe find the answers to some of our questions."

Mr. Rosetti stroked his chin under his mask. "I don't see why not." He thought a minute. "You'll send us a report?"

"Absolutely," Courtney and Hal said at the same time.

Luke and I made eye contact. "Any ideas?" he mouthed under his mask.

"As a matter of fact, I do know one thing," I whispered back, with a lift of my mask. "I know whose body this is, without a doubt. He's been dogging my steps for days. The minute we struck bone, the humming in my head accelerated. And I swear I heard a voice."

Luke pulled me away from the rest of the group. "Are you going to keep me in suspense forever?"

"I can't explain the evidence of the Yankee button and rifle, but I know what I heard."

"What did you hear, Ashby?"

"Beneath the stones," I said.

****

That night I had a surreal dream. I was in a dark place, freezing cold. No windows or doors existed to let in light. Aware of others in the space, I could not see anyone, due to the dense atmosphere. But I could hear them—all of them, their chattering teeth clacking like an oncoming train. I realized I was in Dante's inferno—the dreaded inner circle—the icy space reserved for the worst category of sinners: those who betray their masters. Judas. Cassius and Brutus, eternally tortured by a multiple-headed Satan—frozen together for eternity.

Betrayed. Betrayed. Beeee-trayed-trayed-trayed. The word echoed from the black void. Gradually I became aware of a faint glow from far away—a fire pit? A fire place? An oasis in the frigid, barrenness of this frozen desert? Slowly moving toward the glow, I felt my dream-steps mired in ice. After an eternity, just as I reached the warm, bright spot, I sensed something flying past me, overhead, heading straight for the oasis, now a strong gleaming column of light. With a whoosh, the entity escaped, traveling up the light and out of sight. I awoke in a cold sweat with the sure knowledge I had visited Dante's inferno and had met someone I knew or had come to know: Jeb Stover. Why was he in the frigid Ninth Circle of hell? What treachery had placed him there?

****

We convened in the library for another family meeting. It had been a week since the exhumation and the air was alive with anticipation; Hal had the results.

"We've done exhaustive tests at the museum. The body in the cellar was dressed in a Yankee uniform—a New York regiment. He was buried with a Union rifle. No surprises there." Hal withdrew a folder from his briefcase. "And here's the DNA report." He opened the folder and ran his finger down a page. "DNA shows positive proof that the body contained both Overton and Stover genetic matter."

"Which means he could be either Raeford Overton or Jeb Stover? Or some other blood relative of that line. How frustrating." I cupped my chin in my hands.

"The Yankee uniform? What's that all about?" Dad asked.

"Well, there's more," Hal turned to another page in the folder. "This report shows evidence that the man was killed by a pistol shot to the head." He turned another page. "But here's the shocker. Remember the canteen we found in the grave?"

Jeff chuckled. "I almost gave myself away over that canteen."

"When we examined the canteen at my museum, we discovered something inside."

"Water?" Jeff guffawed.

"Hardly," Hal smiled at my cousin. "Dry as a bone inside that canteen."

We voiced appreciation of Hal's morbid humor with a collective groan.

"Inside we found two perfectly preserved sheets of paper, rolled tight and slipped in, capped off from the elements for preservation." Hal looked quite pleased with himself.

Monica patted Hal's hand. "Enough, Professor Plum—I mean Professor Reynolds. This is not a game of Clue—Colonel Mustard with the knife in the study. Out with it!"

"Sorry. I couldn't resist a little drama. But if I gave each of you a hundred tries, nobody would guess…"

Monica gave Hal a look that was worthy of a murderous Clue character.

"Okay, okay. Here's the first thing we found in the canteen." From the folder, Hal whipped out a photocopy. "Here, Ashby. Take a look and pass it around."

I stared at the paper. "Looks like a crude map.

Hand-drawn." I studied it some more and passed it to Dad.

Dad rotated the map until he'd viewed it from all four sides. "Here's an X—X marks the spot." He looked up and scanned the circle of faces. "Here, Luke. What do you make of it?"

Luke took his turn, with Jeff hovering over his shoulder. "What do you think, Jeff?"

"Hey! It's a treasure map! Looks like a couple of letters under the X." Jeff pointed, bringing his face so close as to touch the paper. "They're really faint, I can't make them out for sure. I think the first letter is *N*. No, it's *M*. And the second letter is either a *Z* or an *S*."

By now everyone except Miss Emma had clustered around Luke and the map.

"*MS*," Miss Emma spoke quietly. "That's the abbreviation for manuscript."

"True," Hal said. "But if I tell you the *M* is for Mexican…"

"Then the *S* stands for silver!" Jeff cried out.

Hal beamed at Jeff.

"It's a map with an X showing where there's Mexican silver?" Mom asked. "Sorry. You've lost me."

"Remember the three silver coins we found at the exhumation?" I could hear the excitement in my own voice. "Our man must have somehow acquired a cache of silver coins, kept a few in his pocket and buried the rest."

"The map shows where," Dad finished. He reached for the paper again. "It certainly appears to show some identifiable local landmarks." He pointed to a square near the left of the map. "Could this be the cottage?"

"If we follow the map—find the coins—we'll be

rich!" Jeff exclaimed.

"Not so fast," Hal cautioned. "Discovering a sack, or rather, more likely, a keg of silver coins—possibly stolen from the Confederate treasury—would be a fantastic find for us—no doubt about it."

"You're going to tell us there's a big problem, though," Miss Emma said from her chair.

"Indeed there is, Miss E. Not just a 'big problem.' What I'd call an insurmountable problem."

"If this map references the 1860s, during the Civil War…" Dad began.

"Then, supposing we could decipher the map—follow it to the X-spot…" Luke piggy-backed on Dad's chain of thought.

Jeff's face fell. "The treasure would be under the lake, wouldn't it?"

Again we voiced a collective groan.

"Yes, the silver is probably forever lost. Even if we could find the landmarks noted on the map—you see one of them is a large tree. One is a boulder. Here's the river. The X is clearly near the river, which means the silver was surely buried in a spot long covered by deep, dark lake water." Hal flashed a sympathetic look.

"Me and Nick can try!" Jeff's voice cracked with excitement. "Maybe we can find it. Maybe it's only *near* the lake, not *under* it. Or it could be buried in real shallow water…"

What an exciting undertaking for a pair of adventurous twelve-year-olds, was my thought.

Hal handed the copy of the map to Jeff. "Go for it! If anybody can find that treasure, it's you and Nick." He turned his attention to the rest of us. "Even if the treasure is forever lost to us, there's more to consider here." He waved another photocopy retrieved from his folder. "Take a look at this—the other paper we found in the canteen."

We grouped ourselves around Hal, peering over his shoulder. Miss Emma had vacated her chair to join us.

We scrutinized the document, reading and re-reading it. I found my voice. "It's signed 'Robert E. Lee.' A hand-written message to Confederacy President Jefferson Davis signed by General Robert E Lee."

"This, along with the treasure map, was inside the canteen." Luke wore a stunned look. "Imagine that."

"A bit of back story might help," Hal said. "The 'Yankee' soldier with Overton-Stover DNA was carrying this communiqué from General Robert E. Lee to the president of the Confederacy. It all involves the last battles of the Civil War, which took place not far from here. With his army starving, Lee had to march day and night to keep ahead of the Federals, but Union pursuers caught the Confederates and devastated Lee's troops. On April 7th, Union General Grant sent a message to Lee, still in Virginia, asking for his surrender. Lee wanted to check with Jefferson Davis before he acted on Grant's request." Hal paused. "Let me read this communiqué out loud. I think you'll be able to connect the dots."

Hal pushed his glasses up on his nose and read:

April 7, 1865.

To President Jefferson Davis

It is with heartfelt regret that I report heavy losses of our troops at Saylor's Creek. With supplies blocked by Union, though I would rather die a thousand deaths, I will be forced to surrender to General Grant at

Appomattox. Unless you advise otherwise, or can assure supplies and the arrival of Johnston's men, I fear the worst.

Robert E. Lee.

"How did this communiqué end up in the canteen?" I wondered.

"Remember Jeb Stover's last letter written just before Appomattox—how he'd been asked by his commander to take a message to General Lee?" Hal asked.

We nodded.

"I can only surmise, of course, but I believe it's logical to assume Jeb delivered the message to Lee and was, in turn, given this one from Lee to deliver to Davis, who was in Danville. With telegraph and railroad lines destroyed, a personal messenger would have been a logical recourse for communication."

"But it was never delivered," Luke breathed.

"A mystery, for sure," Hal said. "Somewhere in route, our man must have encountered a Yankee soldier who had acquired the silver. It was common knowledge that the Confederacy was moving the treasure from Richmond. The woods were full of marauders, many of them Union soldiers, looking to shanghai the transport—snag some riches for personal gain. Perhaps Jeb killed the Yank, took on his overcoat, thinking he would be safer clad as a Federal." Hal thought a moment, then, went on. "And he took the silver with him."

"But he never made it to Danville—to deliver Lee's message," Dad said. "I wonder—if he had gotten Lee's dire news to Jefferson Davis. Would it have altered the outcome of the war?"

"Unlikely." Hal shook his head. "It could only have prolonged battle a day or so, at most. The South was completely outdone by April of 1865." He looked at the communiqué again. "For reasons we can only guess, Stover, ignoring his duty to deliver Lee's message, headed for Overhome. To the cottage, where he buried the silver and made a map telling where."

"Raeford Overton lived at the cottage at the time," Miss Emma reminded us.

We all thought about the possible scenarios. Any way I saw it, the body could be either Raef's or Jeb's. One likely killed the other. I thought I knew the identity of our skeleton, but how could we be sure?

Hal placed the photocopy of Lee's communique in the folder. "The good news?" He did not wait for an answer. "That piece of paper hand-written and signed by Robert E. Lee may be worth quite a lot of money."

"As much as the silver?" Jeff piped up.

Hal smiled. "We just don't know, Jeff."

My thoughts were whirling. "We may have some of the answers. But I'm not completely satisfied. I think we're missing something. We need to go back down there. To the tomb." I didn't tell them about the voice in my head whose words directed me with nagging frequency—the voice which had not let up one bit, even after the exhumation and removal of the bones. I only knew the voice urged me on: "Beneath the stones." We had unfinished business to attend to.

Chapter 24

With each step we descended I felt the stone walls closing in and I found myself taking deep yoga breaths to stifle my claustrophobic panic. What would we find in the ancient tomb this time? Please. No more bodies. Enough already. By the time we reached bottom, I shivered in the chilly air, though my palms were sweaty.

Stepping onto the dirt floor at last, using a long cord, Dad tied a bright flashlight to an iron hook embedded in the arch of the ceiling. It cast an eerie glow as it swung from side to side before settling its arc of illumination to cover a large patch of the floor.

Each armed with our own flashlights, we scoured the subterranean room, with no idea of what we hoped to find. It was upon my insistence that we were here but I could not convey why I felt so strongly that there was more to be found. That dream about Dante's hell flashed before my eyes as I paced off my steps.

Jeff and Nick could not remove their fascination from the vent hole they'd first discovered and the pile of pebbles underneath it. They stood below the vent, alternately shining their lights upward and then turning them off to view the pin prick of light that struggled through, murmuring among themselves in low voices. The room somehow encouraged whispering.

The rest of us moved slowly, exploring the walls a

couple of inches at a time. "Looks the same to me," Luke's voice made me jump. "I wish we knew what to look for."

My attention turned repeatedly to the wood-framed niches recessed at various points in the stone walls. Standing in front of the niche we had deemed the altar, I had the disconcerting feeling I was desecrating the very grave we'd excavated below it. The exhumation had left the dirt as disarrayed as a plowed garden, but I still wondered if I should place my feet on such hallowed ground. Then it hit me. Yes. Sacred ground. I scrolled my flashlight up and down, back and forth, above and below and to both sides of the niche, until I spied something unusual.

"Look here, Luke. Dad, Hal." I ran my fingers over and over one particular spot—a rectangular area about a foot and a half wide and a yard high—above the altar. "I think it's another niche. But it's been covered over. See? If you look closely, the white plaster is a shade lighter than the rest of the area. I think there's something under the stone wall here. Something covered up and plastered over." I knocked on the spot. "Hear that? Sounds hollow."

Following my lead, the men scrutinized the spot. "Let's see what we have." Luke grabbed the pick axe he'd brought along, making several shallow dents in the wall. Plaster chunks dropped to the floor, exposing an air space behind the stones. "Looks like a space covered over, all right," Luke grunted, heaving the pick several more times.

Once the whole carved-out niche was exposed, we stared at what we'd found. By now, Nick and Jeff had gravitated to the spot. Jeff was first to speak. "A metal box. Somebody's hidden it here." With a look at me for approval, Jeff reached for the container, about the size of a candy box. He tried to open it, then, raised his eyes. "Locked." It took only two beats before he cried, "And I have the key!" Reaching into his pocket, he pulled out his rabbit's foot key chain and grasped the tiny key, turning it quickly in the lock, before handing the box to me. If the others were stunned, Nick and I gave each other a knowing look, remembering the key that had been left in the silver baby cup in their clubhouse. Jeff handed the box to me. "You found it, Ashby. Here. You open it."

"Do we dare look inside?" I had the feeling this was Pandora's box. Who knew what plagues and woes might emerge from within? Nobody spoke, but their expressions of curiosity egged me on. My hands shook as I raised the hinged top, half expecting something to fly out and hit me in the face. But nothing like that occurred. Inside was a small leather bag closed with a drawstring and, under it, a sheet of paper, folded like a letter. I looked at my companions. "Which do we look at first? The bag or the paper?"

Jeff was quick to respond. "Maybe it's the treasure! Open the bag, Ashby. Open it! Quick!"

I handed the bag to Jeff. "Go ahead. Let's see if you're right."

With nimble fingers, Jeff pulled open the drawstring, spilling the contents. A dozen silver coins rolled over the floor, settling into shiny piles. "Wow," he whispered. "Look, Nick."

Hal picked up a coin and examined it. "More Mexican coins, all right. But I'll bet there's a lot more buried under the lake if these were stolen from the

Confederate treasury. For transport, we know they were contained in small wooden kegs about twice the size of a football."

"Do you think these are worth much?" Luke asked.

"I'd say a small fortune," Hal answered. "Now, Ashby, how about we check out the paper there."

I reached for it gingerly, still expecting something to bite my fingers. Though obviously old, the paper has been well preserved in the metal box.

"Aren't you going to read it?" Luke's voice sounded strangely hollow.

Unfolding the paper with shaking fingers, I looked it over quickly, then, began reading out loud.

My Dear Sister Angelina,

It is with breaking heart that I convey to you my last words in this life, to tell you what I have done. I know it is my tortured blood that led me to commit the last ghastly deed, and I pray that you, above all people, my beloved sister, will believe it was a mistake. A terrible mistake.

The night was deadly dark. No measure of candlelight could illuminate the cause of the sounds I heard. A clattering in the yard. A repeated thumping on my door. Used as I am to solitude, I gathered my pistol which I had brought home when I deserted. My horse and my pistol, the only remains of my miserable career as a failed cavalryman. My tainted blood from the milk of that slave nurse was ever at fault. It hounded me for the duration of my flawed war service. I had no courage. I gained no confidence from my experiences. My only instinct was to run and hide. To retreat and cower. But that is quite another story.

When I saw the Yankee standing at my doorway in his Union blue overcoat, his rifle at his side, I had but one thought. I would, at last, evidence some courage in the face of danger. Drawing my pistol, I shot, point blank, a mortal blow to his head. Only after he had slumped to the floor and I dared take a closer look, did I realize it was my own dear, honorable and good cousin, Jeb Stover, dressed in Federal garb. Why he would be thus outfitted, I could not fathom.

Weak and losing blood, Jeb managed a brief dying speech. "I shot the Yankee…took his uniform for protection…wanted to see you…tell you that…"

Then, he expired. I know not how long I stood, paralyzed with the consequences of my hasty action. I cannot account for you the hours I cried piteous tears of remorse. I can only say that I buried him and all his accoutrements below this niche and created an altar in his memory. I kneel there daily and pray for his immortal soul. But I could never reconcile my actions, nor could I nullify my guilt. Your brother has been cursed from infancy with foul milk and black blood. I will close off his tomb and seal the vents so that none can find the evidence of my unholy deed.

I will not live much longer, dear sister. I have no desire to live even one more minute in this bleak existence. I will die much as I was born: weak, flawed, unsuccessful in my efforts to reach a worthy and honorable manhood. I have done many, many other ghastly deeds you know not of.

I will take the coward's way out and ask that the family bury me in the Overton family cemetery without any marker or other evidence that ever I existed to do such harm in this world. I hope you will honor this one request when the family decides how to dispose of my miserable remains.

If I had the moral courage, I would see that you receive this missive, give you the bag of coins I discovered after I shot Jeb. But, alas, I am so weak. I will hide this, my letter of confession, above the altar and leave its dispensation to fate. My last act on earth will be to fill in the vents and tumble in rocks and debris to cover the stairwell that leads to Jeb's tomb. Then I shall build a porch to hide the opening. I know not if or when this sacred tomb will be discovered and I cannot predict the fate of my letter to you.

Fair and loving as you are, my Angel, I know you will always do what is best. May God rest Jeb's soul, even though I can expect no rest for my own.

> *Your loving brother,*
> *Raeford*

Silence followed my reading. It was Dad who broke the spell. "If only Raeford knew that his 'honorable and good cousin' was overtaken by greed and actually failed his final duty to his commander-in-chief."

"You're right, Dad." I fingered the letter absently. "It all makes sense now. After Jeb shot the Yankee and discovered the silver, he veered from his path to Danville. He neglected to deliver the critical communiqué from the greatest general the South ever produced." He betrayed his master, I thought.

"He redirected himself to Overhome. To hide the silver, probably thinking he would return at some point to retrieve it," Luke said. "I wonder what Raeford would have thought had he known the truth. If he had looked inside the canteen and put two and two together as we've been able to do."

"Again, that's something we'll never know." Hal ventured another thought. "What if Raeford did discover the map and the message from Lee? What if he knew Jeb had grossly neglected his duty to his general and his nation?"

"Raeford showed some backbone after all to save Jeb's reputation?" I asked.

"As I said, we'll…"

Before Hal could finish his statement, a looming dark dust-devil whirled out of nowhere, careening from wall to wall, down to the floor where it picked up loose dust and dirt, then, curling off the domed ceiling. It gathered size and momentum by sweeping over the remains of Jeb's grave, a whirlpool churning over our heads, emitting the usual foul odor.

"*Never. Never. Never.*" Had the syllables emerged from my own lips in the midst of the tempest? Had I become a medium for Raef's spirit?

"*Yes, brother Raef. Come. Come home to your Angel.*" A woman's wail. Angelina Overton. For sure,

Angelina's spirit was among us.

"*Failed. I am no soldier*," another male spoke. It was the voice in my head that had dogged me day in and day out since our channeling at the cottage. Jeb himself, crying out in tortured tones. "*Failed.*"

"*Come. Come, both of you. It is time*," Angelina again. Her plea was heart-breaking in its intensity. "*It is time. Time. Time.*"

I knew what I had to do and I felt surprisingly strong and clear-minded, even as bits of dirt and gusts of wind swirled about me. Two tortured spirits and an angel who wanted them to move, after all this time, to the other side, fought for direction. My direction.

"Raeford. Jeb. Angelina is right. It *is* time. Go to the light. Search for the light," I implored.

Tasting the dust on my lips, I spoke to my living companions, all of whom stood still as cement watching and listening. "Extinguish your flashlights. Quickly, please."

They hurriedly did so, then, Dad took quick steps to turn off the light he'd suspended from the ceiling hook. Except for the dim illumination from the stairwell, the room was dark as a cavern.

"Find the light," I pleaded again. "Angelina will show you the way. The light is warm, welcoming. Listen to her. Angelina is calling to you."

"*Looking...For so long. So long. So long.*" Jeb's voice echoed.

"Follow Angelina's directions, Jeb. Go with her." The thin image of a man reaching his arms forward, grasping and searching, moved in slow motion toward a faintly glowing funnel of light that shafted from ceiling to floor in a growing cone of illumination.

"*Angelina, I see you!*" A hesitation. "*The light. I'm Jeb, and I've found it at last!*" the transparent image cried out in a quivering voice. The shining cone beamed brighter and stronger just ahead of him.

Jeb's image lurched into the incandescence, turning ice-blue for a moment, before growing thinner, until it faded completely. Silence and darkness ensued. Nobody spoke, but, knowing Jeb had crossed over, I breathed freely. My task, however, was not yet completed.

"*Raeford. Raeford,*" the woman's voice pleaded again. "*Come to the light. Come with us. We are waiting for you here in this beautiful place. For you, Raeford.*"

One huge flash flared in the dark, followed by a cannon boom, and the air instantly left the room— sucked out as if by a strong vacuum cleaner wielded by giant, unseen hands. I felt like something had bowled over me and knocked the wind completely out of my lungs. Gasping for air, I wondered if the others in the ebony depths of the cellar felt the same way. The whirlpool that was Raef was gone. Jeb was gone. All illumination was gone. Surely they had followed Angelina to her celestial light on the other side.

Hal was first to turn on his flashlight. "If I had not seen it…" was all he could muster.

Jeff's face had paled so that his freckles stood out in 3-D and Nick muttered, "*Dios mio,*" and crossed himself three or four times.

"The light," Dad exhaled loudly. "I'd say they found it."

"Does this mean we're clear of spirits in the cottage?" Luke puzzled.

After some deep breathing, I trusted my vocal cords to perform once more. "Angelina has guided her brother and cousin to the other side. But, as for clearing the spirits out—all of the spirits? What about those tortured slaves groaning under the weight of stones and cowering from the overseer's whip as they built our stone wall?"

"Well, I have to point out that Monica first contacted me to help locate the headstones of Overhome's slaves buried under the lake. I have not, thus far, succeeded. There are still a lot of questions out there." Hal looked thoughtful. "Even without Raeford Overton and Jeb Stover, something tells me the Historical Society will still find its share of ghosts here on its haunted house treks." He paused. "What say we gather up our equipment and get out of here?"

Luke put his arms around me, rocking me back and forth, back and forth. "I don't know how or where you found your calling, dear Ashby. But we can all thank you for what you've accomplished today."

"And for leading us to a valuable historic document," Hal put in.

Luke planted a kiss on my neck. "My wife-to-be," he murmured so that only I could hear him. "The ghost buster."

Epilogue

A thin mist hung over the mountains like a delicate bridal veil. A good omen. The sun peeking through promised a clear, bright day for our afternoon wedding. I stood on my balcony breathing in the mild late-summer air, thinking: *Dear Overhome, I no longer worry about your fate; you will surely be financially solid again.* I savored my last look from this vantage point, my last moments as Ashby Overton, thinking: *When next I view the morning I will be Luke's wife. Mrs. Ashby Overton-Murley. A married woman starting a new chapter in life. A long-awaited day.*

Danielle and Aneesh, our wedding attendants, had arrived late last night, having driven together from Northern Virginia. Both had rooms in a hotel in Bradford and I could tell by Danielle's voice on the phone—the two of them had hit it off splendidly. A spark of romance? Weddings lend themselves to that .I was grateful that my best friend and maid of honor would be here any minute to guide me through the day.

The M&M Express was in overdrive—laying out tables, organizing decorations, setting up space for the band, the bar and the dance floor all under a big white tent on the lawn. Sniffing the air from the balcony, I inhaled exotic aromas wafting from the guest house where Mariana was busy preparing the wedding feast. Luke and I had pledged to avoid seeing one another until the ceremony—for good luck.

I stretched my arms to the sky, then, moved them wide in a sun salutation. Taking a moment to meditate, I breathed a few yoga breaths before moving through the French doors into my room. "See you in two weeks, after the New England honeymoon," I told my four-poster. "And dear Luke will be joining me. Namaste." I folded my hands together and bowed.

Opening my door to a light knocking, I hugged my former college roommate and exclaimed, "Danielle! You look wonderful!" And she did. Her long, dark locks had been styled in a chic short bob that accentuated her luminous brown eyes and high cheekbones.

"You're looking pretty good, yourself, Ashby. Did you know at Hollins I always envied the way you somehow appeared beautiful even when you first woke up, with your hair all a-tumble and not a stitch of makeup?" Danielle returned my hug and kissed my cheek. "I am so happy for you and Luke. You're a perfect match—different from each other as you've always seemed."

"It's a wonder, isn't it?" I laughed.

"Let's get busy. We've only six hours to turn you into a beautiful bride."

"Hair a-tumble and no makeup won't get it this time, will it?" I joked.

****

With guests seated in a semicircle facing the gazebo, I walked between my father and mother from the mouth of the maze. Danielle had tamed my hair so that it fell just right beneath my bio-mother's fine wedding veil with its crown of seed pearls. A matching strand encircled my neck, and I swear I could feel her presence. Ever since I had discovered the veil and pearls in her and my father's trunk in the attic, I had known they were meant for me on my wedding day. My satin gown fell in a silky line from the empire waist to the floor, allowing only a glimpse of my silvery sandals. Never one to dress up as a princess, I felt like one at this moment.

Oddly enough, the thorny rose bushes that had refused to bloom all summer were suddenly ablaze, surrounding the gazebo in crimson glory, and offering a striking contrast to the slim white branches of the arched wooden gazebo where the ceremony would take place.

Robbie Mitchell's bluegrass band struck up its own upbeat version of the wedding march, and all the guests stood as my parents and I floated in slow-motion toward my groom and his best man. I had never seen Luke in a tuxedo; I must say it suited him elegantly. But it was the look on Luke's face that spread my lips into a smile. *"You are the most beautiful bride I have ever seen,"* his look told me. *"And you are my one and only babe."*

I cannot say I recall every word the pastor spoke as Luke and I stood, hand-in-hand, inside the gazebo. I cannot say how my voice or even Luke's sounded as we pledged our vows to one another. I do not even fully remember the kiss that sealed the pastor's proclamation: "I now pronounce you man and wife." What can I say, then about my wedding under the bright blue Southern sky?

I vividly recall every face of every guest—the smiles, the tears, the looks that said, *"This is a union that was meant to be.*" I remember my first dance with Dad, a slow waltz, heavy on the fiddle, with his gentle whispering in my ear, "I love you. I will always love you, dearest daughter." And who could forget the toast with cold, bubbling White Rock sparkling wine, given by Danielle and Aneesh, who had practiced a piece with each supplying alternating lines. "To Ashby and Luke: May what you feel today/Last a lifetime and more/Blessings upon your marriage/And your home together." There wasn't a dry eye to be found, until Robbie's gang plowed into a rousing tune that catapulted everyone from chairs to dance floor.

And as the day progressed, whenever I felt my energy flagging, my brand-new husband would kiss my ears and perk me up by whispering his loving, tender reminder of our honeymoon ahead: "Lobster."

Tossed by our guests, rose petals showered us as we ran through the maze to go back to the house and don our going-away outfits and grab our suitcases. Breathless, we got as far as the gate leaving the maze. On the stone step, something caught my eye. I bent to retrieve it, knowing full well what it meant and who had left it for me to discover. I pressed it to my cheek, and then held it under Luke's nose so that he, too, could enjoy its perfumed beauty. A long-stemmed red rose, just out of the bud.

"Rosabelle," we both said at the same time.

A word about the author...

Susan Coryell has long been interested in Southern concerns about culture and society, as hard-felt, long-held feelings battle with modern ideas. She was able to explore these themes in her cozy mystery/Southern Gothic *A Red, Red Rose*, whose fictional setting is based on Smith Mountain Lake, Virginia. *Beneath the Stones* is a stand-alone sequel to *A Red, Red Rose*. Susan is also the author of the award-winning young adult novel, *Eaglebait*.

When she is not writing, Susan enjoys boating, kayaking, golf, and yoga at Smith Mountain Lake, Virginia. She and her husband love to travel, especially when grandchildren are involved.

http://www.susancoryellauthor.com

~*~

Other Susan Coryell titles
available from The Wild Rose Press, Inc.:
A RED, RED, ROSE